A Tale For
MIDNIGHT

FREDERIC PROKOSCH

Of all the star-crossed tales of passion and violence to come out of Renaissance Italy, none is more sinister or more deeply moving than the story of the Cenci. Indeed, it might be said that if the Cenci tragedy had not actually occurred, it would have had to be created by some Elizabethan dramatist.

This is the historic case that provides the central situation for Frederic Prokosch's new novel. Against the rich, tumultuous background of the Renaissance, Mr. Prokosch unfolds a tale of horror and suspense, of crime and punishment overwhelming in its impact.

It happened in the closing years of the sixteenth century, in a country and a time when noble families were no strangers to profligacy and crime, to plotting and to murder. Yet even cynical, worldly Rome was profoundly shocked by the Cenci case.

Was not the beautiful Beatrice Cenci more sinned against than sinning? It was well known that her father Francesco, head of the illustrious Roman family that bore his name, was a lecherous, dissipated, evil man. But what of his wife telling per se and above all."

ALSO BY FREDERIC PROKOSCH

Novels

THE ASIATICS

THE SEVEN WHO FLED

NIGHT OF THE POOR

THE SKIES OF EUROPE

THE CONSPIRATORS

AGE OF THUNDER

THE IDOLS OF THE CAVE

STORM AND ECHO

NINE DAYS TO MUKALLA

A TALE FOR MIDNIGHT

Poetry

THE ASSASSINS

THE CARNIVAL

DEATH AT SEA

CHOSEN POEMS

A TALE FOR MIDNIGHT

A Tale
for
MIDNIGHT

by FREDERIC PROKOSCH

Little, Brown and Company

Boston   *Toronto*

The author wishes to express his indebtedness to the Director of the Vatican Archives, to Signor Paolo Ricciardi, and to the late George Santayana; as well as to the earlier appraisals of the Cenci case by Bertolotti, Guerazzi, Dalbono and Corrado Ricci.

F. P.

Contents

BOOK ONE   *The Murder*   1

BOOK TWO   *The Flood*   89

BOOK THREE   *The Witnesses*   167

BOOK FOUR   *The Plague*   277

BOOK FIVE   *The Scaffold*   337

BOOK ONE
The Murder

I

Our tale begins in darkness and ends in darkness. The dark of the end is an autumn dusk, a withering away of heat and brightness. The dark of the beginning is dawn: a cool, foglit stillness.

One April morning, an hour before sunrise, two pale ladies and a pink-faced gentleman descended the stairs of their palace near the Tiber. An elderly maid in a cloak held a three-armed candle by the door. They set foot in the dewy courtyard. A chubby groom led out the horses. They mounted in silence and set forth for the Sabine hills.

The year is 1595, the month is April. The riders are the Roman nobleman Francesco Cenci with his daughter and his second wife, Lucrezia.

Two menservants accompany them, one on a mule and one on foot. The one on foot carries a lantern and walks alongside a second mule, which is laden with hampers full of food, linen, cutlery.

The mule bells tinkle as they follow the walls of the Ghetto: a tiny echo to the deep iron clanging from San Tommaso. The jet of a fountain traps the lamplight; two black cats go scampering by. The hoofbeats echo in the vaults of a nearby wine cellar. They follow the Botteghe Oscure, where the tiny shops are black and empty, but in the Palazzo Bolognetti a candle is burning in one of the windows. A lonely fishmonger is already wheeling his cart down the alley — sole and shrimp and fresh octopus from the waters by Ostia.

Now in the distance rise the vast pale stairs of Aracoeli. They vanish again, a cool, cascading apparition, and the travelers wind past the Colonna gardens toward the Quirinal. The living horses move close by the marble stallions of Monte Cavallo; the stars flash under the giant hoofs like sparks from an anvil.

Slowly the company rides past the summer halls of Clement the Eighth and past the Four Fountains and the Church of San Bernardo. It moves through the Porta Pia into the open lands outside the walls.

The stars grow pale. The sheep bells tinkle in the dew-peppered meadows. A flock of blackbirds leaps out of a copse and goes wheeling toward Tivoli.

2

"Give me my shawl," said Lucrezia to the groom Pacifico. Pacifico reached into the saddlebag and passed the shawl to his mistress.

Then Lucrezia turned to her husband:

"Well now, this castle of Prince Colonna's. Tell me, Francesco. Is it comfortable, do you imagine?"

Cenci glanced at her cunningly. "More than comfortable, my dear. Luxurious."

"Has it gardens?" said Lucrezia wistfully.

"Ah," said Cenci, crooking his finger. "The Garden of Eden is nothing to the gardens of La Petrella, my sweet. Marble terraces shimmering with fountains as far as the eye can see . . ."

The hills crawled out of the mist as they followed Via Nomentana. A two-wheeled cart full of chickens came clattering along on its way to the city. The dew on the grass began to shine, pearly tints rose out of the ponds. The last shreds of fog faded away in the valleys. A lemon glow tipped the cypresses on Monte Sacro; puffs of smoke oozed up from the scattered farmhouses. Here and there a ruined arch caught the bubbling light, or a broken column entangled in vines.

"Is it cold up there in the hills?" said Lucrezia a little later.

"Eternal summer," purred Cenci. "Nothing but palm trees and peacocks."

She pursed her lips. "Is it lonely, a bit?"

"Ha!" said Cenci. "You've never seen the likes of it. It makes Venice look like a village. Banquets and festivals the whole week long."

Lucrezia loosened her shawl. She looked at the hills with dejection. "Tell me, Francesco. Why are we going to La Petrella?"

Cenci turned on her viciously. "I'm weary of Rome, and that's the end of it!"

They rode on in silence. Cenci's horse was a big bay mare. He was gout-ridden and corpulent but he rode with skill and facility. He wore a doublet of black satin under a sea-blue cloak, and a pair of slashed hose in the Sevillian style. His hat was of felt, a new fashion from Piedmont, and his boots were of a fine iridescent chamois leather.

The two ladies rode sidesaddle, Lucrezia on a chestnut, Beatrice on a black: beautiful horses, well caparisoned, bought from the great Colonna stables. Lucrezia was a tremulous soft-featured woman running to fat: sad of eye, fussy of gesture, apprehensive of tone. Beatrice had the air of a boy, slender and insolent, with an arrowy neck, frail cheekbones, eyes restless and speculative. A girl of eighteen, with the rosy glow of eighteen, but the barren delicacy of a child and the cool self-confidence of a matron.

Lucrezia's garments were black and saffron; Beatrice was all in green. Both of the women wore loose-fitting caps embroidered in gold. The dust welled about them in lazy clouds; it clung to their sleeves and scalloped collars. Their cheeks were shiny with the heat, their eyes were beginning to smart. Lucrezia was sneezing with the fine yellow pollen.

They rode slowly toward the hills. The sunlight fell through the olive groves and a flock of sulphur butterflies came dancing over the fields.

3

From Rome to La Mentana ran the old Roman highway. Soon after sunrise the road was alive with traffic. Peasants on foot or on muleback en route to their fields; mendicant friars, heavily bearded, on their way from the Adriatic; carriers shepherding their donkeys, vintners with their wine carts laden with casks, now and then a young vagabond or a crippled old beggar. Near Colle dei Pazzi they saw a disconcerting thing: two skeletons in tatters dangling

from the boughs of a withered tree. A parchment nailed
on the trunk listed their names and acts of banditry, with
the notary's flourish below and the Papal seal appended.
There was a desolate whiff; a vulture crouched on the
topmost bough. The muleteer crossed himself as they
passed and the party rode on in silence till they saw the
black bell tower of La Mentana ahead of them.

Here the Roman road ended. Their way swiftly deteri-
orated and dwindled into a mule path as it wound into
the Abruzzi.

The sun grew blinding at midday and the party paused
by some evergreens. The horses were watered at a spring
and a damask cloth was spread on the grass. The groom
Pacifico unwrapped two fat roasted guinea hens, and a
bottle of claret was opened; bread and cheese were laid
on the platters. The linnets sang overhead and a hare
skipped by through the thicket. They ate and drank, and
for a while Signor Francesco fell asleep while Lucrezia sat
beside him and fanned the flies from his swollen face.

Beatrice rose and took the lute which lay strapped to
the hamper. She strolled through the trees and sat on a
stone beside the brook and started to play. But soon her
fingers grew listless, her eyes clouded. She stared vacantly
at the locusts which zoomed over the fields.

There she sat when a group of huntsmen went cantering
by. They rode through the glade with their black-hooded
hawks perched on their gloves and the hounds were leaping and darting behind them. One handsome young huntsman was dressed in green serge, his hair was blond as a
Dutchman's and he wore a hat of emerald sarsenet. His
horse leaped over the stream and he came to a halt close
by Beatrice.

She fondled her lute and looked away.

"Play on, why don't you?" said the huntsman.

"Why should I play for a stranger?"

"You're shy?"

"Certainly not."

"Then you're proud."

"What of it?"

The man smiled at her teasingly. He reached up into the leaves and pulled a flower from the bough; he kissed it lightly and tossed it down to her.

"There. Remember me," he said, "when you sing to your lute again, my lovely."

Off he was, riding down through the stony meadow, and Beatrice rose and strolled back through the trees.

"You look feverish," said her stepmother.

"It's the heat of the sun," said Beatrice irritably.

"Ah," moaned Lucrezia. "This country air. It's never agreed with me, and it never will!"

"Come, we're off," shouted Cenci, who had washed his face by the spring, and soon the party was off toward the hills of Nerola. Three black goats and a humpbacked goatherd peered at them wickedly as they climbed the path. They rode through a tangle of ilex trees and emerged on a barren hillside.

"Monte del Lago," said Cenci, wiping the sweat from his cheeks.

The horses came to a halt and the ladies looked around listlessly.

4

A great blue vista spread out as far as the peak of Montorio. A ribbon of sand uncoiling through a web of dust-powdered olive trees; gray-green slopes rising lazily toward rock-crested ranges; and the distant hills, flecked with mist, oyster-gray tinged with silver, and here and there a mountain village with a castle perched over it. Torrents came gushing through the rocks and a solitary eagle hung over the gully. Deep below in the sunlit pasture the ewes were grazing still and golden, but where they rode the clouds were gathering; the air was brisk and capricious.

They climbed a pine-scented path and crossed over the summit and then they rode down again into a great lonely valley. Now they were far indeed from the city; the intrigue and the wicked gossip. Rome seemed strangely remote with its chattering piazzas and fountains. Twilight came. And a tingle of fear crept over Beatrice, as though the world were shriveling away and nothing were left but a vast abyss.

Soon after sunset they saw a town built on the edge of a cliff: it overhung the cold irascible flood of the Turano. This was Posticciola, where the Papal States ended and the Kingdom of Naples began. Ancient battlements loomed over the town, slate-colored and obsolete. It was nearly dark when they came to the Inn of the Stag, just as the innkeeper was hanging his lantern by the gate. The mules and horses were led through the innyard and the Cenci dismounted; they stepped through an arch into a low dark hall.

[9   ]

Flames were dancing in a canopied fireplace, sprinkling their highlights over the panes. The three Cenci came close and warmed their hands at the fire. The sound of singing rose from the taproom; clapping of hands and tinkling glasses.

Cenci sniffed at the air. "We'll dine well here. I smell venison." He snapped his fingers; a shriveled servingmaid came darting through the doorway.

The two women were led to their room and Cenci slipped into the night again. One of the grooms of the inn was alone in the stable, watering the horses.

Cenci stood motionless in the doorway. The lantern swung on its hook, and the light danced lazily on his face. His cheeks were heavy, delicately tinged with a lilac sheen, like a mussel. The nostrils had a fine Castilian curve, richly tufted with blue-black hairs. The lips were pale, weary, pendulous; the hair was powdered with dandruff. But the eyes were brilliant: suave as a cat's, mercurial and mischievous. When he smiled they shone with a penetrating charm.

He glanced quizzically at the groom. "All's well?"

"All's well, signor," said the groom.

"There's a ring around the moon . . ."

"So there is, my lord," said the groom.

"I see fog down in the valley . . ."

"It's a heavy night, signor."

Cenci stood by the stall and put his hand on the young man's shoulders. His voice grew furtive and tense.

"You're a fine-looking lad!"

"Thank you kindly, signor."

"What's your age?"

"Seventeen . . ."

"What's your name?"

"Leonello."

"Lovely name," breathed Cenci. "Here's a coin for you, Leonello."

A little later he strode back into the echoing taproom, plucked a straw from his doublet and ordered wine for the multitude.

Then he stepped into the hall, where kittens were playing in front of the fire. The two ladies stood by the window in the corner, speaking softly. They paused abruptly when Cenci entered. Beatrice turned and stared into the night.

Cenci gazed at her slyly. "Are you tired, Beatricciola?"

Lucrezia sighed. "She's delicate, you know. It's been a long day's riding."

The kitchen door swung open and the innkeeper called softly:

"The meat's ready, my lord."

The candles were lit in the alcove and the coppery roast came steaming on the platter. Cenci was right: venison it was, with pickled cucumbers and currants.

II

The sun was hazy. The dew hung from the naked boughs like a chain of beads. They entered the Kingdom of Naples; the land grew deep and forlorn. They passed stony gray towns huddling on vine-laden terraces, and always the plum-blue mountains rose in the east — the real Abruzzi. Noon came. The sun sharpened. They crossed delicate arching bridges which lay mirrored in little pools, still and shadowy in the heart of the gorges.

Suddenly Cenci muttered:

"There it is. La Petrella."

The cliffs parted. The curtain of trees opened into an S-shaped ravine. The heat quivered over the slime-dappled boulders in the torrent bed. In the distance rose a hill girdled with geranium-red rooftops. And on the peak, bleak and harsh, like a bird of prey, crouched the fortress.

"Cruel and sad it looks, Francesco!"

"Wait till you get there," cooed Cenci.

They walked the horses down a stone-littered path into the valley. The path widened into a road striped with deep muddy ruts. They crossed a moss-tufted bridge and came to the gate of the village and watered their horses at a shady fountain. Once again the sun sank and the ranges flowed into dusk. And suddenly the landscape lost precision and the slopes turned blue and shaggy: they looked like the fur of some huge slumbering animal.

Folk came hurrying from the village and stood whispering by the gate:

"It's the lord of the castle!"

"It's the Cenci!"

"It's the Lord Francesco and his Roman ladies!"

The muleteer led the way through the maze of alleys and archways. They climbed the last steep ascent to the doors of the castle. The horses panted and stumbled; finally they came to a halt. A thick gray wall rose from the edge of the cliff. The door swung open and the seneschal stepped out, brandishing a great copper oil lamp: a towering fellow with a booming voice. His eyes flashed over the swinging flame.

"Welcome," he called. "You're late, signor! The pig's on the spit, all brown and sizzling . . ."

2

The three Cenci followed the seneschal into the castle cloister. Cold, barren walls, like a crater carved out of a cliff. There was a stench of mossy waters, of derelict masonry.

"Plautilla!" called the seneschal.

Footsteps rippled within the house. A candle slid past one of the windows, and a moment later a woman in black came running into the cloister.

"God bless you," she cried, "we've been worrying, si-

gnor! It's dark already, and what with the bandits . . .
Here, this way, signora!" She led the ladies up the stairway and to their rooms on the second floor: three great
chambers, cold, sonorous, with mold-flecked walls and
faded tapestries.

Tall windows looked to the west, where a lonely star
pierced the evening. On the opposite side a tiny window
looked down on the cloister. Plautilla dropped to her
knees and set fire to the logs with her candle. Soon the
flames crackled briskly; tall blue shadows danced on the
walls.

"There's new wool in the mattresses," said Plautilla gently, glancing up from the fire, "and I've put new curtains
around the beds, signora. All we need now is a mat or
two. There's not a rug in the place, I'm sorry to say . . .
Here's the water, signora, and here on the table's a ewer.
Here's the chest for your garments, and here's one for
the linen. I've spiced them with lavender . . ." She smiled
thinly and folded her hands. "It's a cold barren place, but
we'll do our best with it, signora!"

She stood by the hearth and gazed at the ladies with
sudden intensity. There was a grave and long-suffering
kind of dignity about Plautilla: tall, angular, austere, with
jet-black hair and a stony profile, and those huge passive
eyes which caught the firelight like glass.

"Well, I'll leave you now, signora. But hurry, please; the
meat's all ready!"

Her footsteps clicked in the unlit passageway. The two
ladies were left alone.

Lucrezia sank on the bed and buried her face in a fit
of weeping. Beatrice glanced at her indifferently and
walked across toward the inner window.

"It's like a prison," sobbed Lucrezia. "Why in the Lord's name did he bring us here?"

Beatrice kept staring through the window; she drew her fingers across the pane.

"Look — even the walls are weeping!" cried Lucrezia, looking about miserably. "This wet mountain air — it will be the death of me, I tell you!"

A bell rang below. Beatrice glanced into the cloister. Two tiny lights from a chamber opposite stared back like the eyes of a cat. Fumes rose from the kitchen; there was a clattering of dishes. Suddenly Plautilla's voice called: "Olimpio! Come! Quickly!"

A door opened below. The seneschal stepped into the cloister. The light fell on his dark violent face and oxlike shoulders. Instinctively he raised his eyes and glanced up at Beatrice's window. He saw her and began to smile; he stood motionless, waiting.

Beatrice turned from the window and crossed over to the mirror. She looked into the glass and frowned; she touched her cheeks with her fingertips.

Then she lifted the jug and poured out the water and plunged her hands in the copper basin.

3

All was still in the castle. Beatrice set the candle beside her bed and tiptoed out on the balcony which gave from the ladies' antechamber. She placed her hands on the railing and stared at the wilderness below her. Directly beneath the balcony was a heavy thicket surrounded by walls;

outside the walls hung a ledge of rock dappled with thin high grasses. From this the cliff shot down into a great hollow valley — tufts of wood surrounded by pastures, cut by a thin braid of water.

Utter stillness. A stillness such as she'd never known or even imagined. A silence harsh, elemental; unbroken by the trickling of fountains or the ripple of footsteps. A darkness desolate and stony, with not a single candle burning.

"Beatrice."

She turned sharply.

Cenci stepped on the balcony.

"What are you doing here?"

"Nothing. Just looking at the stars."

"They're bright tonight, aren't they?"

Beatrice stood silently, with her hand on the railing.

"I've never seen them so bright," said her father after a moment.

"Nor I," said Beatrice heavily.

"Look. See that one? That's Venus. Venus was the Goddess of Love, my child. A wild and unpredictable goddess," said Cenci.

Beatrice kept staring at a lonely peak that rose directly in front of them. The highest peak in the range: thimble-shaped, pale as ivory.

Cenci lifted her hand from the railing and held it in his own, which felt hot, thick, feverish. A stab of revulsion shot through her. She tried to draw her hand back, but Cenci held it locked in his grip.

"You're afraid of me, aren't you?"

He lowered his head and thrust his dark fiery face in front of her own. His swollen cheeks shimmered like blisters and the hairs were fluttering in his nostrils. She caught the fumes of his breath, rancid, dyspeptic.

"Answer me: Are you afraid of me?"

"No, Father. I'm not afraid of you."

Cenci smiled and dropped her hand. Then he kissed her quietly on the temple. "There. Go to bed now, Beatricciola. All these glittering stars — they're bad for your dreams!"

He turned and walked noiselessly through the ante-chamber.

4

There was a tiny knock on the bedroom door.

"Who is it?"

"Lucrezia!"

"Well, come in . . ."

Lucrezia entered, flushed, foggy-eyed. Her hair hung tangled over her shoulder.

The two women stared at each other without a word, Beatrice crouching on the bed, Lucrezia rigid in the door-way.

Finally Beatrice whispered: "What's wrong?"

"I don't know . . . I'm terrified, Beatrice!"

"You're tired. You need sleep."

"I heard footsteps out on the terrace . . ."

"Nonsense. There's no one there."

"And a shadow lurking at the end of the corridor . . ."

"Hush," said Beatrice, with sudden anger. "It's **your** fancy. Go to bed."

Lucrezia hesitated. She looked at Beatrice with her flat black eyes, glanced quickly toward the window, and drew her fingers over her eyebrows. Then she stepped back into the hall and closed the door softly.

Beatrice licked the tip of her forefinger and deftly tapped the flame of the candle.

III

Now we leave these two ladies for a while in their castle. Two years passed, but nothing happened of particular moment until Francesco one day decided to ride back to Rome. He had certain matters, high and low, to dispose of in Rome. A throng of lawsuits was developing out of the tangled state of his properties. He was planning to sell, for excellent reasons, his several estates in the Papal territories and to purchase some considerably more distant lands, having in mind in particular the Marquisate of Incisa in Monferrato, which belonged at this time to the Lords of Mantua. These and other transactions demanded his immediate attention, and he ordered the groom Pacifico to accompany him back to Rome. This time, however, he decided to stay not in the palazzo on Monte Cenci but in the Hospital of San Giacomo degli Incurabili; this latter house, as it happened, bore immunity from arrest.

A word or two about this nobleman of Rome, Francesco Cenci.

Cenci's father, Cristoforo, died in 1562. Francesco at this time was a husky boy of thirteen, born out of wedlock and legitimatized not long before his father's death. A vast fortune had been accumulated by Cristoforo, who was a functionary of the Apostolic Camera, during a long career of bribery, chicanery and peculation. So it was that Francesco, a lewd and violent boy, found himself in sudden possession of one of the great Roman fortunes. An early wedlock was arranged in view of his precocious ways, and at fourteen he was married to the girl Ersilia Santacroce. The years passed; twelve children were born of this marriage. Of these, seven survived infancy: Giacomo the eldest, then Cristoforo, Antonina, Rocco, Beatrice, Bernardo and Paolo. On Ersilia's death by fever Cenci married again: Lucrezia Velli this time, a bewildered lady with a handsome dowry. Marriage and paternity, however, far from sobered the man. His whole maturity was spent in a series of strange felonies and outrages, almost ludicrous in their multitude, vulgarity and folly. Thrice he was heavily fined for assaulting one of his servants. Thrice more he was fined for physical violence in the streets. At the age of twenty he went to trial in the Court of Savella for sodomy. An abundance of documents, discolored by age and gnawed by mice, still survive in the Vatican archives to enumerate these misdemeanors, with all the fines and litigations, the accusations and testimonies, the interventions and bribes, the absolutions and regularizations. These came to a climax in the year 1594, when Cenci was a stout, irascible man of forty-five. Once more he was hauled before the courts on a charge of sodomy. An elaborate trial took place, and after a host of depositions by a whole parade of leering courtesans, *femmes de chambre,* grooms, scullions, saddlemakers, bootmakers and riffraff from Trastevere, Cenci finally escaped the sodomite's pyre by dint of paying the unparalleled fine of one

hundred thousand scudi, which was half of his fortune,
very nearly.

Thus it was, in order to escape still further risks and
new expenditures, as well as the fumes of notoriety, that
he set forth some months later with his wife and daughter
for La Petrella, a castle which he had leased from Marzio
Colonna, and which lay beyond the jurisdiction of the
Papal States.

These are the circumstances, in their essence, which
precede the opening of our tale.

2

Now it happened that Cenci, before departing from La
Petrella, did a singularly cruel and capricious thing.

Jealous, intemperate, perverse, full of passionate
grudges and acid grievances, he came on the notion that
during his absence the two women might escape. So he
had the windows of their chambers fastened with heavy
green blinds; the entrance to the suite was barred and
bolted and a wicket was built into the door, which the
decrepit butler Santi di Pompa unlocked each time that
he brought them food. Thus the ladies were unable to
leave their rooms at any time: they lived in darkness and
loneliness and a nightmarish boredom.

After his arrival in Rome, Cenci looked about for two
women-servants to be sent to La Petrella, since none were
to be found in the village itself. Finally he found them:
Girolama of Capranica, a garrulous widow of fifty, and
Calidonia of Siena, a lugubrious virgin of twenty-two.

Cenci lured them with promises of abundant pay and sumptuous surroundings, and three days later they were sent on muleback through the hills to La Petrella. There they were promptly locked in the mildewed rooms by Santi di Pompa, and there they stayed, sharing the solitude and squalor of the Cenci ladies.

While in Rome, Francesco avoided his usual nocturnal prowlings and managed to keep his peccadilloes within the walls of San Giacomo. He spent his days in a quagmire of elaborate legal documents: he was up to his neck in a host of lawsuits, as usual. His son Giacomo in the meantime led a merry existence in the Palazzo Cenci, with the bills rapidly mounting and the creditors lurking at the door. And out in La Petrella the months passed in misery. The rooms grew odorous like the cells of a prison, the clothes fell into tatters; summer died, autumn faded and winter was on them, and the listless melancholy of Beatrice crystallized into a hot desperation.

3

She'd sit in her small painted alcove these sunless afternoons, and she'd bring out her lute and start strumming disconsolately. One song she loved dearly; she'd learned it as a child from her nurse Camilla:

> Oh my lord rode by my window
> And his eyes were black with love,
> My lord rode under a laurel tree
> With a falcon on his glove.

[22   ]

THE MURDER

> My lord rode into the mountains
> While the sun sank in the west,
> Oh my lord lay under a sycamore
> With his lips against my breast . . .

She'd sing this little ditty over and over again and her
mind would drift through a world of fancies. She remembered the high flickering torrents and the meadows
studded with thistles, and the green-hatted huntsman who
came riding across the clover. She remembered the fragrance of roast chestnuts that crept through the lanes beside the Ghetto, and the golden mermaid that hung from
the tavern door below her window. She remembered her
early childhood on Monte Cenci, the kittens bouncing
through the courtyard, the logs ablaze in the hearth, the
firelight dancing on the Umbrian tapestries. She remembered the Neapolitan marionettes that jumped about in
the piazza — the blue-sashed bandit and the long-haired
chatelaine, the shaggy werewolf and the red-horned devil.
She remembered the songs from the convent garden and
the songs at night from the nearby inn; the songs of piety
in San Lorenzo and the songs of the fishing boys on San
Bartolomeo. And those furtive glimpses out of her window
in the middle of the night — the drunken soldiers that
came reeling, the silhouetted lovers under the archway.
She remembered how the waters danced and jetted in the
tortoise fountain, and the moss-eyed boar baring his tusks
over the drinking stable boys. She remembered the laughter of carnival and the feasting at Christmas and the line
of coaches that went winding toward the ball at the Orsini
— the masked ladies and gentlemen in great swirling dom-
inoes and the golden coats of arms on the carriage doors.

4

Ten days before Christmas, Cenci returned to La Petrella. Snow had fallen in the Abruzzi and the paths were windy and cold. He arrived at the castle in a venomous mood. He stormed up to the painted rooms, which Santi di Pompa swiftly unlocked for him, strode in noisily and flung his cloak on the floor.

"You're back," said Lucrezia emptily.

"Indeed I'm back," roared Francesco. He stamped over to the chair where Beatrice was sitting with her needlework. "Beatrice, my pet, I wish to speak with you."

"What is it?" said Beatrice coldly.

"You're happy in La Petrella?"

"Why do you ask?"

"I want an answer!"

"Not wholly," remarked Beatrice.

"Did you write to Giacomo in Rome?"

"Not that I recall," said Beatrice.

"Did you write and tell him you were miserable, and wanted to flee from the castle, and that he should come to your rescue? Did you do this, my sugar plum?"

Beatrice looked at him calmly. "Certainly not."

"You're lying," said Cenci hoarsely. He drew a letter out of his doublet and flourished it wildly in front of her face. "Do you recognize your signature, my sweet?" His thickset body quivered with rage. "This is the letter! You've been lying!" He reached for a long leather strap which hung from the wall, drew off his doublet and started lashing about hysterically. Beatrice fell from the chair, the thong struck at her face. She cried hoarsely and snatched at the strap with her hand. It shot through her fingers, ripping the skin and tearing a nail from her finger; the blood started gushing across her palm. She lay motionless on the floor while Lucrezia fluttered about aimlessly.

"There," said Cenci in a low, dull tone. Sweat was pouring from his face. He sat down on a hickory stool and stared indifferently at the women. "When I ask a question I want the truth. I want a daughter I can trust. God damn you for a treacherous little liar, Beatrice Cenci!"

He rose and lumbered wearily into the adjoining chamber. Lucrezia helped the girl into bed with a flurry of little sighs and not a word more was spoken that night in the castle.

5

Three nights later Beatrice was crossing the cloister on her way to the chapel. The seneschal Olimpio happened to cross her path at that moment. He was carrying a tiny lamb flung over his shoulders.

"Good day, signora!"

"Good day."

"There's snow on the hills!"

"Oh. Indeed?"

"You've cut your finger?"

"As you see."

Olimpio grinned; his teeth flashed. "Ah, signora, you look troubled! Nearly Christmas and still so melancholy!"

Beatrice was struck by something raw and primeval

about the castellan; the little lamb looked so terribly frail, so white and foamy as it hung from his shoulders.

She said nothing and hurried on, but as she stepped from the chapel, which faced the cloister from the east, she saw Olimpio once again.

This time he was carrying the lamb by the feet, with the head dangling limply: freshly slaughtered, the little creature, and the blood still oozing from its throat.

He smiled warily as he walked by. No words passed between them, but there was a thrust of intimacy in his jet-black eyes, a hint of something conspiratorial, as though a secret hung between them, and Beatrice's heart beat unpleasantly as she hurried up to her chamber.

I V

THE WINDS came menacing and dark from the Abruzzi.
The streams were frozen; the woods were dead. But down
in the village all the alleys were rustling with expectation.
Sprigs of fir were tied to the doors, gilded walnuts hung
in chains, the fragrance of cinnamon and nutmeg flowed
out of the pastry shop.

It was cold; bitter cold. The nymph in the fountain
wore an armor of ice, icicles dangled from the dugs of the
she-wolf in the piazza. Three nuns had climbed through
the woods from the little convent of Santa Ursula; they
stood huddled in the archway, begging for alms in steaming whispers; and the mules that came down from the
hills glistened with beads of blue ice.

In the castle kitchen a boar was gurgling away on the
spit. Old Santi di Pompa stood by the stove stirring a
sauce for the cheese pudding while the mournful Calidonia
was chopping almonds for the tarts. Olimpio, all powdered with snow, came puffing up from the woods; his
arms were loaded with sprays of fresh evergreen. He
crossed the cloister and started climbing the narrow stairs
to the ladies' chambers.

He met Beatrice halfway up and leaned against the wall to let her pass. A pine twig fell from his arms. Beatrice stumbled; she clutched at his sleeve.

"Forgive me, signora . . . You're hurt?"

"I think not," said Beatrice, recoiling.

Olimpio held her under the arm, and Beatrice caught the odor of pine, and with it the deep wintry smell of Olimpio himself.

"Signora . . ."

"Let me go, please," said Beatrice quietly.

She slid past him and hurried on toward the antechamber.

2

The curtains were drawn. The brazier hissed lazily by the bed. The scent of lavender filled the air, pallid, discreet. Cenci was lying among the cushions, sipping at a glass of hot wine.

Beatrice knocked softly at the door.

"Come in," he muttered. Beatrice entered.

"Where is Lucrezia?" she whispered.

"She's down in the chapel," said Cenci.

A dart of air shot through the pane and set the curtain rippling; an invisible finger went gliding through the folds.

Beatrice turned. "Come," said Cenci. "You look feverish, my child. Let me look at you."

Beatrice stepped closer, then paused and stared tensely at her father.

Cenci reached out and held her cold, narrow wrist between his fingers.

"Beautiful hands you've got, my dear. White as a gull's wing. Just like your mother's . . ."

His eyes were filmy with too much wine. Tiny bubbles shone on his lips. He leaned forward unsteadily; the glow from the brazier touched his face. It seemed that great red embers were smoldering under his cheeks.

"Beatrice," he whispered. "I'm a lonely, unlucky man . . ."

He drew her closer. His arm was trembling. His eyes grew feverish, dilated. Beatrice stood motionless; her face was savage with fright. The light from the brazier hung between them, trembling evasively.

She drew back wildly and swung with her hand; the wine glass fell crashing.

For several minutes father and daughter stared desolately at one another while the wine went trickling over the coverlet.

There was a timorous tap at the door: it was Calidonia, the chambermaid.

"Did you call me, signora?"

Beatrice leaned over and picked up the glass.

"No," she said. "No one called."

She brushed past Calidonia and strode into the corridor, then down the circular stairs that led to the castle kitchen.

The cook Girolama was stirring a thick red gravy.

"Mercy, signora! Have you seen a ghost? Bless your soul, sit down, my lady . . ."

3

On the following night, which was Christmas, they were singing carols down in the village, but up in the castle the three Cenci sat silently in front of the fire. The jug stood empty on the table, the bones lay bare on the platter, and soon Francesco, with his stomach heaving, started to doze in the cushioned chair.

Beatrice stepped through the hall, flung a cloak over her shoulders and tiptoed out on the terrace which lay by the northern battlements. A sheet of snow lay over the flagstones, bright and hard, like chips of glass. The smell of the night was crisp and metallic. She caught a whiff of burning pine logs coming up from the kitchen. Deep in the hills shone a small lonely light from the castle of Staffoli.

A voice purred: "Listen, signora! Do you hear them singing?"

Olimpio was standing close behind her.

"I hear no singing," said Beatrice.

"Listen again!" said Olimpio.

Beatrice cocked her head: there was only the bubbling of the wind up in the battlements.

"There it is!" whispered Olimpio.

A lonely chanting arose; faint, tremulous, uncanny — now it was lost in the woods again.

"It's the winter sprites," said Olimpio gently. "They sing at night to lonely lovers . . ."

"They'll sing no song to me, I think," said Beatrice.

The wind blew a shower of snow on their faces. Beatrice closed her eyes. Her cheeks were stinging. And all of a sudden she felt a rippling in her blood; she felt caught on a ribbon of air, leaping and diving, spinning and arrowing. She had turned into a bird; she was soaring into the night on great black wings. A violent happiness shook her.

"Signora . . . look!"

She opened her eyes. The magic burst. The night shriveled. A ray of light fell through the panes and shone bright in Olimpio's eye. His lips trembled as he looked at her. He reached forward and started to speak.

"Don't touch me," said Beatrice fiercely. There was triumph and cunning in her face as she wrapped the cloak around her tightly: she was trembling with cold.

She hurried back to the flames which played lazily in the fireplace, and crouched on the stones and ran her hand through the ears of the sleeping mastiff.

4

The omens were dark and grim after the holidays in La Petrella. Snow kept falling and the cold was bitter beyond memory in the hills. Lucrezia's mirror went crashing to the floor one miserable morning; and three days later the cat gave birth to a litter of nine dead kittens. The food came burnt to the table, the wine came sour from the casks, and the wind went cackling through the cloister like a horde of goblins.

One day the two servants Girolama and Calidonia suddenly announced that they were leaving the castle for good. Their clothes had fallen into rags and their salaries were still unpaid, and they were weary of Cenci's obscenity and malice. So they went down the hill, clutching their tatters about them, shaking their fists and hurling curses at the black, ugly castle. And in their stead another servant was hurriedly dispatched from Rome — an old Venetian named Giorgio, a gaunt and calamitous individual who made his way over the mountains and finally arrived on the feast day of Epiphany.

The days passed emptily, those wintry weeks in La Petrella. Each morning Santi di Pompa came and opened the shutters and set the glowing brazier by Lucrezia's bed. Cenci was suffering from gout and sat in his pillows till midmorning, and the dour-faced Giorgio would appear to fetch the coins for the day's marketing. When Cenci finally rose they all descended to the castle chapel, where Mass was said by Don Marzio, who was the archpriest of La Petrella. If the weather was clear Cenci would mount his black mare and ride into the hills with Olimpio; if there was rain he sat by the fire, thumbing through sheaves of legal documents. After luncheon he took a nap. After his nap he went for a stroll. After his stroll he would poke about in the recesses of the castle, peering at the wine casks, fingering the cheeses, sniffing the sausages, fondling the silver; and then came dinner, which was usually served in Lucrezia's chamber, in front of the fire. Then he was ready to retire. This was a sordid procedure: the ladies tugged at his riding boots and then Lucrezia drew off his hose and stockings, and Cenci would lie on the bed while Beatrice, tight-lipped with disgust, would scrape his thighs with a linen towel, for Cenci suffered from the "itch." His body was covered with sores and rashes from the waist to the ankles — some sort of eczema, or maybe an illness picked up in the stables of Trastevere. The closestool was set in front of the fire and here Francesco relieved himself, naked and gross and shameless in front of the ladies. Then he rolled into bed; the shutters were closed; the bed curtains were drawn; the screen was set in front of the embers. The bolt was dropped and all was still when Beatrice took up her candle and stole back to her room, which looked over the starlit cliffs.

V

CARNIVAL CAME: a cool crackling day, sharp as a diamond. All day long they were hanging the garlands from the doors and archways, and when night came the village fiddlers gathered in the piazza and the dancing began.

Beatrice, standing on the balcony, could hear the music down in the village. She listened awhile; then suddenly she flung a shawl over her head and took her cloak and crept down through the empty cloister. Out she slipped through the castle gate, which Giorgio had forgotten to lock that night. She climbed down the path from the castle and made her way to the edge of the piazza, and there she stood in a narrow alley and stared at the wild-eyed merriment.

The peasants were dancing and singing under a row of lanterns — broad-hipped girls and tousled plowboys kicking their heels in the air. Nearby, Marzio the tinker was strumming away on his lute. All wore masks — trolls and dragons, galloping fiends with twisted horns, a mincing stag with gilded antlers, a muttering boar with blood-stained tusks. One young fellow beat on a kettledrum while the rest clapped their hands, and the village cobbler, all in red, turned great cartwheels in front of the fountain.

"Bravo, Baldassare!" cried the ragamuffins, standing around in a circle.

A row of stalls was set by the walls of the church — taffy and nougat were for sale here, and long pink sausages, dripping with oil. Under the arch the old puppet-master set his Punchinello leaping. Dorotea, the fishmonger's wife, was ladling the cider.

Beatrice stood motionless in the shade of the alley with the shawl over her cheeks; only her eyes could be seen — dangerous black eyes, like a gipsy's.

The boys clapped their hands; the music grew quicker. The dancers broke into a loud tarantella.

Beatrice turned and walked back up the path toward the castle.

2

A great shape stepped out of the cloister — it was Olimpio the seneschal.

"Signora!" he whispered.

Beatrice halted beside the gate.

"What are you doing?" said Olimpio softly.

"Nothing," she said, "that need concern you."

"You've been in the village watching the carnival?"

She shook her head. "I need no carnivals."

"I saw you," muttered Olimpio. "Down in the shadows, signora!"

"Very well. You saw what you saw. Good night," said Beatrice viciously.

"Wait. Signora!" said Olimpio.

She turned her vast brooding eyes on him.

"Please, signora," gasped the seneschal.

Her voice grew gentle: "What do you want?"

"Only to help you, signora."

"Help me? How?"

"However you say!"

She placed her fingers on his hand; the flesh was hot, like a hand in fever. A sickening dizziness, bordering on nausea, took hold of Beatrice.

"Wait," she said in a thin, dry voice.

"Why?" said Olimpio, half desperate.

"Give me time. I must think . . ."

"Why? Why?" said Olimpio, shivering.

She turned quietly and crossed the court and made her way to the winding stairway.

When she reached her room she sank on the bed, with the shawl wound sharply around her neck. She lay absolutely motionless; her eyes were closed tight. Finally she rose and stepped into the adjoining room, which was the antechamber to Lucrezia's bedroom.

A double door opened on the long wooden balcony. Under the balcony lay a rank and inaccessible thicket, which rose toward the castle prison and was surrounded by high gray walls. Beatrice stepped out; a gust of wind came out of the west. It tore at her shawl, which shot loose and went fluttering through the air. It looked like an enormous bat as it loped into the night — she could see it circling and swirling toward the thicket below.

"There," she thought. "Now it's lost."

She looked for a while at the stars, which seemed unnaturally near that night: blue-hot embers from an invisible fire.

[36]

She reached out with both hands, feeling the night drift through her fingers.

She felt dizzy quite suddenly. The darkness below seemed to suck at her, to draw her down like a magnet toward the dull black pit of the elder thicket. She clutched at the balcony railing, which trembled under her grip. A sharp tingle slid through her, cold as an icicle.

How easy it would be! Simply to glide into the darkness, to vanish away forever in the gulf of the night. She felt no fear of the woods, of the windy gloom. She had something in common with the wilderness, the stunted trees, the arid cliffs. Her blood-beat echoed to the hissing gullies where nothing was alive except the birds in their passage and the wild boars roaming among the oaks.

The wind grew violent — she touched her cheeks and they felt like porcelain, smooth and rigid. She closed the door again stealthily and tiptoed back to her room. The candle was guttering; long-legged shadows danced on the ceiling. She stood for a while in front of the mirror, staring back into her eyes. Sly and impenetrable, birdlike: like the eyes of a bride. With a brooding curiosity she drew off her garments, one by one. For a moment she stood naked, china-smooth in the shuddering candlelight. She drew the night robe over her arms, dipped her wrists in the ewer, drew them slowly over her brow, and slipped through the curtains into her bed.

3

The next day, toward midmorning, Cenci strolled out on the balcony to have a look at the clouds that were gathering in the north.

He stepped back into the room, walked toward the fire and called to Beatrice.

"Yes?" said Beatrice. "What is it?"

"What's this thing I see in the thicket?"

"Which thing?"

"Like a shawl, my cuckoo."

"I've no idea what you mean."

"Go and look, Beatricciola. There's a thing down in the elder bushes."

Beatrice stepped warily across the room and out on the balcony.

"Do you see it?" called Cenci.

"Yes," said Beatrice. "I see it."

"Would it be that lovely shawl that I brought you from Pisa?"

"I can't tell," said Beatrice heavily.

"You're lying, my dear," purred Cenci. "It's your shawl, and you know it. How did it get there, do you suppose?"

"Well, a wind might have blown it."

"Come here, Beatrice. A bit closer. Here by the fire. Stand still, please."

He swung out with his hand and slapped her violently on the cheek.

"Now you'll remember, my fine young lady, that it's better not to lie to me. Go. Tell Giorgio to reach down

from the prison with a fishhook and fetch the shawl. And
see to it, please, that no wind blows it down again, and
that no daughter of mine tells ridiculous lies again."

Drops of sweat hung from his temples. But his fury was
spent; he smiled benignly and sat down by the fire with
his thumb-worn documents.

4

And Beatrice, with her cheek still throbbing, walked
aimlessly through the cloister. It was a dark, treacherous
day with the clouds green and ugly. She paused by the
gate; she thought of begging old Giorgio to unlock the
doors. There was a ring on her finger, a braid of gold
with a pointed diamond: she thought for a moment of
bribing Giorgio to fetch a horse from the village.

A voice called softly: "Olimpio!"

Plautilla was leaning from a window, calling for her
husband. A door slammed shut and Olimpio appeared,
carrying a freshly cleaned saddle and a great black bucket
in his dripping hands. Beatrice passed him with lowered
eyes; but instead of entering the door to the stairway, she
went on and entered the dark stony tunnel that ran under
the kitchen. This tunnel lay on the way to the castle
prison, which looked down on the thicket below the balcony. She opened a creaking door and found herself in
the wine cellar. She forgot why she had come but her
breath came tense and urgent; she leaned against the
wall and stared through the shadows, cold with panic.

A small oil lamp hung from the wall, dim and dusty

with years. It shed a velvety light on the row of casks with their shining spigots, the black stains of wine, the little clouds of old cobweb. The scent of wine-soaked mortar and antique dust filled the place.

She leaned down and dipped her finger in a pool of wine. She tasted it gingerly: a queer mineral tang. Then she drew her finger along a wall, through a silky wisp of cobweb. The spider dangled in mid-air. It shone like a tiny ruby.

The door squeaked as it opened. It was Olimpio who spoke first.

"Signora. Let me help you . . ."

Beatrice glanced at him casually.

He stepped up and took her hand, which was trembling with excitement. She could hear the pulse of his breath whistling curiously in his throat.

"What will you do for me?" said Beatrice.

"I've said already, signora: anything."

"You swear?"

"Yes," he panted.

Now she knew it must happen: it hung in the air, ready to burst. She closed her eyes. She felt the breath from Olimpio's mouth on her cheek, and then the wiry tangle of his beard brushed her neck. The fumes from the great wine barrels closed in like a drug. Olimpio kept whispering but she hardly listened. Suddenly he picked her up lightly and carried her to a heap of empty sacks, and there he laid her on the ground beside him.

"They'll know!" whispered Beatrice.

"No," said Olimpio. "No one will know." And he kissed her under the chin while his hands went rippling over her. He plucked clumsily at the strings and buttons, and

[40]

then suddenly she lay back and drew him on her and said hoarsely: "Do you love me, Olimpio?"

"I love you," chanted Olimpio, "my blood of my heart, my lovely darling . . ."

They lay motionless for a little while: until desire grew sharp and torturing, and when she opened her eyes for a moment she saw him kneeling astride her, his shirt flung wide open, his jerkin loosened, and the whole dark mass of his body struck her as bestial and horrible; a shape in a nightmare. She closed her eyes instantly and all the power flowed out of her body; she felt him penetrate her gently and suddenly she cried: "Stop! I'll bleed!" But he whispered, "Lie still, Beatrice," and then nothing more mattered: a great sea of indolence heaved around her on all sides and neither pain, pride nor terror survived in this sea. Time passed. She heard the drops clicking rhythmically from a spigot. The smell of wine, the scent of burlap, the pungent scent of Olimpio — they wove a dark separate world, safe, secret, profound.

When she opened her eyes again the light shone soft on the copper hoops; the gray cobwebs hung in the crannies like small ghostly handkerchiefs. She turned her head and saw Olimpio kneeling on the floor beside her, his arms wet and quivering, pressing his face in the palm of her hand.

VI

Spring crept up from the valleys of Campania and Basili-
cata and the hills changed from a dull, furry blue to a
budding emerald. The rains sent ribbons of foam-flecked
water through the gullies: a cloud of leaves, frail as thistledown, hung floating among the boughs. Tulips and
daffodils started to bloom in the village flowerpots and out
in the woods, in the mossy shade, gleamed the lilies of
the valley.

But in the castle the days grew more and more shadowy.
Clouds hung churning over the mountains like dust from
a stampede. Beatrice's mornings passed empty, aimless and
somnolent. Only at dusk for a moment the sun pierced the
clouds and a rush of light shot through the valley, like a
torrent of gold. Rocks and trees came to life, grave, startled,
like a dawning dream. The distant shepherds turned their
heads, the blackbirds circled over the crags, and a far-off
voice, low and loving, stabbed her heart like an ice-cold
needle.

Then the daylight vanished and a dusky awe took hold
of her. The shadows closed in like the walls of a lair. Night
came, and with it a kind of nightmare lunacy. Life lost its

balance and shape. Monstrous forms rose from the horizon — shaggy snakes, blood-eyed bulls: she was paralyzed with terror. She felt her strength seep away from her, and a sudden frenzy took hold of her; she crept down the stairs with her shawl over her head and crouched motionless among the wine casks, listening for Olimpio's footsteps . . .

2

One warm day Olimpio went sauntering down to the village piazza and saw the tinker Marzio Catalano sitting in the shade of a chestnut tree.

"Good morning, Marzio," he said.

"Good morning," said the tinker, plucking at his lute.

"Everything's well with you these days?"

"Well, the sun is out," said Marzio plaintively. "But my larder's empty, my clothes are worn and I need new heels on my boots."

Olimpio lowered his voice: "I have something to say to you, Marzio."

"Yes? What?"

"Listen, Marzio. I've heard you're friendly with certain bandits."

"Bless my soul! Which bandits?"

"The bandits in Marcatelli."

"Well," said Marzio, scratching his chin, "I know Lattantio, with the broken nose, and I know Scarapicchia, who hails from my home town, Ascrea."

The tinker Marzio felt no shyness at revealing these intimacies: he knew quite well that Olimpio himself some years back had dabbled in banditry, and had been a friend of the notorious Caccia, who was later beheaded.

"Look," said Olimpio, "I have an idea for you. And if you ever breathe a word of this, I'll beat out your brains with an ax. So listen carefully, my good fellow."

"I'm listening," said Marzio. He was a tall, sad-eyed man, weak-chinned and hollow-cheeked, with a high, melodious voice.

"It's about Signor Francesco Cenci. He's treated you badly, Marzio, hasn't he?"

"Oh, not really," said Marzio cautiously. "Once he struck me. But that's long since."

"If you'd care for a bit of silver, my dear Marzio," said the seneschal softly, placing his hand on the tinker's shoulder, "you'll do what I tell you. You'll go and speak to Scarapicchia, do you understand? And he'll give the appropriate orders to his band of cronies. And they'll pay a little visit to Vallecupola one fine day and there they'll wait in the bushes until Signor Francesco comes riding along. And then they'll seize him, bag and baggage, and carry him off to the hills."

Marzio picked at his nostrils. "How will they know when he'll come riding?"

"That's a thing I'll handle myself," said Olimpio affably. "Let me continue. When this bandit Scarapicchia has seized Signor Francesco, he'll demand a clear ransom of five thousand scudi, which the ladies of the castle will hasten to send him. This ransom you and I will share with the bandits . . . What do you think of it?"

"And what do we do with Signor Francesco, after the ransom is paid?"

"After it's paid," said Olimpio with a wink, "we'll leave

our friend Scarapicchia to dispose of Signor Francesco
in the usual manner."

"Ah," said Marzio, frowning slightly. "It's ugly work,
Olimpio. Isn't it?"

"Not more than plenty of other things," said Olimpio.
"Signor Francesco's an ugly fellow."

"It's a risky business, I think, Olimpio."

"No riskier than any good day's earning!"

"And clumsy too, if you ask me."

"Not if we handle it cleverly!"

Marzio stared at the sky and scratched his left ear, and
the men strolled into the tavern for a glass of wine.

3

The following day the tinker Marzio came to the castle
after sunset and waited below the battlements for a signal
from one of the walls.

Soon Beatrice appeared on the terrace; she leaned over
and beckoned to Marzio, who came closer discreetly and
stood in the niche of one of the buttresses.

She said softly: "Olimpio's been chatting with you?"

"Yes, signora. He mentioned a matter."

"Listen, Marzio," said Beatrice rapidly, and her eyes
grew thin and birdlike; "listen and I'll waste no words
with you. I'm weary of living in this miserable manner.
If you're sensible, Marzio, you'll do as I say. I have some
silver here in the castle, one large ewer and three candlesticks, as well as some fine Tuscan linen and three lovely
golden rings. They'll all be yours to share with Olimpio,
if you do what I tell you."

[45   ]

"I'll do it," said Marzio faintly.

"Then speak with the bandits."

Marzio nodded his head obediently.

"You swear it?"

"I do, signora."

"Then God speed you," said Beatrice, and she hurried across the terrace and Marzio went back to the tavern by the piazza.

4

Things were easier said than done, however, especially for a wayward-minded tinker, and Marzio allowed the days to go by. First a week, then a fortnight, and finally a month. Marzio was timorous by nature, and he saw the utter ineptitude in these projects, and he put off his visit to the camp of the bandits.

One day he finally set out. He borrowed a mule from the apothecary and followed the lonely mule paths through the cliffs of the Cicolano. Late that evening he arrived near the caves of Marcatelli. He rode hither and thither, calling. No sign of life. Not a murmur. Charred stones and broken boughs and bits of refuse, but no bandits.

So he scratched at his armpits and sat down on a hollow tree trunk; then he reached into his pocket and drew out a coal-black sausage. The light of the sun rose from the cliffs like darts of flame from a caldron, and the elder trees hung floating like a cloud of smoke, coppery bright.

An old man in a tasseled cap came limping by with a bundle of twigs.

He called to the tinker:

"Are you looking for Scarapicchia, by any chance?"

"I am," said Marzio bluntly. "Has he gone from these hills?"

"Indeed he has," said the wrinkled woodsman, fondling Marzio's little mule. "His men left here three weeks ago and they headed for the south, and they carried everything with them, because of a thing that's been happening."

"What thing?" muttered Marzio, nibbling glumly at his sausage.

"Well, I'll tell you," said the woodsman. "They've sent a fellow up from Naples to clean out the hills and get rid of the bandits, and that's the truth, whether you like it or not. His name is Captain de Sanctis and his soldiers have come to Cittaducale, and when our jolly Scarapicchia got wind of this business he packed all his hampers, and I'll tell you this, my friend, he's far in the south and he won't be back again!"

Marzio shrugged his shoulders and spat out the pepper seed. Then he mounted his mule and started wearily down the mule path. Dusk fell and he spent the night in an empty wood hut, and the following day he rode back to his house in La Petrella, where the wistaria was already beginning to bloom on the balcony.

5

That was the end of Beatrice's plan with regard to the bandits. Soon she came on a second, more plausible scheme; but one day a distressing bit of news reached the castle.

A letter arrived from Prince Colonna, ordering the seneschal to shift his lodgings. Olimpio was requested to leave the castle at La Petrella without delay and move down with his wife to the baronial house at the edge of the village, which likewise was a property of the family of Colonna.

Olimpio sensed instantly, and not inaccurately, that this letter had been written at the instigation of Francesco Cenci, who suddenly desired, either from pique or some vague sort of inkling, to see the big seneschal thrown out of the castle.

So this was done; but before it was done Olimpio met Beatrice in the wine cellar, from which a stairway skirted the kitchen toward the terrace which adjoined her room.

"Beatrice, sweet," whispered the seneschal. "I have orders to quit the castle."

"I know," said Beatrice quietly, opening the door to her bedchamber.

"I'm leaving tomorrow with Plautilla."

"Yes," said Beatrice, folding her hands.

"But I'll come and see you nonetheless," said Olimpio, stuttering with anger. "Listen, my darling. Every night I'll come and see you in this castle . . ."

And he told her how that very evening he had taken a long wooden ladder and hidden it in the grass outside the walls of the thicket, and had hidden another ladder in the thicket itself, directly beneath the window of the prison, and had pried open the bars of the window with a chisel, so that he could climb from the rock outside into the castle at night and make his way through the wine cellar up to the terrace by Beatrice's chamber.

Beatrice listened attentively.

"I see," she said.

"What do you think of it?"

"I'm not sure," she said calmly.

"Not sure!" growled Olimpio.

"It's dangerous, this thing of the ladders."

"Dangerous — of course it is! What of it?"

The orange glow from the little oil lamp shone on Beatrice's face, which grew luminously transparent, like a parchment mask, as though some secret inner face were shining through, desperate, terrified.

"Olimpio. I have something to tell you."

"Yes, my swan."

"Something that concerns you."

"Well, what is it?"

"A tiresome thing."

"Come. Tell me."

"I'm with child."

Olimpio grew thoughtful; he plucked at his ear lobe. In moments of meditation such as this, Olimpio's face grew gross and heavy. The eyes grew foxy, clandestine; the lips sagged unpleasantly.

But an instant later he smiled and a sudden radiance flowed through him. His eyes shone with a pleading, cherublike sweetness.

"Well," he said, "there it is. Worse things might have happened."

Beatrice's eyes gleamed like needles. "Worse indeed, I dare say, but I'm at the end of my patience, Olimpio. You swear to help and do nothing. I'm weary of all this shilly-shallying."

Olimpio kissed her on the neck. "Don't fret, my swallow. I swore what I swore."

"Now look," said Beatrice. "You'll do what you promised, and you'll do it before it's too late. If my father should wander along one fine day and see me sitting there, all pale and swollen, he'd kill me for it!"

"You exaggerate, my pet."

"And he'd kill you too . . ."

"Well, I'll think about it."

"No need to think," said Beatrice flashing. "There's no time to be wasted. Go to Rome. Speak to my brother Giacomo. He'll gladly help in this little plan, if I know his real feelings. Ask him to give his approval and make himself useful. Go and do this, Olimpio, and stop hemming and hawing."

Olimpio glanced at her sharply: "Tell me, Beatrice. What's the truth of this?"

"What do you mean?"

"This hatred of yours."

Beatrice darkened. "Is there anything odd in it?"

"He's your father. Remember that."

"I do," said Beatrice.

Olimpio looked at her dully. "There's something, I think, that you haven't told me."

Beatrice's voice grew ominously gentle: "Will you do it, Olimpio, or will you not?"

"Oh, I'll do it," groaned Olimpio. "Don't worry, my hummingbird."

He closed his eyes and laid his shaggy black head on her lap.

6

She drew her fingers dreamily across his forehead. The skin felt glossy and vibrant, like the hide of a stallion. The eyes seemed to twitch uneasily under their lids: glittering and centaurlike when awake but now masklike in sleep, curiously marine, as though dimmed by the depths of the sea. The lashes lay long on his cheeks, damp and wistful; the centaur had turned into a slumbering Triton.

Suddenly he awoke and whispered hoarsely:

"You're returning to Rome? When it's all over?"

"Yes," said Beatrice absently. "I'll go back to Rome."

"You'll take me with you, my darling?"

"Yes," said Beatrice. "I'll take you with me."

"There'll be gossip . . ."

"No matter."

"And Plautilla?"

"She'll come later . . ."

His eyes gleamed, he smiled drowsily, and a moment later he was asleep again.

A heavy fog, blue and clinging, seemed to ooze out of the walls. It crept like a film between herself and the man beside her, chilling the flesh, blurring the contours. She knelt on the edge of the bed and stared down at his face. He was sleeping like a child. His naked chest rose and fell. She could hear the hiss of his breath; she caught the musk of his skin, like rock moss. Her eyes wandered along his body — the heavy lips half parted, the powerful tendons in his throat, the tufts of hair, black and curly, between his nipples and mighty loins . . .

And all around this chasm of silence! The twinge of tenderness in her body dissolved, like a whisper, in the limitless folds of stillness. Not a sound; not a breath of air. A single star shone through the window. It peered down at her with a burning intimacy, like a green, savage eye. It seemed to beckon to her suddenly, like a light at the end of a tunnel, a ray of hope piercing the cold black abyss of her life.

VII

SOME DAYS later the seneschal informed his wife Plautilla
that he was off on a four days' journey to a manor of Prince
Colonna's, near Viterbo, to bring some bolts of fresh silk
to the ladies who lived there. And then he mounted his
horse and rode off into the hills.

The day was hot and a pinkish haze floated over the
valleys. The streams were dry, the dust sizzled and steamed
under the hoofs. White butterflies went skipping over
the glades like drifting pear blossoms, and a tiny snake,
ruby-red, wriggled across the path near Monteleone.

Olimpio stopped by a spring and sucked at the cool clear
water. A shepherd came strolling through the trees and
knelt beside him in the moss.

"It's hot, isn't it?" he muttered.

Olimpio nodded. "Yes, it is."

"There'll be a storm soon, I think."

"There might be," said Olimpio.

"Let me tell you something," whispered the shepherd.
"I saw three shooting stars last night. All in a row, right
to the east. Do you know what it means?"

"No," said Olimpio. "I don't."

"Death," said the shepherd. "That's what it means. Bloody death. There's no question about it."

Olimpio smiled grimly and wiped the drops from his chin.

"Death by violence," hissed the shepherd. "Wait and see: there'll be murder in the hills. Three shooting stars foretell a killing, and so it's always been, and so it is this time, and it's the truth of the Lord Himself that I'm telling you!"

The shepherd dipped his face in the spring, called his dog and went off again, and Olimpio mounted his horse and rode on to Monteleone.

2

He arrived at the Palazzo Cenci the following evening. He was led up to the loggia, where Signor Giacomo sat at a table, playing a game of cards with the boys Bernardo and Paolo. Olimpio laid his hat on the stool and introduced himself to Giacomo.

"Yes. I've heard about you," said Giacomo, with a curious look at the seneschal.

"Favorably, I hope."

"Excellently."

"I'll say the same," said Olimpio, bowing. "A man of wit, style, subtlety — that's how your sister has always spoken of you."

"You've come for a visit?" clucked Giacomo.

"Two short days," said Olimpio.

"Well, then," said Giacomo, scenting the approximate

point of the occasion, "you'll stay for dinner, I trust. Come, join us at cards for a while, and then we'll gossip a bit in the loggia."

The night was hot and the airs of the street crept in through the windows: the fish sizzling in the *osteria,* the whiff of dung from the nearby stables, the strange pungency of the warm, loud, sensual Roman populace. It was good, Olimpio thought, to hear the clatter of carriages again, and all the rush and flurry of the marvelous city. He sank back in the enormous chair; he felt mellow, astute.

"Well?" said Giacomo, filling his glass and lighting the candle beside them. The servants had left them, only the boy Bernardo stayed on. The forks and knives lay scattered about, the silver plates were pushed aside, and Olimpio was sucking at a large nectarine. "You've brought news from my sister?"

"I have," said Olimpio.

"She's well, I hope?"

"Not altogether," said Olimpio. He placed his elbows on the table and stared meaningly at Giacomo. "She wants your aid and approval in a rather delicate venture, Signor Giacomo."

"Indeed," said Giacomo, with furtive eyes. "I am deeply fond of Beatrice."

"And she of you," declared Olimpio. "And for that reason she feels that you'll probably see eye to eye with her in this enterprise."

The cool airs from the Tiber flowed up through the loggia. Olimpio gazed at the walls, which were decorated with frescoes: views of cities for the most part, Naples and Florence and Siena, with all the palaces and churches carefully etched in black and gold. Nymphs and satyrs, tipped by the candlelight, disported themselves in the upper corners.

A dreamy smile played in the curves of Olimpio's great lips. He raised the glass, held it poised, and stared probingly at Giacomo.

"Your sister, the Signora Beatrice," he said, "is a most unhappy woman."

"Ah," sighed Giacomo. "Poor Beatrice. Poor little creature."

"Her life is miserable beyond all reason. She spends her days sobbing and praying. She longs to escape to a nunnery." Olimpio paused significantly. "She has even toyed, I regret to say, with the thought of flinging herself from the battlements. She is close, very close indeed, Signor Giacomo, to desperation."

"I'm sorry to hear it," murmured Giacomo.

"And I'll tell you this, Signor Giacomo. There's one person and only one who's behind all this misery."

"There is nothing," lamented Giacomo, "that I wouldn't do to help poor Beatrice."

"Well," said Olimpio, licking his lips, "your sister Beatrice has a plan."

"I'm glad to hear it," said Giacomo, with an earnest expression.

"She needs your fine judicious hand, however," averred Olimpio, "for the execution of it."

"Quite," said Giacomo, running his finger around the edge of his glass.

"She tried one thing before," remarked Olimpio, "but it failed to materialize."

"What was that?" inquired Giacomo.

Olimpio pursed his lips. "Bandits."

Giacomo looked into his glass and meditated a little. He was a lean, bony fellow with a cast in one eye; handsome in a fashion, with deep-set eyes and a certain elegance of profile. But somehow weak, a bit shifty; not a man to inspire confidence.

Olimpio saw this quite clearly and proceeded accordingly.

"Signor Giacomo, please forgive me but let us come to the point. Your sister Beatrice has sent the message which I'm bringing you now. Will you participate in this matter, which is advantageous to both of you, or will you not? She wishes the courtesy of an unequivocal answer."

Giacomo lifted his luminous, poetic eyes. "I will. Naturally."

"Good," said Olimpio. "Have you any suggestions?"

"Have you thought of poison?" murmured Giacomo.

Olimpio's face relaxed pleasantly. "Well, now, I'm glad we've come to the core of it. Poison, you say? To tell the truth, I'm not sure the signora hasn't thought of it. But you know how it is in these tiny villages; one can't obtain the rarer specialties."

"It doesn't surprise me," said Giacomo. "Still, don't let it disturb you. I don't doubt that I can make some discreet little purchase . . ."

The boy Bernardo was listening silently all the while. And the two older men, who by instinct despised one another, filled their glasses and clicked them lightly and smiled tenderly across the table.

3

Three nights later Olimpio made his way into the castle by means of his ladders; he trod cautiously through the empty prison, crossed the cellars and passed through the cloister, climbed to the terrace and slid noiselessly into Beatrice's room.

The sirocco was blowing, hot and humid, and he threw his clothes off impatiently. He hurled himself on his lady like a man athirst in a desert; his lips moved ravenously across her body, sipping the savor from her skin.

"Well?" said Beatrice, after a while. "What did Giacomo have to say?"

Olimpio reached for his jerkin and drew out two little objects which he held under the moonlight: a thick yellow-ish pellet and another thing, like a tiny carrot.

"And what are these?" said Beatrice coldly.

"The pellet is opium," said Olimpio. "Dissolve it in wine, the chemist told me, and it leaves the drinker sense-less."

"And this other thing?" said Beatrice.

"Most effective," said Olimpio, beaming. "Grind it carefully and powder his meat with it. It was quite ex-pensive, said Signor Giacomo. It came all the way from Tartary in a caravan of camels."

Beatrice's voice was hard and dull. "Wasted money. And utter folly."

"Why? What's wrong?" growled Olimpio.

"Listen, my love. I've told you before. Such a mood of suspicion has come over the man, he sees conspiracies in the very air. And what's more, he is obsessed with a fear of poison. I test his food for him daily — right at the table, in front of his eyes. This notion of poisoning, I tell you, is quite grotesque, my sweet fellow."

Olimpio was mournful: "It was a most ingenious scheme, said Signor Giacomo."

"Giacomo is a dreamer," said Beatrice. "Giacomo's head is in the clouds."

"Well, at any rate," said Olimpio, "he has given his blessing in the matter."

"Precisely," said Beatrice. "And now it's you who'll finish the thing." She tugged gently at his ear lobe. "Do you hear me, my bully?"

"Yes, I hear you, my dear," said Olimpio wearily.

And then Beatrice, running her fingers through his hair, sketched out her scheme for him. Bandits and venom had proved impractical: one thing was left and that was violence. In cool and tender, deliberate tones the naked girl who lay beside him told Olimpio precisely when and in what manner he was to do this deed: namely, the murder of her father, the Roman nobleman Francesco Cenci.

VIII

ONE SIMMERING NIGHT — it was the sixth of September, to be exact — Francesco Cenci retired in an irritable mood. Things went badly in the castle: Santi di Pompa had left without notice; the girl from the village had fallen sick; new servants from Rome had failed to arrive. Only old Giorgio, glum and cadaverous, still lived in his room by the castle gate.

And then, aside from these matters, Cenci felt curiously wretched. Age was swiftly creeping over him; his gout grew worse daily. The itch on his legs was spreading like gangrene. And now the south wind had come again and the air was damp and sickly. A violent depression, almost suicidal in its force, was taking hold of him.

He left his papers beside the window, peered into the hot, uneasy night, then drew off his clothes and lay down on the bed.

But he left the candle burning: the thought of the dark filled him with horror — that great quagmire of faceless and half-remembered phantoms.

Finally he turned and whispered to his wife who lay beside him:

"Go fetch Beatrice . . ."

Lucrezia rose and returned with the girl, who looked pallid and breathless.

"Rub my legs, Beatricciola."

So Beatrice took the towel from the hook and sat at the foot of the bed and started to scrape Cenci's thighs. Her hair hung over her forehead and her face was cold and hard; but Cenci saw that a strange alertness had come to life in Beatrice's eyes.

"Are you well, Beatricciola?"

"Why do you ask?"

"You look pale."

"I'm always pale."

"You're panting."

"It's the sirocco," said Beatrice.

Cenci looked at her craftily. "Is that all? Are you sure? I shouldn't like it, my dear, if any scandal should come to you."

Beatrice glanced over the bed. Her eyes caught Lucrezia's. A tiny gleam passed between them; she lowered her eyes quickly.

"No danger of that," said Lucrezia daintily. "The girl's thoughts are on the nunnery."

Cenci chuckled. "Oh really? Is it true, my kitten?"

Beatrice glanced at him calmly. "Why shouldn't it be true?"

"The nunnery! For a pretty girl like you?"

"I wish I were neither a girl nor pretty!"

Cenci gazed at his daughter with a quick, sly tenderness. "You love me a little, don't you, puss?"

"Yes, of course," said Beatrice slowly.

"There's a lot I've done for you, dear."

"Yes. I know there is, Father."

"Life's a miserable farce," he whimpered. "I keep trying to help people. I give money left and right. And what do I get? Lies and slander. Plots, conspiracies, lawsuits . . . It's a nasty world, I'm telling you."

"Yes. I know it is, Father."

"Beatrice," said Cenci. "Tell me something. What do you think of Olimpio?"

"You mean the seneschal?" said Beatrice carelessly. "I've hardly thought of him, Father."

"He's a handsome fellow," said Cenci.

"Is he?" said Beatrice. "I hadn't noticed."

"I've seen his eye when he looks at you. It's a hot greedy eye!"

"Indeed?" said Beatrice blandly. She drew the towel across his ankles.

"And that, my mouse," remarked Cenci, "is why I've sent him down to the village. I'll have no seneschal scheming about to lay his paws on my daughter. You understand what I'm saying? Look, Beatricciola — if I ever find you've favored the scoundrel, I'll rip open your throat with my own unlucky hands!"

His eyes sparkled. He looked at his daughter with a delicate mockery. There he lay, with the light shining faint on his face, deepening the sour blue lines, tipping the puffy little pouches, glazing the delicate long nose, deadening the gluttonous lips. His eyes rolled under their lids and peeped wearily at the ceiling. And the mockery gave way to a kind of impenetrable desperation, something like panic at this gathering flood of decay. But then that too faded. He closed his eyes and sighed a little, and all that was left was a dreadful loneliness.

Finally Beatrice folded the towel. "Good night, Father," she whispered. She leaned over and kissed him lightly on the temple.

"Good night, my child," said Cenci; and he rolled on his side with a little moan.

2

Beatrice sat in her room by candlelight, drawing the thread through the needle. The warm light floated in the room like a cloud of vapor, brightening the silver bowl and the glass decanter, doubling its flame in the laureled mirror.

The door opened; it was Lucrezia, with a shawl of silk over her head.

The girl raised her eyes.

"Am I bothering you, dear?"

"Not at all," said Beatrice.

Lucrezia peeped over her shoulders at the petit point: it was an elaborate chair cover. A fluttering cupid, with his bow and arrow, amidst a wilderness of butterflies.

"Lovely," said Lucrezia. "You'll be finished in a week."

"Or less, even," said Beatrice.

There was a stealthy little pause while Beatrice plucked at the needle.

"Listen, Beatrice."

"I am listening."

Lucrezia leaned down and whispered: "Beatrice, think of what I'm saying. We've suffered, both of us, and bitterly. We have a right to a bit of happiness. But I tell you, my child . . ."

"Yes?" said Beatrice.

"There are things more important than happiness!"

"What are they?" said Beatrice.

"An easy conscience," said Lucrezia.

"Well," said Beatrice witheringly, "go and keep your easy conscience."

"And patience," said Lucrezia tensely.

Beatrice laughed. "Till the hair grows gray?"

Lucrezia pressed her hands together. "No," she pleaded. "It isn't that. We must see this thing clearly. Beatrice, I tell you, I'm terrified!"

"Wait till it's done," said Beatrice idly. "You'll feel no terror when it's done."

"It's all this waiting," said Lucrezia hoarsely. "It's like standing on the edge of a cliff — day after day of suspense . . . I haven't slept for three nights!"

"I can't help it," said Beatrice.

She drew the needle through the cloth, biting her lower lip gently. Lucrezia kept watching with her small, gliding eyes. She plucked at a wart which clung to her cheek like a small, withered huckleberry.

"Beatrice, I warn you. Don't do it."

Beatrice drew the thread languidly.

"Or if you insist, against my advice . . ."

Beatrice's eyes grew bright and fierce. "Lucrezia, stop playing a role, please. I know exactly how you feel."

"Very well," said Lucrezia with a filmy look. "Do as you wish."

"I shall," said Beatrice, lowering her head over her needlework.

Lucrezia stood and looked at the girl with a mesmerized expression; liquid eyes, sagging chin, head lolling on the soft, fat shoulders. She sighed, then nodded faintly and went shuffling back to the antechamber.

3

The moon was nearly full: a great silver melon. The leaves hung damp and leaden in the icy light. The village was fast asleep, not a light was burning, and no one saw the two men who met beside the great trough and stood whispering in the shade of the castle tower.

Finally they came to the high gray wall that surrounded the thicket.

"Is this the spot?" whispered the tinker.

Olimpio didn't answer. He groped busily among the bushes and drew out a ladder of hickory wood and leaned it against the wall. He climbed first and then Marzio; they stood astride the thick wall and then they drew up the ladder and dropped it carefully on the other side.

Now they stood in the thicket. Rank weeds came up to their waist. The ground was peppered with rabbit holes and they had to step cautiously. An ugly stench rose from the heap of refuse under the balcony, which hung forty feet above them, like a little cage.

Olimpio followed the thicket wall until he came to the wall of the castle. He ran his hand along the stone; it was still warm with the long day's sun. He glanced up quickly, then knelt by an elder bush and drew out the second ladder, which was of pine wood and considerably longer than the first. This he leaned against the wall: it reached within a foot of the prison window.

He glanced quizzically at the tinker. "I'll go first," he said gruffly.

He started climbing. The ladder quivered and squeaked under his weight. Finally he came to the top and Marzio saw his body poised on the edge of the window, twisting laboriously through the opening, then vanishing in the gloom of the prison.

Some minutes passed; Marzio waited; Olimpio's face peered from the window.

"Come," he whispered, "and be quick! Carry the other ladder with you!"

So Marzio followed him up the ladder, trailing the smaller ladder after him, and when he'd entered the deep-set window he drew both of the ladders after him and laid them stealthily on the dungeon floor. Then he followed Olimpio down the foul-smelling passage. Utter blackness: and a trickle of nausea crept over the tinker; he thought of the prisoners who had died here, half-naked specters with long beards trailing; he could feel their scaly fingers snatching wispily at his ankles. He groped gingerly with his feet, running his palm along the wall. The ugly aroma of the dungeon gave way to the fresh, crisp scent of the wine cellar.

Now at last a faint light shone at the end of the passage. The wall curved, and suddenly they stood in the moonlit cloister.

Marzio glanced at the hollow windows. "There's no one that might see us?"

"There's only Giorgio, that old idiot, and he sleeps by the gate," grunted Olimpio.

Marzio hesitated. His voice grew pleading: "I don't like this, Olimpio."

Olimpio snapped: "Don't be a donkey. Stop chattering and follow me."

He led the way to the door of the kitchen and they climbed the narrow stairs. Once the tinker slipped and stumbled. Olimpio snatched at his arms: "Idiot!" Finally they came to the hexagonal terrace below the battlements.

The great valley spread beneath them. They could see the blue slabs of cliff, and the torrent piercing the heart of the gorge like a white-hot needle. The great hills lay smoldering uneasily in the moonlight; even the sky seemed to throb with a huge, pristine watchfulness. But not a sound rose from the village and the tangle of dusty walls looked white and dead, like a heap of bones.

Olimpio tapped at the terrace door; it opened softly; he disappeared.

Once again Marzio waited. A chill of ghostliness crawled over him. He kept staring at the moonlit mountains and the black massive battlements. An owl cried from the elder thicket, and then, an instant later, came the hollow ding-dong from the campanile.

The thought occurred to Marzio of sliding down the buttress and hurrying off into the woods beyond. But a queer inertia weighed him down, like that of a man trapped in a nightmare. He stood motionless and stared at the mottled hills by Ascrea.

Beatrice stepped suddenly through the door in her pale green cloak and beckoned to Marzio.

"Here," she said, "take this candle." He followed her down the stairway. She flung open a door and whispered rapidly: "This room was Santi di Pompa's. You'd better sleep here. The bed's been taken away but you can sleep on the table."

She tossed a blanket over the table and looked at him calmly. "Good night. Sleep well." And she closed the door behind her, very softly.

And once again the sad-eyed tinker sat and waited, all alone. He watched the flame of the candle slowly burning away the wax. He held his hand in the air and made shadowy patterns on the wall — an imp, a bird, then a crocodile; and finally he saw the last flutter of pale-blue light dart from the wick.

The room was utterly black. He lay back on the table and fell asleep.

4

And Cenci too was sleeping. Who knows what he dreamed?

Lost in the jungle of his obsessions, beating his way through his secret swamp, gasping with thirst, wet with fever, swollen to a frenzy with insect bites — or was it more like a prison corridor, long and narrow, sickeningly barren, blank doors opening imperceptibly on immense rusty hinges and a dingy gray light seeping over a nest of foul bed linen, here and there a face grinning with a subtle half-familiarity — the pimply cheeks of a barber's apprentice, the boarlike profile of an innyard harridan? More and more of them, some of them lovely with a hard, antagonistic beauty but most of them tainted, foul-featured, bestialized: adventurers in lust, pimps and slatterns, dabblers in blackmail and thievery. And then suddenly the walls shrivel and he stands alone in a twilit valley surrounded by black, inaccessible ranges. Smoke rises from the highest peak in a frail, drifting feather; it widens and darkens, it flows into a huge migrating cloud. Voices call out of the stillness like a tinkling of little bells, but the words are unintelligible, the voices inhuman. He climbs and keeps climbing, devoured by a last crazy urgency; the air grows choking and luminous, his blood-beats echo, his feet grow leaden, and he opens his mouth in a sharp, thin scream . . .

He wakes up suddenly. The bed curtains are stirring beside him gently. Lucrezia touches his fingertips:

"What's wrong, Francesco? Another nightmare?"

5

The next morning Plautilla, the seneschal's wife, rose early from her bed and lit the fire under the kettle. She kept glancing through the window at the dawnlit hills. Her heart was clouded and confused. Olimpio had failed to appear that night, and now it was daylight and there still was no sign of him.

Plautilla too had once been lovely — slim and keen-eyed and glowing. It was eight years ago that she had married Olimpio, and she had loved him passionately ever since. Many a time he'd ridden off for a night or two in a neighboring town, and come back with the telltale luster of casual love-making in his eyes, but then his tenderness for Plautilla had always come back to him, and though she suffered and wept, her love for the rascal was deep and powerful. And all in all it was a life as happy as she could expect, with moments of heartbreak to season it, until the Cenci came to the castle.

Then came the evening when Plautilla scented the change in her husband, the dreamy glance and the wayward manner, and she knew he'd fallen in love. But she knew well enough that her own loveliness had faded; her body had aged, her face had thinned, the lines of labor lay dark in her cheeks, and patience was gradually taking the place of pride. So she said nothing to Olimpio and prayed that this passion of his might cool, or that the lady would finally tire of him, or that events would come to her rescue.

And then one day when they were told by Prince Colonna to lodge in the village, she too sensed the irritable hand of Cenci behind this order. But soon she realized that Olimpio still had access to the castle, and many a time he came home two hours or more after midnight, and she caught the faint musk of Beatrice Cenci on his skin. But still she said nothing and hoped that time would bring an end to it; and her love for Olimpio was unaltered, it was even strengthened by this misery.

Then she suddenly detected something new in the air — a dark look in Olimpio's eyes and a sheen of purpose about him. He had mounted his mare one morning and ridden away for four days, and she knew that he lied to her when he said he was off to Viterbo. Something ominous was in the air, something subtle and shadowy. And a thousand suspicions came fluttering about her like a cloud of gnats.

So this morning, when Olimpio had failed to appear in the house, and the hours went by and the time had come for the noonday meal, a desperate nervousness came over Plautilla. She sat by the window with her long-lidded eyes fixed on the castle, and her fingers moved through the flax as she tried to sing to her children: the girl Vittoria and the curly-headed boy, whose name was Prospero.

Finally she rose and slipped a pink cotton shawl over her head and started off toward the almond trees which grew on a slope over the castle gate. There she sat on the ground and hid for a while in the shade of the foliage, keeping an eye on the great doorway. But no one came and no one left, so she climbed a little higher, toward the eastern side of the hill, and finally she came to a rock which jutted out over the trees, and from here she could look straight down on the castle battlements.

Suddenly she saw Olimpio emerge from one of the doors — it was the door to Beatrice's chamber — and there he stood in a niche talking to Marzio the tinker. Something about the whole scene filled her with a sickening presentiment, and at that moment Marzio caught sight of her and tapped Olimpio on the elbow. Olimpio turned and stared at the rock where Plautilla was crouching. He raised his finger in warning, and she could sense from afar that his coal-black eyes were burning with rage. So she hurried down the hill and ran back to the house. There she flung herself on the bed and drew the bed curtains around her and she started sobbing; for now she was sure that something ugly was afoot.

6

An hour later she heard Olimpio's footsteps down the path, and he flung open the door and came stamping into the bedroom. He came to a halt by the bed and tore open the curtains.

Plautilla stared at him wretchedly and said: "Olimpio! What's wrong?"

His face was purple with fury. "You fool! You old busybody! What business did you have up on the hill there, spying down on the castle?"

He struck her savagely in the face, and she turned away and wept silently until she heard him go off down the path into the village.

It was dusk when he came back again. She could smell the wine on his breath, and she knew that he'd been with his friends in the tavern. He tore a sausage from a hook in the kitchen and went about glowering.

"Olimpio," she whispered timidly.

He kept lumbering about with stormy eyes.

"Olimpio!" she cried to him finally. "What's this thing that's happening in the castle?"

But he threw his crust in the fire and snatched his knife from the table.

"Oh, Olimpio," she whispered, "may the Lord protect you!"

And Olimpio strode through the door into the night without a word.

IX

A MISERABLE NIGHT — hot and heavy, like the breath
from a cave. The whole village is caught in the grip of
insomnia. At the monastery the young men twist and turn
in their dreams while the old ones lie limp, with the moonlight shining on their pates. The pigeons keep rustling
uneasily in the cotes, the hens cluck in their sleep, the ewes
bleat softly. Down in his den the old apothecary goes poking among his vats, counting the pills, pouring the pow-
ders, shaking the little pink vials . . .

The vintner Polidoro lies sweating and blubbering in
his sleep — he is dreaming about the apothecary's daughter, Filomena. Filomena herself has a rendezvous with
Ambrogio the pastry cook — they meet in the cemetery
among the cypresses and there's rustling and moaning.
Tino the latchmaker is a nimble fellow, with a face like a
frog's: he has climbed into a eucalyptus tree by the house
of Baldassare the cobbler. There he sits astride a limb,
peeping at the widow Pomona, who lies naked in her bed,
squirming in the heat like a stranded jellyfish. Down in
the piazza the iron nymph sends the water spraying from

her breasts, and up in the copse there's an owl with a field-mouse in its claws.

The butcher's wife, Maria of Aquila, sits in her kitchen by the fire; she is rolling out the dough for tomorrow's *lasagna*.

"Well," she says, "I don't like the looks of it, and I'll tell you so frankly."

"Where there's smoke there's usually fire," mutters her aunt, Simonetta, an elderly virgin with a delicate, pearl-gray goatee.

"Wait and see," says Maria of Aquila. "I saw Olimpio up on the hill again. He's paying visits every night now. It's going to end up in trouble."

"Well, I tell you," says Simonetta, "too many plums kill the plum tree. He's going too far, mark my words. Signor Francesco will soon be on to it."

"And mind you," says Maria, "there's more to it than just the naughtiness. She's a weird young lady, Signora Beatrice, and there's nothing I'd put past her."

"Too many chains set the mastiff growling," says Simonetta, reaching for the wine glass, and the bell starts tolling in Santa Maria.

2

And in the meantime Marzio the tinker goes prowling through the village to ward off any suspicions that might spring from his absence. He sits by the fountain and plays his lute; finally he wanders home to sup with his wife.

All the lanes were deserted when he crept up the rock and met Olimpio once more by the castle walls.

"Look, Olimpio," he whispered. "I've been worrying about this business."

"Why? What's wrong?"

"All this delay . . . The omens are bad, I can't help feeling."

In point of fact, he had waited throughout that same morning as well as the previous night: nothing at all had been achieved, as luck would have it. Cenci had kept a small oil lamp burning beside his bed and in the middle of the night he had risen and bolted his door, and after that he had sat in his cushions running his thumb through his documents, and Lucrezia couldn't leave nor could Beatrice enter. The man seemed actually to sense some vague unpleasantness in the air. Even Olimpio had wavered a little; but Beatrice herself was adamantine, and now once more the two men were to wait on the terrace for the signal.

"Look here," said Olimpio, thrusting his wine-smelling face close to Marzio's, "you're a part of this thing and you'll do as I tell you."

Marzio hesitated. "But what if . . ."

"What if what?" snapped Olimpio.

"It's a crime," breathed Marzio.

Olimpio sniffed. "Well, what of it?"

"What if we're caught? What will happen?"

"You're an ass!" snarled Olimpio, and he drew the ladder from the weeds and placed it firmly against the wall. "Who's to catch us? The angel Gabriel? Come, my man, let's get it over with!"

So once more they made their way over the walls into the dungeon, and then stealthily through the cellars toward the terrace beside the battlements. Once more the dark seneschal knocked at the door to Beatrice's chamber and Marzio was left on the terrace to gape at the moon.

A little while passed; then the door opened softly and a pale, plump figure came rustling across the flagstones. It was Lucrezia with her night robe fluttering about her. She beckoned feverishly to Marzio.

"Are you still awake?" she whispered.

"Awake enough," said Marzio hoarsely.

"Be patient," she said, with a glance at the door.

"What are they waiting for?" said Marzio.

Lucrezia looked at him dolefully. "Signor Francesco's wide awake. I brought him some wine but he wouldn't drink it. God knows what he's thinking. He keeps moaning and groaning . . ."

"I don't like it," said Marzio.

"Nor do I!" wailed Lucrezia.

They looked swiftly at each other. For a moment neither spoke. Marzio's face hung in the darkness, desolate and drooping, like a bloodhound's. And Lucrezia looked like a doll left out in the rain: cheeks blurred, hair tangled, eyes dull and askew.

She clasped her hands and whispered tensely: "Marzio . . . It's a horrible thing we're planning!"

"That's the truth," quavered Marzio. He plucked wistfully at his lower lip.

"It's a murder!" snapped Lucrezia. "It's worse than a murder!"

"I'm only doing it for the money, signora," pleaded Marzio.

"What an absurdity," said Lucrezia, tightening the robe about her hips. "What money? There's no money in this wretched castle, my poor fellow!"

"Ah, signora," groaned Marzio, "I wish I'd never been caught in this!"

"Speak to Olimpio," hissed Lucrezia. "Tell him you're out of it. Tell him it's lunacy . . ."

And she dipped through the doorway and disappeared in the antechamber.

And Marzio stood leaning over the terrace wall. The moon was low; tiny clouds went skimming over the hills. They looked like tatters from a witch's cloak, a wicked blue edged with fire.

Faint shadows, no larger than gnats, were stirring on the slopes above Ascrea. Marzio's eyes were sharp as a bird's: Wolves, he thought, and it's not yet autumn!

But then the tang of ripe fruit and yellowing leaves rose out of the orchards, and a cool, quick gust shot forth from the Salto. The elders rippled in the moonlight, filmy, ecstatic, like a flock of elves.

Marzio crouched on the flagstones; a moment later he started snoring.

3

Finally, just as the moon was sinking, Olimpio stepped on the terrace. The tinker sat slumped in the corner with his head in his arms. Olimpio shook him by the wrist.

"Come," he grunted. "It's time."

Marzio staggered to his feet. His eyes were bleary with wine and weariness.

"Olimpio . . . listen . . ."

Olimpio's hand felt like iron on his shoulder: Marzio's

will sagged under the impact, and he lowered his eyes and said nothing.

"Here," said Olimpio. "Take this. And be sure to use it when I tell you."

He held out a wooden rolling pin with black metal handles, such as the Neapolitans used for making their noodles. He himself was carrying a two-faced hammer, one end blunt and one end pointed — a Lombardy hammer as they called it.

"Now," he muttered. "Come. Follow me."

Marzio followed him meekly down to Beatrice's bedroom. Beatrice was waiting by the window with a muslin turban around her head.

"Quick," she said, pale and cool. "He's fast asleep. We'd better hurry."

She took the candle and they tiptoed down the hall toward the master's bedroom. But suddenly they saw Lucrezia stepping through the door, brandishing a chamber pot.

"Is he sleeping?" whispered Beatrice.

Lucrezia's chin shook with terror. "Oh Beatrice, darling . . . Wait a moment!"

"Why? What's happened?"

"We're out of our minds!"

At that moment, as it happened, the bell went tolling in Santa Maria.

"Listen," said Lucrezia, rolling her eyes. "Do you hear? It's the Feast of the Assumption! Let's all pray to the Madonna! It's a day to be begging for forgiveness!"

But Beatrice's eyes were hard and contemptuous; she pushed Lucrezia aside and made her way toward the door, leading Olimpio by the hand. At that moment Olimpio burst into an uncontrollable fit of coughing. He clutched at his throat, his chest heaved, the blood rushed suddenly to his cheeks. "Wait," he gasped; he went lunging down the hall toward the ladies' antechamber and out on the terrace, where he leaned by the wall and stood quaking.

Marzio hurried out after him. "In the name of Christ," he said, "what's ailing you?"

"It's a fishbone," gasped Olimpio.

"It's an omen!" moaned Marzio.

Now Beatrice stepped out on the terrace and strode fiercely up to Olimpio. Her whole body seemed to seethe, phosphorescent with fury.

"What's this nonsense?" she demanded.

"It's a bone in my throat," croaked the seneschal.

"Bone indeed. It's sheer pretense. You're a miserable coward," she said passionately. "You're a liar! And worse! I'll never trust you again!"

Olimpio was stammering with rage. "If I'm a coward, my fine lady, I'll tell you what you are! You're a fiend out of hell! You've brought me nothing but trouble, and you'll bring me nothing but ruin!"

Beatrice laughed in his face. "It's a beautiful way to keep promises."

"Yes! Promises to murder," said Olimpio, spitting with excitement. "I've been following you like a lamb, my little she-wolf, and a fool I've been!"

Beatrice stood close in front of him; her lips started twitching. She swung out with her hand and slapped him viciously on the cheek.

"Very well. Go your way. This is the end of it," she said.

And she slipped across the terrace and vanished in the darkness.

4

So once more their plans crumbled and their plots came to nothing, and the tinker and the seneschal climbed over the walls and sauntered homeward: Olimpio sweating with indignation, Marzio limp with relief.

"I'm done with it," Olimpio muttered as they crept down the path. "There's no point in being ruined by the whims of a woman, now, is there?"

"Certainly not," agreed Marzio.

"And a madwoman at that!"

So Olimpio bade the tinker a surly good night and opened the door to his house and came tiptoeing into the bedroom. He stripped and crept into bed; his breath came hoarse and uncertain. He kissed Plautilla on the temple, very tenderly, almost imploringly.

"Where have you been?" whispered Plautilla.

"Off on an errand for the prince."

"What kind of errand, Olimpio?"

"I rode to Poggio to fetch a stallion . . ."

"God bless you, darling," said Plautilla, who knew he was lying; but she felt a passionate relief to feel him safely beside her.

Olimpio lay motionless for a while, but the night was a troubled one. His dreams were hot and ugly and soon he woke up again. His heart was pounding with anger and his face was burning with humiliation; but his flesh ached with longing as never before. He rose and stepped into the courtyard and looked at the stars, and he saw the castle high above him, perched on the rock like a vulture. He grew dizzy with desire. "Beatrice, my lovely," he whispered. And he stepped into the room again and slipped on his jerkin.

"You're getting up?" whispered his wife.

"It's a sultry night. I can't sleep."

"Well," she said, "it's nearly dawn. I have work that needs doing . . ."

So Plautilla rose likewise and made ready to comb her flax while Olimpio fetched his mare to let her out to the pasture. He stood for a moment by the house and the shutter swung open. His face, at that instant, looked dreadful and leonine: blunt, far-eyed, heavily furrowed, with a feverish stillness about the mouth. There was a sinister dignity about him, like that of a man condemned to death.

Plautilla sat at the window watching him. The candle shone on the silky flax. She said nothing but her eyes were full of a cold, still terror.

X

Everything was dark in La Petrella. Not a window was lit. Olimpio strode through the village till he came to the tinker's hovel.

He pounded at the door. "Get up, Marzio! There's something I want to tell you!"

Marzio peered through a slit in the pane. "What needs telling, Olimpio?"

"Come with me," whispered Olimpio.

"No," said Marzio. "I'm not coming."

"You're frightened?" said Olimpio quietly.

"Look," said Marzio. "It's nearly dawn. All these comings and goings, all these whisperings and so on — I tell you, Olimpio, the whole village is seething with suspicion!"

"Nonsense," said Olimpio, shaking his fist. "Come and don't be an idiot!"

And the strangest thing in this sinister comedy of procrastinations is surely this: each new coming and going, each new squabble and delay, far from exhausting the will, served only to deepen the compulsion, as though its victims drifted away from the heart of the whirlpool only to be sucked back again each time into a narrower, quicker circle. So that this fretting and fuming, this whole parade of hesitations in the end merely deepened the real and dreadful inevitability.

And so poor Marzio, far from rebelling at this ill-tempered order, merely submitted once again by sheer force of habit and followed Olimpio up the path that led to the thicket. This time the two men hardly concerned themselves with secrecy; they had gone this way so often that they gave no thought to the matter. They climbed the walls and crept through the cellars and once more arrived on the terrace. The first haze of dawn hung over the hills when Olimpio knocked at the door.

2

All was still. A peculiar fog was in the air that morning. Like sunset: a misty glow from an unseen conflagration. The sheep down in the pasture floated softly, like phantoms. The trees, even the cliffs looked like shapes in a Chinese shadow play. Everything pointed toward that powdery incandescence beyond Staffoli; a secret gesture, as it were, toward an inaccessible dream.

Beatrice turned from the window and walked slowly to the door. Her hair was streaming over her shoulders and her eyes were red with exhaustion.

"Well," she said, looking at Olimpio without expression. "What now?"

"We're here to do it," said Olimpio bluntly.

"You've shed your cowardice, I see," said Beatrice.

"Come," said Olimpio, "no more chatter; let's get it done once and for all." And he led the way through the ladies' antechamber, where he picked up his Lombardy hammer and took the rolling pin from the shelf and tossed it casually to the tinker.

Then the three of them went stalking down the hall to the master's bedchamber.

"Wait," said Beatrice. "The sun's rising. I'll tell Giorgio to go to market . . ."

She threw the cloak over her shoulders and hurried out into the cloister. They could hear her calling to the butler's window: "Here's your money for the marketing, Giorgio! Hurry up . . . We'll be eating early!"

Three minutes later she was back in the hall again, pink-cheeked and panting. "Now," she said.

She tugged at the knob but the door was bolted. She knocked softly, then a little louder.

Footsteps rustled across the floor. Lucrezia slid the bolt from the door and peered mistily through the crevice.

"God have mercy," she whispered.

3

Now they knew that the time had come, the crime was ripe for the doing. The evil fruit was beginning to fester. It had to be plucked; now or never.

Olimpio flung open the door without further ado, and they all rushed into the bedroom helter-skelter. Beatrice ran to the side of the bed and snatched at the curtains; then she hurried out of the room with Lucrezia behind her and shut the door.

The two men stood by the bed and peered down at Francesco Cenci, who grunted and blinked, then raised his head with a look of dreadful presentiment. "Hello," he stammered. "What's this?" But Olimpio was on him already; he flung his weight on Cenci's chest and swung at his head with the hammer — first with the blunt end three times and then, in a kind of frenzy, with the pointed. Marzio kept pounding at the feet and ankles with his rolling pin. Cenci's bones hissed and crackled; his arms flailed blindly at the air. A great shudder ran through him and he crumpled into a heap.

Olimpio strode into the antechamber. "Well, it's done now," he muttered.

Beatrice stood frozen by the window but Lucrezia sank into a chair, all aquiver.

"Look," said Olimpio. "Is anyone passing?"

Beatrice glanced through the window. "No one."

Olimpio stepped on the balcony and peered down at the thicket. The sun was creeping out of the hills; all was heavy with dew. The shrubs were veiled in a pearly web and the crows were chattering in the elders. But nothing stirred on the mountain road. The fields were empty and still. So Olimpio tugged at the railing, trying to tear a great gash in it. But the wood held fast; it bent a little but refused to break.

"It's no use," he called into the room.

"Try the other way," said Beatrice swiftly.

Olimpio crouched on the floor of the balcony and started ripping at the boards. They were soft with decay and came asunder more easily. Then there was trouble. A long narrow hole had been torn, but two rafters held solid as rock on each side of it.

"Try the other end," said Beatrice, leaning out of the window.

At the other end of the balcony lay the usual sort of aperture: a circular hole sawed in the floor which might serve as a privy. So Olimpio went with his hammer and hacked busily at the edges, widening it little by little until the thing seemed sufficient.

He kicked the splinters into the shrubbery. "Now," he grunted. "We'll have to dress him."

So he and Marzio returned to the bedchamber and gathered up the dead man's garments. Cenci's blood had flooded the sheets and seeped down into the mattress. His head hung dangling with the eyes wide open, peering through a dark, glossy mask. The two men leaned over the bed and set to clothing him clumsily — stockings and hose and the blue-black jerkin, and finally the boots and the velvet doublet. A hasty job and a slovenly one, like all else that was done that morning.

"Look again," called Olimpio. "Is anyone passing on the road?"

Beatrice looked a second time. "Not a soul. Come. Bring him."

So Marzio took one end of the sheet and Olimpio the other and they carried the corpse through the antechamber and out on the balcony. There they raised the ponderous body and placed it upright in the crevice: Cenci was stout and the hole was jagged, and there was quite a bit of trouble. His arms kept flapping about and his head jerked aimlessly, sending a spray of thick red drops over the railing. But they tugged and squeezed and prodded until finally he slid through and the corpse went hurtling into the thicket. They heard it land with an ugly crackle as it ripped through the twigs and sank in the thick dark mud underneath.

So now the thing was finally done; all that remained was to cover the traces.

4

Lucrezia was back in the bedroom, trying to tidy up the bed. She was dazed with terror, cooing and twittering to herself like a halfwit. She plucked aimlessly at the mattress, which was spattered with stains, and finally Olimpio pushed her aside and carried the mattress into the antechamber, where he tore it wide open and started to pull out the wool. All four at this point were seized with a frenzy of inefficiency — Olimpio snatching at the blood-soaked wool, Lucrezia tucking it into a basket, Marzio gathering the wayward tufts, Beatrice folding the spotted sheets. A superficiality of order was finally restored: the sheets were thrust behind the chest in the antechamber, the bloodstained wool was dropped in the kitchen fire, the clean wool was rolled in a parcel, the hammer and rolling pin were tossed in a toolbox. None of them paused to consider, none of them troubled to calculate, and all through the house they scattered the telltale hints of their crime.

Now Beatrice peered through the window and saw Giorgio returning from the village, a bundle of carrots in his basket and a leg of mutton under his arm.

"Quick. Hide by the gate," she murmured.

The men went stumbling down the stairway while Beatrice screamed into the cloister: "Giorgio! Hurry! For the love of God . . ."

The old butler came running, and while he was crossing the cloister the two murderers slipped through the castle gate. And not long after the seneschal was quietly leading his mare through the pasture while the tinker, witless with panic, was hurrying off into the hills.

BOOK TWO
The Flood

X I

It so happened that a wandering wood carver, Claudio
Crespi by name, was passing toward Rome on his way from
Rimini, on the Adriatic. He was a sprightly little man
with a wart on his cheek and a black goatee. Being penniless, he had spent the night in a stable, and soon after
sunrise set out through the woods. He paused by a spring
to quench his thirst and sprinkled his face with the mossy
water. Then he sat under an almond tree and started to
gnaw at a crust of cheese. The sky was dappled with ruddy
clouds, the air was dull and oppressive. The sirocco was
astir; even the insects were listless.

As Claudio sat in the almond grove, gnawing away at his
purple cheese, he saw the smoke rise from the chimneys
and the monks at work in their vegetable garden. Crows
were circling about over the castle thicket. He glanced up
toward the balcony and caught sight of a curious thing:
two men were carrying a heavy burden on a long white
sheet, and they lifted the burden, which looked like an
enormous painted doll, and rammed it laboriously through
the floor of the balcony until finally it fell and went plung-
ing into the thicket. Rather odd, thought Claudio; what

sort of business was this? But at that moment a large juicy frog skipped past him, and Claudio leaned over, cupped his hand and trapped the creature, which was a beautiful glossy green, crisply dotted with black. The frog gaped at Claudio and plucked at the air with his tiny fingers, and Claudio popped him briskly into his doublet pocket.

Then he finished his cheese, throwing a crumb or two to the linnets, and finally rose with a groan, brushed a leaf from his sleeve and started casually down the path to La Petrella.

He came to a neat little cottage just behind Santa Maria, and poked his head through the kitchen window. A young housewife in a yellow apron was standing by the oven, kneading her dough.

"Good morning," said Claudio breezily.

"I wish you the same," said the housewife.

"Excuse me," remarked Claudio. "Do I see some olive oil in the pan there?"

"Indeed you do," said the housewife.

"Do me a favor," said Claudio, dangling the frog over the window sill. "I'm dizzy with hunger. How about frying me a bite or two?"

So the housewife took the frog, chopped it neatly in four, seasoned it deftly and dropped the quarters in the bubbling oil. A subtle aroma, like roast quail, flowed out through the kitchen window.

The housewife eyed Claudio inquisitively: "Here's a glass of wine for you, and a bit of bread . . . What are you doing here in La Petrella, by the way?"

"Nothing special," said Claudio. "I'm down from Rimini. On my way to Rome."

"Rimini . . . Hm. What sort of town is it?"

"Very smart. Very fashionable."

"Pretty girls, too, I suppose?"

"They're the loveliest in the land!"

The housewife bridled. "Oh, indeed? Then why did you leave it, may I ask?"

Claudio chuckled. "There's nothing like change for a man like me," he said spicily. He peered at the curly-headed housewife, who was plucking the frog's legs out of the pan, and added: "You're as sweet as any I've seen in Rimini, by the way."

"Oh," said the housewife. "I don't need flattery."

"It's God's own truth," whispered Claudio, and he started nibbling at the juicy meat.

"Good heavens," exclaimed the housewife, rushing to the window. "What's all this hubbub?"

There was a clattering and shouting out in the street all of a sudden. The men were running up toward the castle as fast as they could; the women were scurrying into the piazza, wiping their hands on their aprons.

Claudio gulped down the rest of the wine and went loping down the lane.

"What's happened?" he said, stopping a boy in a checkered jerkin.

"He's dead, he's dead!" shouted the boy.

"Who's dead, in God's name?"

"Signor Francesco! He's fallen from the balcony!"

Claudio scratched his head thoughtfully and followed the crowd up the path, toward the long black trough by the castle gate.

2

Plautilla sat by the window, combing her flax in the dull gray light. She was telling a tale to the boy Prospero, who sat at her feet with a ball of wool. It was a tale about the bandits from the hills of the Cicolano, and how they robbed an old abbess in the town of Pendenza. One of the men had come to the abbey disguised as a friar, and while he was gossiping with the abbess, telling her the latest news from Rome, the rest of the men crept into the kitchen and stole her eggs and her butter, as well as a fine pink ham that was dangling from the ceiling . . .

"Was she a nice lady?" said Prospero.

"She was kind in her way," said Plautilla.

"Was she pretty?" said Prospero.

"Not very," said Plautilla.

Prospero ran his little hand over his mother's knee. "Tell me about the queen who turned into an owl," he said softly.

At that moment a girl cried from the neighboring house: "Oh Plautilla!"

Plautilla leaned through the window with a pang in her heart: "What's wrong, Paolina?"

"Come! Quick! There's something dreadful going on up in the castle!"

So Plautilla ran from her house, one shoe off and one shoe on, and joined the throng that was hurrying through the lanes up to the castle. She entered the gate and stood in the cloister, looking this way and that, and then she saw Signora Beatrice's face at a window, white and stricken.

Beatrice beckoned to her desperately. "Come," she cried. "Help us, Plautilla!"

At that moment the fishmonger's wife Dorotea came rushing by. She seized Plautilla by the arm. "Mother of God," she gasped, "he's killed himself!"

"What? Who?"

"Signor Francesco!"

Plautilla turned and caught sight of the village priests rushing through the gate, with Don Marzio in front, followed by Don Francesco and Don Domenico; they went scampering across the court and up the circular stairway.

So Plautilla followed the priests and made her way toward the antechamber. Outside the door stood the butler Giorgio, gaunt, aghast, like an apparition.

He was wringing his hands. "Oh Mother of God! What a day!"

"What's happened, Giorgio?"

"The master's fallen!"

"Heavens. Where?"

"From the balcony!"

"Is he dead?"

But all that Giorgio could say was: "God protect me! What a day!" So Plautilla squeezed past him and ran straight into the antechamber, where Signora Lucrezia stood by the table with her hands over her face.

"Mercy, signora," moaned Plautilla. "What's this terrible thing that's happened?"

"Oh, I told him again and again, the poor man," wailed Lucrezia. "I told him the wood was all flimsy and never to go on the balcony! Time and again I used to tell him! But he kept on going, and now you see . . ."

And she broke into a loud and shuddering lamentation.

Plautilla loosened her stays and led her to the chair with the cushions; she sprinkled wine on her face while Lucrezia kept jabbering.

"Oh Plautilla, I can't believe it! Time and again I kept warning him . . . He'd go in the morning and make water from that flimsy old balcony, and I told him again and again. But he just wouldn't listen . . . And then I heard the wood splintering and I heard him shouting 'Jesu!' Just once, like that: 'Jesu!' And I ran out on the balcony . . ."

And once more the poor woman dissolved in a great loud shudder while Plautilla kept fanning her with a sheet of parchment.

In the neighboring hallway Beatrice was talking in a somber tone to the archpriest, and down below a great crowd was gathering by the wall of the thicket.

3

"Here! This way!" cried the butcher, whose name was Sinibaldo, and the boys carried the ladder and set it swiftly against the wall. Everyone kept shouting and gesticulating, offering advice and encouragement, and finally the cobbler Baldassare climbed cautiously up the ladder, followed by Nanni the tailor and Ambrogio the pastry cook. The three men drew up the ladder and let it down on the other side. They stepped into the thicket and made their way toward the corpse, twisting their way through the waist-high weeds and the thorny underbrush. Heaps of refuse lay all about, overgrown with thick-leaved shrubbery.

Finally they came to Cenci's body, face down in a clump of elders.

"Have you found him?" shouted the butcher from the other side of the wall.

"Yes! He's here," squealed the tailor.

"Dead, is he?"

"Dead as a doornail!"

"Hurry up! Bring him out!"

"Well, we'll try," croaked the tailor.

The three men took hold of the body, all stained as it was and all bedraggled, and dragged it gingerly to the bottom of the wall. But the corpse was heavy and limp, most unpleasant to the touch; it kept slithering through their fingers as they tried to raise it.

"He's too slippery!" shouted the tailor.

"Do you want a rope?" called back the butcher.

There was a mutter of consultation. Finally the tailor cried hoarsely:

"Tell old Giorgio to hurry up and bring a rope and another ladder!"

So a second ladder was hoisted over the wall and flung into the thicket. To this they tied Cenci's body with a thick black rope, and finally they tugged him over the wall and slowly down on the other side; thus they carried him to the castle gate and laid him down beside the trough.

There the villagers and peasants gathered about in a wide-eyed circle, watching the cobbler and the pastry cook draw the clothes off the corpse; torn and bloody they were, streaked with dust and dereliction. One by one they were stripped away — the boots and the hose, the jerkin and doublet, and two of the women were chosen to wash clean the victim: first Lucia, who was a widow and excessively pious, and then the fishmonger's big bosomy wife, Dorotea.

The three priests stood by the trough to supervise the ablution — Don Marzio grim and thoughtful and Don Francesco fussing and fidgeting; Don Domenico kept his eyes fastidiously averted. Towels were brought and the blood was cleaned from the evil-looking body; the great wounds in the head started bleeding afresh.

"Just feel him," said Dorotea, "he's cold as ice already!" And she turned a lurid eye on the horde of bystanders.

Lucia sat still and solemn in her long black dress but the fishmonger's wife kept chattering away briskly:

"God's mercy! Just look at him . . . Suffered from the gout, the poor man, not to mention that other thing . . . And those wounds! The thorns of the elder bush, could it have been?" She thrust her forefinger deep into the wound by Cenci's eye. "Look," she said, raising her hand with a look of triumph. "Did you ever see such a wound? God protect me!"

And the peasants cast dark, queasy glances at one another.

Finally the washing was done and the corpse was clad in a clean white shirt; then it was laid on the bier on a linen sheet. Don Francesco leaned over and gently folded the dead man's hands and the archpriest Don Marzio led the procession to the church.

The butcher and the tailor carried the bier, together with the pastry cook and the village cobbler; they followed the path down the rock and passed through the maze of alleys and finally they came to Santa Maria, and the body was laid before the altar.

It was nearly noon and the clouds had drifted away to the north. A surly haze hung over the hills, not a breeze was stirring. Claudio, the wood carver from Rimini, stopped in the piazza and drank from the fountain, and then he crossed over the bridge and was off toward Nerola.

XII

Up in the castle a host of villagers went thronging
through the chambers, peeping at the beds, fondling the
tapestries, sniffing and fumbling about in the kitchen.
Even the plowboys came clattering through the rooms in
their dusty boots, plucking a sausage from the wall or
maybe a spoon from the cupboard, and one and all had a
fine industrious look at the fatal balcony. They leered inquisitively at the parapet, visualizing the fall in their own
bright fancies, arguing and fussing about the broken timber and peeping down at the shattered elder bushes, and
the air was filled with a veritable swarm of speculations.

However, the seneschal Olimpio put in an appearance
at this point, and promptly and vigorously took charge of
the situation. He ordered the folk out of the castle and
sent old Giorgio down to the church to see that candles
were burning beside the dead man's body, as was proper.

A bit later he paid a visit to the archpriest himself. Certain glances and murmurings had created uneasiness in his
mind. He urged Don Marzio to make haste with the obsequies and see that the body be buried swiftly, and he
brought the necessary garments, chosen from Cenci's own
wardrobe.

Plautilla in the meantime stayed on with the ladies, tidying up and setting the table and offering carefully chosen words of condolence. Lucrezia was growing calmer; she lay on the bed in Beatrice's chamber. Beatrice, bland and aloof, sat down at the table and wrote a letter:

Dear Giacomo:
   Our father Francesco died this morning in a terrible fall. Please come to La Petrella immediately and arrange to accompany us back to Rome.
                                        Your sister,
                                        Beatrice

Finally, at six in the afternoon, Francesco Cenci was quietly laid in a sepulcher in the small, bleak church of Santa Maria della Petrella. The ladies did not attend; only the seneschal was there, restless and irritable and glowering, to see the body into the grave.

2

That same evening, by candlelight, dark rumors passed through the village. There were hints in the little piazza, there were mutterings beside the fountain. There were grim speculations in the little black lanes.

In the tavern the cobbler Baldassare was having a drink with his friends.

"That hole in the balcony," he said softly. "Did you have a look at it, Nanni?"

"Yes, I did," said the tailor. "It looked queer, I thought. Handmade, if you ask me."

"Mighty narrow, that hole," said Baldassare, "for a man like Cenci to tumble through!"

"And I saw some bloodstains on the railing. What do you make of it?" said Nanni.

The tavern was steeped in the scent of wine-soaked wood and plowmen's boots. The candle flickered; the eyes were glowing. Sinibaldo tugged at his beard.

"Where's Marzio tonight?" he muttered heavily. "I haven't seen him all day."

"I saw him hurrying off to the hills this morning," said the pastry cook brightly.

"He's been acting a bit odd these last few days, don't you think?"

"You're dead right! And the seneschal too, now that I come to think of it . . ."

The men emptied their glasses and stared grimly at the yellow jug.

"You saw that wound?" said the cobbler quietly. "No thorn, I tell you, dug a wound like that."

"If it wasn't a thorn it must have been a hammer, or maybe a chisel," growled the butcher.

"What do you think, then?" whispered the latchmaker Tino, a spindly man with watery eyes.

"I think what I think," snorted the butcher. He spread his meaty hands on the table. There were clots of blood still caught in his fingernails.

"I tell you," said the vintner Polidoro, the fattest man in the village; his voice was like a tempest bubbling away in a vat. "It's not for nothing that Olimpio's been creeping at night into the castle. He's a hard one, that castellan. There's not a thing he'd shrink away from."

"You're dead right," piped Ambrogio. "He was one of the bandits some years back."

"Up in Poggio," nodded the butcher. "In the days of Caccia and Cocumela."

"He's killed before, it's a fact I'm telling you," said the vintner profoundly.

A new jug was set on the table — fine fresh wine from the nearby vineyards. Nanni poured. The wine came braiding out of the snout like a string of rubies.

"Well," sighed Piero the hatmaker, and the lamplight danced on his shiny pate, "forgive me for saying so, but there's many a worse thing he might have done. There was darkness and doom in the heart of Signor Francesco."

"He was a cruel one with his ladies. Locking them up the way he did . . ."

"And using the strap on Signora Beatrice . . ."

"Ripping the nail from her thumb, I've heard . . ."

"And forcing his lust on all the shepherds . . ."

"And leaving his bills unpaid, what's more . . ."

"I'm not lamenting him, may the Lord forgive me!"

There was silence in the tavern. A rat came darting out of a crack: it sat staring at the table with its wild little eyes. Polidoro picked up a glass and hurled it violently across the room. The rat shot up like a bullet, then lay quivering and grinning, like a tiny demon.

3

The tinker's wife, Porzia, was sitting by the hearth stirring a sauce — a frail, wispy woman with haggard features and small green eyes.

The door opened. It was the butcher's wife, Maria of Aquila.

"Is he back yet?" she said softly.

The tinker's wife shook her head.

"Well, don't worry," said Maria. "He's gone on an errand in the hills, no doubt."

"A bitter errand," sighed Porzia.

"Bless you, my dear," burbled Maria. "It's a lonely time you've been having. A careless husband and a weak one. But it's lies they've been whispering by the fountain, I'm sure of it."

Neither of them spoke for a minute or two. The steam came hissing out of the pot — a floating fragrance of tomatoes and leeks and mushrooms.

Porzia sprinkled the salt into the *fettuccini* and looked sorrowfully at Maria.

"I'd rather have a weak sort of husband, I think, than a faithless one."

"You're thinking of the castellan?" said Maria eagerly. "Well, you're perfectly right. It's an outrage, and it's not only Signor Francesco I'm thinking of. And I tell you another thing, Porzia, they're absolute fools down at the fountain if they think that the ladies had nothing to do with it!"

"There's a certain strangeness about Signora Beatrice," said Porzia tentatively.

"Indeed there is!" chirped Maria. "There's nothing soft about the lady. She's like a boy in a woman's dress. Tall and slim, no hips at all, and that low dark voice of hers . . ."

"There's a mystery in her eyes," said Porzia thoughtfully.

"You've noticed it too?" cooed Maria, resting her powerful breasts confidentially on the table. "Let me tell you something, my dear. The day I saw her I told Sinibaldo, 'Look, there's a curse in her eyes, Sinibaldo!' That's what I said. He thought so too."

"God protect us," said Porzia thinly. "What will be the end of it all?"

"And the way she was acting today up there in the castle!" said Maria vengefully. "You'd never think it was her own dear father that passed away . . ."

"And Signora Lucrezia . . ."

"Oh, she's a cunning one," put in Maria, sniffing at the sauce. "Whimpering and moaning away in her chair, when her heart's as hard as a rock . . . Did you see the bed in the master's bedroom?"

"Well, I thought there was something odd . . ."

"The mattress was missing!" said Maria, glittering. "I have my own private notions, and I'll keep them to myself out of plain decency. But all the same, say what you wish, dear, there's been a murder up in the castle, and what's more, Olimpio's the man who did it!"

"The noodles are ready," murmured Porzia, wiping the sweat from her brow. "You'll have a bite or two, won't you?"

"I don't mind if I do," said Maria rapidly, "and it's good to keep you company, my poor lonely pet. Mercy me — it's a terrible time we've come to live in, isn't it, with nothing but profligacy and murder, and even worse, I don't care if I say it, right here in the village of La Petrella . . ."

4

Up in the castle in the meantime all was curiously still. The clatter of footsteps had vanished; the cloister was empty and the gate was locked.

Beatrice sat by her window and looked out at the misty hills. Deep and calm: not a leaf was stirring. The vines hung motionless from the battlements. It was a stillness that seemed massive, unalterable, complete, like a huge green cavern carved out of the Apennines; and she herself was only a tiny insect climbing the wall, with thin white claws . . .

The light faded. The immobility changed into a dark, mysterious tension. The slopes rose like the crest of a huge single wave — it moved closer and closer, it reared higher and higher, the whole range hung in a passionate, electric suspense. She kept climbing desperately; the walls quivered under her touch. Streaks of light, clear as cobalt, played on the glassy-smooth hollows and a ripple of foam went twisting along the peak, like a fiery worm. Nearer and nearer; vaster and vaster. The stillness echoed like thunder.

But the wave didn't break. The terrible silence remained intact. One last facet of light still hung in the cliffs by Ascrea — a single point suspended in chaos, like a great dusky emerald.

XIII

Night came and the candles were lit in the upper chambers, and Plautilla stayed on with the ladies to keep them company in their distress. The dead man's clothes had been brought from the trough and left to soak in a wooden basin, and the master's bedroom was tidied and locked for the night.

But all the while a terrible suspicion was growing on Plautilla. She went down to the kitchen and set the kettle on the fire and dropped the fish in the frying pan, but her mind was far away, driven by a cloud of anxieties.

It was a cavernous room, this kitchen, with a vaulted ceiling black with fumes and a great array of copper shimmering beside the oven. A marble table stood in the center, covered with bowls and wooden ladles. There was an alcove beyond the oven and here hung garlands of thyme and rosemary, chains of onions and chives, loops of black and purple sausages. A huge tortoiseshell cat lay sprawled on a cushion beside the fire.

There was a knock on the kitchen door. It was Plautilla's sister Artemisia: a lean, leathery spinster with a face like a corporal's.

She put her arms around Plautilla. "My poor angel," she muttered.

"Why have you come, Artemisia?"

"I've come to help you," she said. "Giorgio let me in through the gate." She looked deep into her sister's eyes. "There's much to be done here in the castle, I'm sure."

"You needn't have troubled," said Plautilla.

"I don't want you to be alone here, Plautilla."

"Where's Prospero?"

"I left him with Lucia . . . You look pale, Plautilla."

"I'm weary and worn, Artemisia."

"Look, my darling," said Artemisia in her deep throaty voice, flinging an apron around her. "I'll do the cooking tonight. Sit down. Have a glass of wine . . . It's been a terrible day, hasn't it?"

"It has indeed," said Plautilla.

Artemisia rolled up her sleeves and shook the seasoning into the pan.

"Listen to the wind blowing outside."

"It's turned cold all of a sudden."

"There's a storm in the air."

"Yes, there is," said Plautilla.

There was silence awhile: only the hiss of the oil in the pan and the velvety patter of the cat drinking her milk.

Plautilla said faintly: "You'll be sleeping here, will you?"

"It's better," said Artemisia. She flicked at the trout and turned them over. "They've been gossiping in the village," she added.

Plautilla was silent.

"Nasty whispers," said Artemisia.

Still Plautilla said nothing.

[108   ]

"About Signor Francesco's death . . ."

Plautilla stared at her sister desperately. "Artemisia! What are they saying?"

"He didn't fall. That's what they're saying."

"What do you mean, Artemisia?"

"He was killed. That's what they're saying."

"Oh Artemisia! I'm frightened . . ."

"Hush, my lamb," said Artemisia. She folded her arms and her voice grew gentle, but her eyes were cold and sharp as a lizard's. "They say he was murdered, and they say that Olimpio was the murderer. That's what they're saying, my dear, and you might as well know it."

Plautilla sat by the kitchen hearth; her lips were trembling but she didn't speak. Two great tears rolled down her cheeks, but then her face grew calm as a mask. She rose quietly and washed the lettuce and tossed it lightly into the salad bowl, and then she took out the glasses and set them on a tray.

No more words passed between them, but Artemisia glanced at her sister and there was triumph in her eyes as she poured the wine from the jug.

2

The table was set in front of the fire and the glasses were filled with the white Abruzzian wine, and soon Plautilla brought in the trout still sizzling on the platter. But neither of the ladies was hungry; they nibbled listlessly at the salad, but the fish lay untouched, the wine stood untasted. Soon the dishes were taken away again and the candle was set on the night table, and then a mattress was laid on the floor for Plautilla and Artemisia. Not a word was uttered and soon the ladies drew the bed curtains; the two sisters lay by the fire and stared desolately at the flames.

Little by little the fire grew fitful and Artemisia closed her eyes, and Plautilla lay gazing at the blue, clicking embers.

Far away, on the floor below, she heard the rustle of stealthy footsteps. A door opened and closed. Plautilla rose softly. Some instinct told her who it was, and she took the candle from the table and went tiptoeing down the stairs till she came to the room of Santi di Pompa.

She paused for a moment; her heart was pounding, and she listened carefully outside the door. Familiar sounds — the click of a belt, a heavy boot tossed on the floor. She opened the door quietly. Olimpio was sitting on the table, one boot off and one boot on, scratching his chest with a vacant stare.

"Olimpio! You've come to sleep here?"

"I thought I'd better," he growled. He looked at her touchily. "What's wrong, Plautilla?"

"Olimpio . . ."

"Well, what is it?"

"I can't sleep!"

"Don't be a goose."

Suddenly she flung herself against the table and gripped his arm passionately. "Tell me the truth, please, Olimpio!"

"What truth is there to tell?"

She looked deep into his eyes, which were black, hard, petulant; and her voice grew dull and thin. "Olimpio, listen to what I say. There are rumors down in the village. They're saying that Signor Francesco was killed."

"Idle talk. What of it?"

"You had nothing to do with this death?"

"Sheer absurdity. Why should I?"

"You did nothing, nothing at all? . . ."

"Utter fiddlesticks," snapped Olimpio. "What do you take me for? A murderer?"

"No, no," pleaded Plautilla.

"Then be still and go to bed!"

For a moment Plautilla stood close beside him with her hand on his shoulder. Then she kissed his tangled hair and slipped softly from the room.

Up in Beatrice's chamber the last embers shone in the hearth. Plautilla lay down by her sister in front of the fire. No one stirred but she knew that all three women lay wide awake, and when she glanced at Artemisia she could see her eyes glittering through their lashes.

3

The next morning at dawn all four of the women rose promptly, and they set to work packing the bags and getting ready to leave the castle. The clothes were carefully folded and laid in a hamper; the blankets were sprinkled with balsam and stowed in the cupboard. The cutlery and the silver were wrapped in little jackets of pea-green felt. The two sisters went scampering up and down the winding stairway, and Olimpio helped Giorgio set the storerooms in order — tightening the spigots of the wine barrels, laying the bottles on the shelf, locking the rooms in the servants' quarters, bolting the shutters above the terrace. Likewise Olimpio took the ladders which were lying in the empty dungeon and carried them off and locked them carefully in one of the cellars; and he hammered the bars in the dungeon window back into shape as best he could.

Plautilla was folding an empty mattress when she noticed a long black stain. And a little later, as she was laying away the pillows in the antechamber, she caught sight of a blood-soaked sheet behind the chest. Her first notion of the moment was that these were menstrual stains, but then she drew out the sheet and saw that the blood was thick and massive.

"Signora Lucrezia!" she cried, stung with dread. "What's this I see?"

"Hush, Plautilla," said the lady sharply. "Go soak the sheet in a copper basin."

And a little later she called Plautilla to her side and said graciously:

"Look, Plautilla. Here's a petticoat of mine you can have. And the dishes there on the shelf, the ones with the dolphin — they're yours too, if you have use for them. But be careful not to break them . . . There's a parcel down in the hall, by the way. It's clean wool for a mattress. Take it along to your house, my dear. They're all things that I'll have no use for."

Plautilla's voice trembled. "Thank you, signora . . . tell me, signora . . ."

"Yes?"

"There are tales, signora . . ."

"What tales?"

"Down in the village they're telling them! Strange tales about this death of Signor Francesco."

"Hush, don't talk about it, my dear."

"There's only one thing that frightens me, and this is it, signora! Was my husband Olimpio a part of the killing?"

"Mercy, no," said Lucrezia rapidly. "Don't fret, Plautilla. He had nothing to do with it . . ."

Plautilla knelt on the floor and started to wrap up the dishes: beautiful things they all were, these Neapolitan platters, with a golden dolphin in the center framed in a delicate wreath of sea shells.

XIV

Two days later all was finished, the bags and the hampers were packed, and the ladies sat by the window listening to the buzzing of the wasps. A lovely autumn day: the scent of cider was in the air. The grass in the hills was warm and lustrous, like chinchilla.

There was the sound of a horn; Beatrice looked down at the valley and saw a party of horsemen crossing the bridge.

"They're coming," she said, tapping Lucrezia on the wrist.

"At last," said Lucrezia in a dry, leafy tone.

Not long after, the four horsemen halted at the trough and watered their beasts, and Giorgio opened the gate and the visitors entered: Giacomo Cenci and young Bernardo, together with two others, somberly clad — their cousin Cesare Cenci and the family tailor, Orazio Pomella.

They entered the hall. Beatrice kissed her two brothers austerely.

"We were deeply shocked," murmured Giacomo.

"It was a terrible thing," said Beatrice.

The brother and sister looked calmly and profoundly at one another, and that was all that was said that evening about the death. No visits were paid to the little sepulcher in Santa Maria, no gifts were submitted to the priest for the saying of prayers, and a strange unreality pervaded the air of the castle. A sultry stillness took the place of all the panic and lamentation. Dinner was served in the lower hall, where the fire was lit though the day was steaming, and not long after they all went up to their beds; the four visitors were led by Giorgio to the upper story, which had once been the dwelling of the seneschal and his wife. And long before midnight all was dark in the castle, the little windows were barred and all the candles were snuffed.

2

Soon after sunrise two mules were laden with bundles and baskets, and the muleteers and servants followed behind on foot. Two horses were hired in the village and the party set out: Lucrezia and Beatrice on the Cenci horses, Giacomo and Bernardo on the mares from the village. The cousin Cesare and the tailor Pomella came following after, and last of all rode Olimpio and his little daughter Vittoria, who was the apple of his eye and whom he vowed to take with him.

One little contretemps occurred, however, before they left that sunny morning, and that was the unforseen arrival of the tinker Marzio Catalano. He came shamefacedly to the castle gate and requested an interview with Olimpio. But Olimpio was down in the village bargaining about the mares, and Beatrice came to the gate instead.

"What do you want?" she said to the tinker.

"I want what was promised," said Marzio sullenly.

"What was promised?" said Beatrice gently.

"You know, signora, the silver and linen."

"There's little silver and not much linen, Marzio, and it's packed in the hampers."

"I shan't leave here, signora, without the things that were promised me!"

So Beatrice hurried into the castle and begged Giacomo for some coins — a small handful of testoni — which she slipped into a bag. Then she went to her father's bedchamber and unlocked the great chest and took the cloak which still hung there, and she hurried back to Marzio.

"Take these," she said quickly.

The tinker looked glum. "It's little enough," he muttered.

"Very well," said Beatrice sharply. "I'll send you some money from Rome, and some clothes. But this is all I can find now and that's the end of it, Marzio."

"My wife had a dress," ventured Marzio. "A purple gown that I gave one day . . ."

"Yes?" said Beatrice impatiently.

"As security on a loan from Signor Francesco. He took the gown and laid it away. Give me that gown, Signora Beatrice."

"Wait," said Beatrice, and she went once more to the master's bedchamber, for she remembered having seen the gown in a lower drawer among some blankets. She found it and rolled it carefully and gave it to Marzio by the gate.

"Here you are. And now go. You'd better leave La Petrella."

So Marzio wandered off again, clapping his hat on his long lean head, slipping the coins in his pocket and tuck-

ing the garments under his arm; his eyes were mournful
and his heart was bleak, but he sang quite sweetly as he
went along.

3

Olimpio led the horse forward and held the stirrup for
Beatrice. Then he vaulted to the saddle of his own gray
mare and gathered up the reins.

And the party was off at last on the road to Posticciola.
All the way to the bridge they were followed by a host of
curious children, gaping peasants and village simpletons
who peered at the ladies with foolish eyes. But one by
one they straggled away and the silent riders entered the
woods; only the birds and slinking foxes peeped through
the leaves as they clattered by.

The wind had veered. A glory of clouds hung in the sky
by Caprodosso. The great beeches shone like satin, the waters tinkled like silver bells. Beatrice was riding in front. A
jay went shooting over the path and his wings were bright
as a gentian. Two great butterflies went waltzing side by
side over the goldenrod and the leaves fell from the tiger-
striped laurel, flame by flame.

The song of a thrush dropped through the boughs, clear
and deft as a copper button. A spider dangled from a tree
and drew his thread across her cheek, and once a ladybird
dropped out of the sky and lit on her glove.

"Make a wish, signora!" cried the muleteer who was
walking beside her.

"I've made it," said Beatrice.

[117   ]

The muleteer smiled at her. "Don't tell anyone . . ."

She leaned forward and stroked the warm chestnut silk of Pino's ears, and at that moment the whole world seemed to be born in iridescence. The past was a sea and the future a cloud; only the present leaped and sparkled. The hoofs drummed crisply against the pebbles; a locust went zooming at the turn of the path. Three low blasts came echoing from the heart of the wood, and a moment later a lonely huntsman went galloping through the glade. The stream sprang over a cliff like a long glassy tongue and the towers of Posticciola loomed in front of them, sudden and menacing. The road dipped and they entered the States of the Pope.

They came to an inn soon after sunset, not far from Monteleone. There was a smell of bulging cheeses; a soup of leeks squirmed in the caldron. An old witch in a tattered bonnet came shuffling up to their table. "Wine!" cried Giacomo, and she started pouring from a great jereboam. The wine danced in the fluted glasses, which blazed like great opals, and little by little forgetfulness clouded their eyes. Soon they went to their separate beds and Beatrice sat by the pane and listened — the horses stirred in their stalls, a groom made water against the wall, and a moment later the night was still and pure as a crystal. Not a sound, not a footstep; the long Apennines were sleeping and only the air was still awake, all spicy with pasturelands. There was an orchard beyond the wall, the moon shone cool on the misted plums — now and then a fruit fell hissing into the deep black grasses.

X V

THE HILLS below them still huddled under the shawl of the night — a series of smooth blue folds, like a herd of buffaloes.

But then the sun scattered the fog. The day grew brilliant and cloudless. They passed Nerola and they smelled the rich black ooze of the trodden grapes, and when they came to Monte Libretti they smelled the freshly smoked sausages dangling in long black garlands over the butcher's alley.

Near Tre Ponti they saw the boars nuzzling among the oaks looking for truffles; blue-black, dolphin-snouted, with the golden dust spraying about them.

The hills sank toward Mentana and they stopped in a grove to breathe the horses. They could see a brook flashing through the branches; sun-tanned boys were floundering in the shallows. An old peasant strolled by with a pair of freshly caught trout, and they paid him two paoli and started roasting them over the flames while Pomella tucked the wine jug in the cool, hissing water.

Finally they rose and started off again, lazy and limp with wine. The breezy slopes melted gradually into warm roll-

ing meadows. Flocks of sheep crossed their path and peacock butterflies came skipping along, and then the road
widened suddenly, the carts came clacking, and finally the
rooftops of Rome rose out of the haze like a field of pop-
pies.

Giacomo drew alongside of Beatrice as they approached
Monte Sacro.

"Well," he said. "Tell me about it."

"There is nothing to tell," said Beatrice.

"How did it happen? Exactly?"

"You've heard from Giorgio already."

"The balcony crumbled; was that it?"

"Yes," said Beatrice. "That was it."

Giacomo looked at her slantingly. "Don't be aloof
with me, Beatrice. I'm the head of the family, please remember."

Beatrice smiled. "Bravo, Giacomo."

"Look," said Giacomo venomously. "I don't know what
you've been up to. You and that rascal of a seneschal. I
don't know and I don't wish to know. But watch your man-
ners, please, Beatrice."

And suddenly Beatrice grew red with fury. "Say whatever you like, Giacomo. But remember this, if you please
— what's been done we've done together. You as much as I
or Olimpio. Listen, Giacomo — do you know what it's like?
Month after month of filth and imprisonment? No, you
don't. You lived merrily in Monte Cenci, my dear, and
when you gave your approval — oh, don't deny it, please,
Giacomo — you didn't give it out of pity or indignation.
You gave it out of avarice. I loathed my father, I tell you,
Giacomo, and yet I loved him more than you did!"

The sun was low. Treacherous clouds were seeping out

of the west, raw and ruddy. They rode silently over the Ponte Nomentano and the goat bells tinkled beneath the arches.

2

They entered Rome by the light of dusk. They passed wearily through Porta Pia and made their way past Santa Susanna toward the walls of the Quirinal. The chandeliers were already bright with flames in the great palazzi. They rode down past the house of the Antonelli and entered a tangle of twisting lanes.

It was night now; the torchlight played on the arcades. They followed the Street of the Dark Little Shops. The lamps were glowing in the tiny dens, which looked like a row of secret caverns. The bootmakers were hammering away on their little stools, and the great heraldic volumes shone on the bookseller's stall. They paused by a fishwife's cart and sucked at the fresh juicy sea urchins. A little girl was rolling a hoop down Via Paganica.

They could hear the thin, lilting music of the Tortoise Fountain, and then they turned the corner and Beatrice's heart beat with excitement. The light from the ironmonger's shop shone on the lovely wet statues. The water sprang from the leaping bodies, the great shells gleamed like phosphorus; the spray danced over the basin like a swarm of fireflies.

Finally they arrived at Monte Cenci. They climbed the dusty slope, entered the court of the palace and dismounted wearily. The groom ran up from the stable while the maid Bastiana flung open the door with a little cry.

She held up her lamp and peered at Beatrice. "Ah, my lovely signora! It's a long, long time you've been away!"

"And a sad time," said Beatrice.

"God bless you," whispered the maid. "Come. Everything's ready."

Beatrice climbed the marble stairs to the dusty flickering of the pendent lamps and the vague, familiar odor of the great blue tapestries. A lighted brazier was in her room. There was an aroma of incense pastilles. She drew the curtains from her bed and lay down fully dressed. For a long time she lay there, staring emptily at the walls. Then she rose and stepped to her window. Nothing had changed. Nothing whatever.

Voices rose from the Ghetto and a cool gray mist came up from the Tiber. The same gilded mermaid hung over the tavern door. The same little crucifix burned over the archway, and the same smell of leather and salted fish lurked in the air. The bells that rang from San Salvatore had the same singing ripple; the bells from San Tommaso had their old gloomy echo.

The door creaked. She turned quickly. A broad shadow hung in the doorway.

It was a moment before she recognized him. "Please," she whispered. "Be careful."

"No one can hear us," he said.

"The walls can hear us," said Beatrice.

He came closer, with a sidling animal stealth. She could hear the hiss of his breath; she caught his warm, rootlike fragrance.

"Beatrice. Come. I've been waiting . . ."

Beatrice stared at him icily. "And you'll keep on waiting. We're in Rome now, Olimpio."

"What do you mean?" growled Olimpio.

"We'll forget what has happened. That's what I mean."

Olimpio's eyes grew sharp and narrow. "I'll never forget what has happened . . . Nor will you, my darling. I'll see to that."

Beatrice stared through the window. The smoke rose from the Ghetto in slow blue spirals, mingling with the fog. The dark scrollwork above the gate shone damp and scaly; the iron torch-holders along the wall looked like great, clinging bats.

She drew her hair back from her forehead. "Listen, Olimpio," she said. "You'll do what I tell you, and I tell you this. There's an end to this thing between us."

For a while neither of them stirred. The room was entirely dark now. There was only the cherry-bright eye of the little brazier. Olimpio tiptoed toward the window and stood behind her without moving. She could feel the heat from his body. His breath came more quickly.

Finally, ever so daintily, he put his hand on her shoulder and placed his mouth on the nape of her neck.

She wheeled around furiously. "Did you hear what I told you?"

He held her firm. "Yes, my darling. I heard."

His face froze into fine gray furrows, like a slab of rock. He took her wrists and pressed them against the wall, then leaned over her gently. The pain grew sharp but she said nothing. Finally she sank to her knees in front of him.

"Now," he whispered. "You'll do as I say, my dove."

3

An hour later the family was sitting at the long black table — Giacomo now at the head of it and his wife Ludovica behind the candles, and between them Lucrezia and Beatrice, young Bernardo and little Paolo. Facing Beatrice sat the cousin Cesare, a thin, steely man with a profile sharp and heavily dented, like a saw.

Lucrezia had drawn up her hair under a small green toque. Her eyes were bright and nervous as she chattered away briskly.

"There'll be a ball at the Lancellotti," said Ludovica, "next month."

"Don't speak of balls!" exclaimed Lucrezia. "I haven't a dress to my name . . . And then a month will be too soon, don't you agree? You know perfectly well what these people expect of us."

"I dare say," said Ludovica, a lean, dark girl with a provocative squint, not unattractive aside from this trivial blemish, but with a hard, clanging voice which set Beatrice's teeth on edge.

Beatrice said in a dull, flat tone: "You look well, Ludovica."

The girl blushed furiously. "Ah, Beatrice — praise from you is praise indeed! But I'll return it, my angel — I've never seen you so ripe and lovely . . . Tell her what we're thinking, please, Giacomo."

But Giacomo merely raised his brows.

"It's time you thought of a husband, sweet," blurted Ludovica crudely. "You're as fine a match as any to be

[124]

found here in Rome . . . Now there's that boy of the Odeschalchi and there's Guido Caetani, not to mention that little hunchback Frangipani — what's his name?"

"Hush, hush, Ludovica."

"There's no point in being funereal," went on the woman, "now is there? Let's be candid. There's not one broken heart at this table, I'm bound to say." Her eyes glittered maliciously. "Still, it must have been dreadful. Tell us about it, Beatricciola. Your poor nerves — mercy me! Did you swoon away when you saw him lying there, down in the bushes?"

"Strange thing, the way he fell," said Giacomo curtly.

"It certainly was," put in Lucrezia. "Time and again I used to tell him, 'Don't go on that balcony, Francesco, my love, it's all rickety and flimsy!' But he just wouldn't listen. He was dreadfully stubborn . . ."

"Well, it's nobody's fault," said Giacomo, holding his goblet under the light.

"Still, I keep blaming myself, I really do," wailed Lucrezia. "I should have seen that the thing was mended. Little, of course, did I dream . . ."

"There's no use fretting," said Giacomo.

"No," sighed Lucrezia, "I suppose there isn't." She added thoughtfully, with a glance at Beatrice: "Still, you know how it is. One keeps dreaming up reproaches out of the air, somehow or other."

"Quite," said Giacomo sardonically.

"But there is this," said Lucrezia. "He was suffering dreadfully these days. The gout, you know and that other thing . . ."

"Please," said Beatrice savagely.

"Nonsense, darling, there's no mystery about it. He lay

in anguish, I don't mind telling you. Fussing and fuming and moaning and piddling the whole day long, just like a baby. So in a way, after all . . ."

"You're perfectly right," said Ludovica. "When life's a series of groans and agonies, what's the use of prolonging it?"

"That's what I thought," said Lucrezia softly.

"Listen," said Beatrice, raising her forefinger.

The black spaniel by the door pricked up his ears and growled softly. A low hiss came through the windows, like a rustle of taffeta. And then the drops came drumming against the panes, sharp as gravel.

"The storms are coming," said Ludovica.

"They're starting early," observed Giacomo.

There was a powerful clap of thunder. The windows shook and the candles shivered, and the red wine leaped in the narrow goblets. The tapestries rippled along the wall as though a rat were darting beneath.

And a moment later the rain came clattering in a breathless rush. Beatrice rose from the table and looked through the middle window. The roofs were cascading, white as foam under the stabs of lightning. Rivulets scurried down the alleys, dogs ran scampering for shelter. A lonely carriage went skidding toward Via del Portico.

And that was the beginning of the catastrophic rains.

XVI

FOR FIVE DAYS it kept raining — a gray gusty rain that sent waterfalls from the Palatine and torrents gushing from Monte Mario. The Piazza Navona was a quagmire. The coaches floundered in the mud and the vineyards beyond the Vatican were afloat in a mighty pool.

Then for a while the downpour ceased. A pale green sun oozed through the clouds, and with the coming of October all was well in the city. The great balls were beginning; sheep were roasting on the spit and battalions of plum tarts came rattling out of the ovens. The little bow-legged tailors sat with their shears in a flood of satin. New felt hats in the latest style were ordered from the Florentine hatmakers. Slippers with beaded toes and gold-leafed heels were brought from the cobblers, and the candlemakers molded their wax in the shape of porpoises and pineapples. The towering hedges of the Colonna were clipped and hung with painted garlands; in the court of the Orsini the sculptors were setting a bright new fountain.

And for a while the city was merry and all went well on Monte Cenci. Olimpio the seneschal and his daughter Vittoria had settled for good in the palazzo, and he spent his days strutting lazily through the smart piazzettas. He wore a diamond ring on his finger which he showed to all and sundry — "A token of love from a noble lady," he said with a wink: it came from Beatrice. In the late afternoons, if the sun was out, he climbed the Aventine with young Bernardo and there in the fields by Santa Sabina they played at *pallamaglio,* which was a kind of tennis. He'd ride about on his fine gray mare with his sword dangling beside him, paying visits to the neighboring courtyards, where he'd sit and gossip with the dandies. And back in the Palazzo Cenci he'd go roaming about the rooms, ordering the servants to and fro, babbling with Beatrice, teasing Lucrezia, bullying Giacomo and leering at Ludovica. Finally it reached a point where he dined at the table with the rest of the family, and there were vicious little scenes of innuendo and recrimination, so that Giacomo soon developed a detestation for this castellan, this great bully who filled the house with his blasphemies and scandals.

2

Ugly rumors had crossed the hills and finally seeped into Rome, village gossip from La Petrella that spread its poison through the piazzas and finally burst out openly in the great palazzi. Curious glances followed Beatrice when she rode through the streets. There were whisperings and nudgings when Olimpio played on the Aventine. And the day came when the authorities were compelled to take notice, and certain measures were taken in the Vatican as well as the Kingdom of Naples.

But as yet the family of the Cenci lived in idle indifference. Bernardo would play in the tennis fields while Giacomo went riding in Via Appia. Lucrezia lolled in her
cushions nibbling wafers of almond paste. And Beatrice
sat by the window with her lute, singing song after song,
and her world little by little grew totally unreal: the darkness and violence were exterminated from her mind, and
she lived in a succession of drowsy imaginings — a huntsman galloping through the woods, an eagle circling over
the waterfall; and nothing troubled this little limbo except in the late afternoon, when the candles were still unlit
and Olimpio came blustering into her room with his bar-
barous kisses and caresses.

Sometimes in the stillness of the siesta hour, when the
whole palazzo lay dozing, she'd sing Camilla's old song,
which still brought tears to her eyes.

> Oh my love rode over the meadows
> While the sun sank in the west,
> Oh my love lay under the cherry tree
> With his lips against my breast.
>
> Oh my love climbed out of the lily pond
> And he drew my limbs apart,
> But now he lies in Portugal
> And the blood flows from his heart . . .

And sometimes in the late afternoon she'd go sauntering to the Campo dei Fiori, where the stalls were laden
with autumn fruits and all sorts of pumpkins and cabbages.
There were baskets and brooms and copper kettles, earth-
enware jugs and burnished ewers, and cage upon cage of
doves and guinea hens, Spanish magpies, African parakeets.
One young fellow carried about a bright red vixen on a

chain. Another had a swan that followed him around like a spaniel. The ruddy market folk went milling about, the auctioneer's cry mixed with the squeals of the fishwives, and the whole aroma of the populace filled the air, acid and leathery. She'd walk down the long narrow lanes of the artisans — the Street of the Keymakers and the Carpenters, the Street of the Basket-weavers and Latchmakers, and then back past the walls which enclosed the Ghetto like a separate city, locked and bolted at sunset and opened again after dawn.

3

Or she'd stroll to the nunnery of Montecitorio and sit in the cloister, chatting away with her old schoolmistress, whose name was Sister Ippolita. And if the sun was still warm she'd climb through the groves of the Gianicolo and visit the Church of San Pietro Montorio, which was the home of her confessor, Fra Andrea Belmonte. Fra Andrea was a fat little man with a high-pitched voice and the soft, impenetrable gaze of a eunuch. He'd sit by her side under the pines as the sunlight slid from the rosy rooftops, and his voice would flow over her consciousness like waves over a beach.

Or she'd wander over the Bridge of the Four Heads which led to the island of San Bartolomeo. Here she'd linger among the willows, watching the fishermen float past with their nets. Sometimes she crossed over the Ponte Sisto into the jungle of Trastevere, where the *popolo* held sway in all its clamor and sensuality. Voices came screaming out of the kitchens, laundry swayed on a thousand lines, children rolled in the alleys, witches crouched in their hovels. Dogs, cats, mules and roosters, pigs and goats ran helter-skelter; the flavor of wine and sizzling olive oil danced through the air. The little urchins gaped as she passed with their great doelike eyes, and the fine young bucks in their bulging breeches cried out: *"Che bella donna!"* And she felt her senses dissolving in this seething promiscuity; the rest of the world melted away in this hot, hoarse earthiness.

There was a broad stone stairway near the Porta Settimiana, and here the blind used to gather and sit in the sun. There were seven of them that came every day and sat in a row — the youngest only a youth, the oldest a white-bearded patriarch. They'd whisper little jokes and anecdotes from ear to ear, and strange shadowy smiles would go flitting from face to face. Tiny gifts would go traveling down the aisle from hand to hand — a bead, or a shell, or a feather — and each would fondle it curiously. Beatrice was stirred and fascinated by this desperate human poetry, and every time that she passed she'd drop a *paolo* in each palm.

And down by the doors of San Crisogono the cripples would congregate — little monsters clattering along on wooden stumps tied to their knees. They wore tall, tufted hats, and each wore a dog's tail sown to his sleeve. There they'd sit, cackling away, plucking the lice from their seams, and when Beatrice passed they flicked at their shirts to show their wounds. "Signora! *Per carità!*" And she'd toss them a coin and hurry on.

Late at night, when all the others lay asleep in their beds, she'd go and peep through the window into the cool autumn night. Once she saw a bright carriage following a

line of helmeted horsemen, torches flashing on cloaks of
carmine and netted gems in the ladies' hair, and she heard
the deep croaking of trumpets beyond the Tiber. Then
everything grew still again, a foggy disk hung over the
towers, and only the cats went hissing through the lanes by
Monte Cenci.

4

One sunny day in mid-November, Beatrice went shopping with the girl Vittoria. They rode in their coach to
Monte Giordano, and there they turned and followed the
lanes toward the teeming arcades of Via dei Coronari.

The great ladies from the palaces were rustling about,
toying with fabrics and bric-a-brac. There were luminous
pearling silks of green and saffron from Como, and scarves
of Venetian lace patterned with centaurs and unicorns.
There were marble boxes from Bergamo, copper caskets
from Brescia. Mirrors from Padua caught the sun, framed
in intertwining serpents, and there were candlesticks from
the illustrious Sienese workshops. There were goblets
from Burano and slippers from Mantua, sculptured ivo-
ries from Zanzibar, stilettos from Damascus. Tufts of er-
mine from Muscovy, obscure spices from Tibet, jars of
incense from Djiddah and the subtle teas of Colombo. The
air was pungent with pigskin and Milanese brocade, and
the Northern cloakmakers stood gesturing with cataracts of
satin. Here and there a bearded goldsmith stood hovering
by his treasures — tiny dragons and basilisks tucked in trays
of green velvet. The perfume-makers minced along with

their wicked little bottles — attar of roses from Bulgaria, powdered lilac from Languedoc. And toward dusk the famous courtesans sauntered past with their lackeys, and willowy boys with hennaed hair stood lisping beside the fountain.

Beatrice bought an agate box and some fine coal-black velvet: this last, she thought, as a gift for Olimpio — a splendid suit could be made of it. As she sauntered back to her coach she caught sight of two ladies, the Princess Orsini and her cousin Giulia, dabbling casually among the laces. Beatrice smiled at them and beckoned, but they quickly turned away, and she rode back to the palace with a sting like poison in her heart.

5

It was twilight when Olimpio came lumbering into her room.

"You look tired," he said. He took her chin in his fingers, like a goblet.

"I was shopping," said Beatrice bleakly.

Olimpio's eyes began to glitter. "Ah," he said. "What did you buy?"

"Trifles," said Beatrice with a shrug. She tossed the agate box on the bed.

Olimpio plucked it from the pillow. A dreamy smile hung on his lips. "Charming. Whom is it for?"

"Paolo," she said. "It's his birthday tomorrow."

Olimpio looked woebegone. But a moment later his eyes began to flicker.

"Come, sweetheart. Let me kiss you."

Beatrice glanced at him carelessly. There he stood: a huge child, vain, vulnerable, greedy. She felt touched all of a sudden.

"Here," she said. "This is for you, dear." She flung the velvet across the chair. It went coiling among the shadows, sleek and swarthy.

"Lovely," purred Olimpio. He knelt on the floor; he was blushing with delight. His thick brown fingers crawled over the cloth and stroked it tenderly, as though it were alive. Then he sniffed at it quaintly and drew it cautiously over his cheek.

She looked away. The whole room was filled with the odor of exile — raw and stinging, like ammonia; it drew tears from her eyes.

Olimpio clutched at the velvet and stared at Beatrice with puzzled eyes.

"Beatrice . . . You love me a little, don't you?"

Her face was dull and expressionless.

"What's wrong? Tell me," whispered Olimpio.

"Nothing at all," said Beatrice drowsily.

He crouched close beside her and raised her palm to his lips. "What have I done? Why are you angry?"

But she scarcely heard him. She was listening to the dusky sounds down in the piazza: muted cries, bawdy laughter, the sly gavotte of a fountain. The night was rolling over the Ghetto, glossy and tense, like an enormous wave.

Olimpio frowned. "Is something troubling you?"

Beatrice smiled at him, amused.

"Beatrice! I don't understand you! You're like a bird,"

muttered Olimpio. "Some day you'll fly through the window and leave me forever . . ."

And he buried his head in her lap with a little cry.

6

She drew her fingers dreamily along the back of his head. His hair was rich and sinuous, like a setter's, ending in a crisp little curl on the nape of his neck. It seemed to squirm under her touch; it uttered a tiny dry hiss. His shoulders heaved very gently, the heat of his mouth clung to her hip.

"Are you asleep?"

He didn't answer. She slid her thumb along his ear lobe, which felt soft and velvety, like a kitten's paw.

The night deepened. A lamp was lit in the opposite wing of the palazzo: a parallelogram of gold lit on the wall above her bed.

"Olimpio! . . . Wake up!"

But he kept on sleeping. She felt his heart beating feebly against her knee. She leaned over and kissed him on the temple, very lightly: his skin felt coarse and feverish beneath her lips. He seemed at that moment hopelessly remote, a lost soul. And for the first time she felt a pang of something close to real love.

XVII

A<small>ND IN THE MEANTIME</small> the wheels of justice were beginning to move; slowly at first and lethargically, but then
more and more ominously.

In view of certain unsavory tales which had reached his
ears, the Prince Colonna, who owned the castle, found it
expedient one day to send an auditor to La Petrella and
investigate the death of his tenant Cenci. This auditor
was a man, Biagio Querco, from Frosinone, a lively fellow
with broken teeth and jaded eyes like a turtle's. He set up
lodgings in the castle and proceeded to interview the villagers — the butcher, the cobbler, the fishmonger's wife,
as well as the widow Lucia. He examined the balcony;
he searched the closets; he poked in the thicket; he
prowled through the dungeon. He even paid an unex-
pected visit to the house of the druggist Gasperini, who
happened to be a close kinsman of Plautilla's, and there he
found under a bed a parcel of wool and some mattress
covers, scrupulously laundered but still perceptibly stained.
And some days later he compiled a full report of his find-
ings and sent it by messenger to his employer in Rome.

And not long after, in view of similar distasteful rumors

that had reached the Kingdom of Naples, a royal commissioner was sent by the Viceroy Don Herzio de Guzman,
Count of Olivares, to ascertain if it were true that Francesco Cenci had been murdered. This royal commissioner
was an individual named Carlo Tirone, a tall and satur-
nine man with a nose like a vulture's. Tirone likewise in-
vited the confidence of the villagers of La Petrella, and he
promptly searched the castle from cellar to roof. He found
that the tinker Catalano, who had returned from the hills
not long previously, had hurriedly fled from the village
some three hours after his arrival; and he forthwith proceeded to examine the tinker's wife Porzia. And that same
day he made a gratifying discovery in the castle cellar.
First of all he found two ladders, of precisely the type that
he expected. And then he came on a dusty toolbox in a far-
off corner; he flung it open and found, all tangled among
some ropes, a long wooden rolling pin and a Lombardy
hammer.

And thereupon he had the body of Francesco Cenci ex-
humed from the sepulcher and had the head removed by
a surgeon for a more meticulous examination. Two days
later the experts gave it as their mellowed opinion that
this head bore certain wounds which derived from the
blows of a powerful implement — some kind of hatchet,
perhaps, or hammer; no elder thorn could have produced
them.

And after further private interviews the commissioner
Tirone issued a proclamation in which he stated that a
murder had been committed in La Petrella; that the victim was the noble Roman Francesco Cenci; that the perpe-
trators of this crime were the seneschal Olimpio and the
tinker Marzio; and that the conspirators involved were

the Signora Lucrezia and the Signora Beatrice, who were respectively the wife and the daughter of the deceased.

2

But Rome lay far from La Petrella, and news moved slowly and circuitously, and for a while life went on in all its indolence on Monte Cenci. Evil tales made their way into the stables and kitchens, but on the *piano nobile* the folk spoke little and discreetly, and the family took its meals in a mood of dreamlike isolation.

The boy Paolo, the youngest in the family, fell sick with fever one day; he reeled on the stairs and a thick yellow flood poured from his mouth. Two maids came running and carried him up to his room, where he lay groaning and shivering the whole night long.

And some days later the weather grew ugly and dark again. The wind kept blowing from the south with peculiar insistence, and the fortunetellers up on the Viminal muttered of doom and desolation.

And so the weeks went by and the leaves fell withered from the poplars. The days grew drearier, the nights grew deeper, and the smell of charcoal filled the courtyards.

In mid-November — the fourteenth of the month it happened to be — a representative of the Papal prosecutor called on the Cenci. A casual visit, thoroughly discreet, apologetic indeed; and a cursory examination of Giacomo and Beatrice ensued. Two days later the authorities repeated their visit and interviewed Signora Lucrezia. All three gave their customary versions of Francesco's fall from the balcony, and the testimony was duly signed in the presence of a notary. Then they were courteously informed that a guard would be placed at the outer door, and that they were not to set foot outside the precincts of the palace until further notification, under a forfeit of fifty thousand scudi.

3

That night no rain fell, but a heavy mist rose up from the river. Beatrice stood by the window and saw the streets lost in a vapor, the tiny lights piercing the dullness like stars in the early morning. The dome of San Carlo shone thick and blunt in the fog; the whole city looked shapeless and prehistoric.

The door opened and Giacomo entered. For a moment the two stood facing one another, eyes tense and defiant as they tried to pierce this vague oppression.

"It looks evil," said the brother.

"So it does," said the sister quietly.

"It's Lucrezia I'm worried about. She's a fool. She'll speak carelessly."

"I've told her to admit nothing. To be ignorant of everything."

"She should never have known in the first place.'

"That was impossible. God knows she favored it."

"And now," said Giacomo, "look at the woman. An agony of remorse."

"No," said Beatrice. "Not in the least. An agony of fretfulness, that's all."

As they stood there in the candlelight they looked almost like twins: the bitter chin and high cheekbones, with the eyes deep-set and smoldering.

But it was Giacomo who looked like a woman: the subtle lips, the elusive glance. Beatrice's face shone with a hard and bellicose brilliance.

"And so it is," said Giacomo slowly. "How can we tell our fears from our conscience?"

"Have you a conscience?" said Beatrice dryly. She drew her fingers across her eyelids.

"Well, I hope," replied Giacomo, "that my feelings lie deeper than lust or vengeance."

Beatrice looked at him with infinite weariness in her eyes. "Listen, Giacomo. I felt neither lust nor vengefulness at La Petrella. Disgust, yes. Fear, yes. Anger, yes. But that's all."

"As you wish," said Giacomo icily. "All things are possible to justify."

"To the world, if one is lucky. But there are others," said Beatrice heavily.

"You will carry this thing for the rest of your life, then," said Giacomo.

"Very well. I can bear it. I'm not afraid of loneliness," said Beatrice. Her eyes grew distant, indifferent. "And you," she added listlessly, "you'll forget. You'll forgive yourself. Your mind will end by drawing a veil over it. And for that, my dear, I feel nothing but pity."

The heat was gone out of the room; a dull chill crept in through the window.

"Good night, Giacomo."

"Good night," said Giacomo, and he walked into the dark, echoing hallway.

4

She felt herself shivering. A spasm of nausea shot through her. The membranes behind her eyeballs were burning like pepper. She sank down by the table and ran her fingers along the candle. In the mirror another hand moved slowly, searchingly along the wax.

She saw her face staring back at her, suddenly alert, as though listening. For an instant she scarcely recognized it. Strange highlights played in the eyes, caressed the bold, arrogant cheekbones. The neck looked lean and brittle, the forehead icy, ascetic. The curves in her face had frozen into cold, pale angles. Appalled by the feverish, almost lunatic look in her eyes, she crushed the flame with the palm of her hand. Then she folded her arms and sat motionless, staring into the darkness.

She abdicated all thought; she postponed all decisions. She closed her eyes and slid softly into a haze of bygone dreams. A cloud-dappled sky; balconies mirrored in the water; the golden light on the arches; ripples trembling beneath a bridge. A hooded boat drifted past, there was a stranger in green velvet . . . Yes, there still was a chance of happiness, even of love! There still was a chance of freedom, if only she could plan it all carefully: gather the money, bribe the groom, set out in the darkness for Perugia, or Pesaro . . .

The dream faded. The wet air flowed in past the curtains. Her silhouette, dark and featureless, hung in the octagonal mirror. The tension, the dread were invisible. All she saw was a shaggy head, like an ape's, slightly bowed, as though in obedience to some inexorable law in her being.

XVIII

TIME PASSED, the rains kept falling, the clouds churned over the hills. Christmas was near, and in spite of the weather there was an air of celebration: the news spread through the city that the Pope was returning. Seven months had been spent by Clement VIII in Ferrara, which had recently been captured from the family of the d'Este by his nephew, the adroit and indefatigable Cardinal Aldobrandini. Five days before Christmas, after a month spent en route, the Pope came riding from Viterbo and the streets were fluttering with banners.

All month the rains had fallen, but that morning the sun came out; throngs were pouring into the Corso to witness the illustrious procession. A stream of cardinals moved past on horses sumptuously caparisoned, followed by a flood of lesser clergy and canons and choristers. Then came the officials of the militia in brilliant red braided with gold, and finally a horde of knights and ambassadors in fur-fringed brocades. They met the company of the Pope on the slopes of Via Cassia and then rode back into the city through the Porta del Popolo. All ablaze and ashimmer they came clattering down the Corso, followed by a long string of mules and two silver-reined camels. Rugs, tapestries and pennants were hung from the balconies; twigs of fir and gilded ilex were tucked in the eaves. All the way to San Marco the great company went riding, and then they wove through the tangle of lanes that led to the bridge of Sant' Angelo. Folk came seething from the hills to have a peep at the Holy Father: a mountainous man, immensely stout and peculiarly pale, towering a foot or more over the surrounding bevy of cardinals. There was a blowing of fifes as they passed the Palazzo Montalto, and when they came to the Tiber there was a pounding of great tambours. Finally they arrived at St. Peter's, and there His Holiness dismounted. He knelt by the threshold and pressed his thick white lips to the crucifix, and then the choir began to sing as he entered the basilica and moved toward the altar in a slow, gargantuan tread.

That night the whole city was deep in festivity. For once there was starlight, and the air was sweet with burning wood. The Piazza Navona was lined with tinsel-draped stalls, the lamps shone softly on a host of tiny mangers. There was a bleating of horns and a roasting of sausages; there was prancing and pirouetting by Santa Maria della Pace.

2

But again the next morning the rain fell in torrents. A curse and a punishment, said the witches, tightening their tattered shawls, and the prophets predicted a hideous plague throughout the peninsula. Streams came gushing from Monte Mario and went plowing through the vineyards, and the caves of the Colosseum were lost in a giant pool.

That same day, on Monte Cenci, there was a knock on the kitchen door. The cook peered out and saw a quaint sort of rogue on the steps — a rain-soaked vagabond with a glint in his eyes and a good-sized wart on his cheek.

"Well," said the cook, "what's up, my fellow?"

"I've come with a message," said the man.

"A message from the devil, it looks like."

"We'll see," said the man with a leer. "It's for Signora Beatrice, and it's a matter of considerable urgency."

"She's asleep," snapped the cook. "She's dreaming."

"What?" said the fellow. "On a day like this?"

"What's this message of yours?" said the cook.

"It's confidential," said the bright-eyed fellow. He took off his cap and wrung it dry; a thin blue stream wormed its way toward the oven. "I'll have to see her, dreaming or no. Tell her it's a message from La Petrella."

"What's your name?" said the cook.

"Claudio Crespi of Rimini."

"Well, I'll look."

"And look quickly!"

So the cook climbed the stairway and Claudio sat down on a stool by the fire, squeezing the drops out of his jerkin and spreading his doublet in front of the flames. A beautiful kitchen it was, all tidily whitewashed and gleaming with ewers and vats and great silver magnums. On the table lay two pheasants freshly plucked and disemboweled, with the bread and seasoning for the stuffing close beside. There were jars full of spices, thyme and rosemary and bay, and a jug of sweet Sardinian wine to be used for the cooking. Claudio knelt on the floor and raised the jug to his lips. Then he glanced at the door and snatched a sausage from the ceiling. He listened, no one came, and he took the knife from the table and carved a fat slice of cheese and tucked it deftly under his shirt.

The cook came waddling back into the kitchen. "The signora's waiting for you," he said. "She's upstairs, in the room with the tapestries."

The pantry boy Pasquale stepped out to lead the way. Claudio climbed the great stairs and followed the boy to the *piano nobile*. He peered with wonder at the massive chairs, the oaken chests and the chandeliers; he touched the tapestries as he passed and fondled the marble-topped tables. Pasquale simpered, "Wait here, please," and Claudio stood by the window. He could see the rain cascading from the rust-red walls of the Ghetto, and beyond, coiled and swollen, the powerful rush of the Tiber.

A curtain stirred and Beatrice stepped into the room. She was all in black, but a bright golden chain shone on her neck.

Claudio blinked; he was startled by her crystal-clear loveliness.

"What brings you?" she said curtly.

"A delicate matter," said Claudio.

"Yes? Who are you?"

"Claudio of Rimini."

"And who is that, may I ask?"

"Alas," said Claudio, "nothing but a poor young wood carver who's come to Rome to ply his trade."

Beatrice stepped toward the window to look more closely at the stranger. A slim and wiry sort of fellow, with a black goatee and dancing eyes — there was a secret exultation, a tinge of mischief about him.

He looked steadily at Beatrice; he saw the depth in her brooding eyes, the drawn skin which was pale and sickly, and the cool defiance of the bones. He saw the gold of the chain which shone heavily against her throat, finely hammered into a row of little oak leaves and acorns.

"I am not interested, unfortunately," said Beatrice, "in either carvings or the men who carve them."

"Indeed, signora?" said Claudio sorrowfully. "I could make you a lovely little stool . . ."

"I need no stool, nor chair, nor bed."

"Or a fine big candlestick, perhaps?"

"We have candlesticks aplenty."

"Or a mirror? Ah, signora," and he breathed a deep sigh, "there's marvelous loveliness you'd see in a mirror!"

Beatrice crossed the room slowly and came to a halt by the great armchair. She ran her fingers over the carving — the head of a faun with shining horns and two bright-pointed ears, like the ears of a wolf.

"Thank you," she said. "Now be off."

Claudio hesitated a moment. Then he whispered, "Or an ebony jewel box? Neatly cushioned for a golden chain? Or for a ring with a diamond, maybe?"

Beatrice turned her glowing eyes on him. Her voice came patient, deliberate:

"You have your choice. Be off instantly, or be hurled out of the window."

Claudio's face grew pained and reproachful. "It's a pity, signora. The diamond ring that you gave Olimpio would look lovely in ebony . . ."

Beatrice stood without stirring; a great fatigue crept into her eyes.

"Before I leave," said Claudio gently, "may I tell you a

little tale?" There was a dry, thin smile in his foxy counte-
nance. "One fine day, last September, a young wood carver
set forth from Rimini. I forget his name, it might have
been Curzio or Candido or even Claudio. He crossed the
hills and came wandering through the woods of the
Abruzzi. He paused to drink by a stream, signora, and
when he glanced through the trees he caught sight of a
lonely castle on a black, barren rock. And that same moment, as luck would have it, two men stepped out on the
balcony. One was a seneschal and one was a tinker, and
they were carrying a murdered body. They thrust it
violently through the balcony, and it fell into a high-
walled thicket. All this the wood carver saw with his
own sharp eyes. And he saw the ladies of the castle
weeping and crying from the windows. And he came to
Rome by and by, this wandering wood carver, and he
heard quite a number of odd little rumors. He heard that
the tinker had fled to the hills, and that the ladies were
living in Rome, and one day he saw a ring on the hand
of the seneschal . . ."

"A pleasant tale," said Beatrice quietly.

"And edifying, too," remarked Claudio. His voice grew
suave, apologetic. "Forgive me, signora. I'm poor and I'm
hungry . . ."

"State your sum, please," said Beatrice.

"I could ask for a fortune, I think," said Claudio. "But
why should I, after all? I bear you no malice, signora, I
assure you."

"State your sum," repeated Beatrice.

"Well," said Claudio demurely, "give me the chain on
your neck, signora, and my little tale will remain a secret."

Beatrice stood motionless with her eyes fixed viciously

on the wood carver. Then she took the chain from her neck and walked toward him serenely.

"Take the chain," she said with a smile. "Take it and go, my good fellow. I wish you luck with your trade and I trust it will take you back to Rimini."

"You are infinitely gracious," said Claudio, bowing. "And wise as well, Signora Beatrice."

"One last word," said Beatrice casually. "All good things have their limit. If I hear from you again, I will most certainly arrange that . . ."

Claudio chuckled. "No need, signora. No need, I promise you. I'm a man of honor as well as sense and I'm off to Rimini tomorrow . . ."

"God speed you," said Beatrice.

"The Lord protect you," said Claudio.

And he slid through the room and went skipping down to the kitchen. The cook was rolling out the noodles with a long white rolling pin.

"Well, I'm off," said Claudio merrily, and he kissed the cook on the cheek, slapped the pantry boy on the buttocks, and went dancing into the rain.

3

Still it rained and kept raining, and the torrents from the Abruzzi came roaring down through the hills into the Tiber. The river rose ominously; a frenzy of whirlpools seethed past and the foam was tufted with roots and branches. Sheep, swine and newborn foxes lay drowned in the tea-green current. Inch by inch the great tide rose to the brink of the embankment.

Two days before Christmas the Tiber slid over its banks. Only a little at first, then more and more powerfully. It seeped into the lower cells of the prison of Tordinona; half-naked criminals hung wailing from the iron-grilled windows. It came trickling into the cellar of the Osteria dell' Orso, swirling darkly among the wine casks and drenching the charcoal bins and the flour sacks. The great gardens by Via Giulia were covered with yellow lakes, the whole island of San Bartolomeo was a maze of canals.

That night the great flood rolled out in all its fury. All the way from the Ponte Milvio to the Porta Portese it seethed over the banks in great dull sheets. The tiny lanes of Trastevere were knee-deep in water and black rivulets ran gurgling down the aisles of Santa Maria. The little shops in the Botteghe Oscure were turned into grottoes. The seas went scurrying toward the Campidoglio laden with baskets and barrels, loaves of bread, bottles of wine, squealing bird cages and empty cradles. All the insignia of the festival were ripped from the doors; banners and wreaths and gilded dolls went rippling down toward the river.

All night the devastation roared through the city — there was shouting and screaming and cackling and neighing, a bursting of timber and a rumble of bricks, and in the morning the whole heart of the city was under water. The streets were foul-smelling tributaries which churned their way into the great palazzi, drowning the ovens in a mighty hiss and lapping at the high marble stairways. Cataracts came rippling into the convents and the nuns went wading toward Aracoeli, where the steps were soon crowded with prayers and lamentations. The streets were impassable to horses, who lay floating in their stalls. Little rafts were hastily improvised and launched on the noisome waters to rescue the drowning and carry food and wine to the needy.

Christmas Eve saw the water steadily rising. People went swimming and paddling down the alleys toward the Esquiline. A large raft from one of the monasteries capsized next to the Colosseum, and the monks clambered frantically among the colonnades. Night came and there was a ceaseless tolling of bells; folk prayed from their rooftops for the malediction to be ended, and the princes and cardinals flung open their doors and set hampers of bread on the lamplit stairways.

XIX

Christmas Day finally dawned. The rains had stopped falling but the waters still rose and a sickening dread seized the city. Things fell into ruin. The stores of food were rotting away and the stables and pens were littered with corpses. The whole glory of Rome lay festering under the sea. The Temple of Vesta rose from the waves like a floating umbrella and the Arch of Constantine mirrored its frieze in a pool of amber.

And high in the Apennines the snows kept melting in the breath of the sirocco, and still more torrents came sickling into the Tiber. The rich and powerful houses — Colonna, Orsini, Aldobrandini — sent parties of rescue roaming on rafts through Trastevere; victims were plucked out of windows and carried safely to the palaces. Great fires were built in the palace halls and the folk were gathered together; they hung their wet clothes and huddled naked in front of the flames, passing the wine and the cheese while the mothers suckled their babies. The Castel Sant' Angelo rose on its bank like a small peninsula, with ropes and ladders cast from its battlements to guide the swimmers to safety. The little hovels which clung to the

old Roman walls were ripped away, and the ruined caves of
the Palatine were filled with muleteers and stable boys.
Along Via dei Coronari the roofs were covered with populace, all drenched and shivering and bedraggled, wringing their hands and crying for rescue.

And once again twilight came, the skies grew clear and
the stars appeared and the moon shone calm on the flooded
columns. Tiny skiffs moved in silence through the shadowy
lanes and tall figures in black climbed the dripping stairways. There was looting and murdering in the derelict
houses; now and again a great cry pierced the watery stillness. Lamps shone faintly through the windows on the
whirlpools and eddies. Here and there the blaze from a
palace danced gaudily in the flood.

But most of Rome lay in darkness. Courtyards echoed
like cisterns. Marble transepts were filled with invisible
chortlings and gurglings. Only in Santa Maria Maggiore all
the flames were aflicker and the nave was crowded with
wet, weary slumberers. The moonlight shone on the circular lagoon in the Colosseum, mirroring the huge black
corridors and multiple arches. Waters lapped at the stairs
of the basilica of St. Peter's. The great palazzi — the Farnese, the Montalto, the Cenci — emerged from the sea like
geometrical isles. A waterfall fell from the edge of the
Pincio, and the savage shrubs shone in the moonlight like
some dismal vista in the African jungle.

Folk lay sleepless up on the Esquiline, listening to the
walls slowly crumbling. There were rumors that the world
was finally coming to an end, the second flood had arrived
and the sins of the city would see their punishment. The
old witches on the Strada dei Serpenti shook their fingers.
Sin, sin, they kept wailing: vice, debauchery and retribu-

tion! Rome lay ruined once again, and this time for eternity. The harlots listened and shuddered; they vowed
they'd enter a nunnery. The thieves and miscreants got
down on their knees and begged for forgiveness. Even the
spies and hired assassins and the sodomites from Portugal
looked deep into their souls and prayed for purification.

2

That night all was still and subdued on Monte Cenci.

Lucrezia kept to her bed, nibbling away at her almond
patties and shuddering at the sound of the fearful deluge.
Giacomo and Bernardo sat by the fire playing at cards with
Olimpio. The light from the high candelabra fell on the
seething waters below the window. The cook and the pantry boy Pasquale set up quarters in the *piano nobile,* and
there they boiled a large fish, seasoned with capers and
anchovies. The child Paolo lay gasping in his room, deep
in delirium, while the maid Bastiana sprinkled water on
his forehead. The groom Pacifico was praying and shivering in his garret while the laundress Simonetta went scampering from room to room, laying felt around the windows
and dragging the tapestries upstairs. Beatrice sat alone in
her chamber, drawing the needle through the silk. A candle burned by the mirror and the room was scented with
lavender. All was still, nothing stirred; the curtains hung
motionless. She looked in the mirror and drew her fingers
across her forehead — she had grown intensely pale,
drained and flaccid with pregnancy, and her eyes were
deep and dull in their sockets.

And all this while the great flood went crashing through the Ghetto, and up at the Piazza Trevi the stallions were floundering in the mire.

3

It was a melancholy Christmas; no candles were burned, no Masses sung. The little churches were empty, waist-deep in water. The beautiful roasts, the hams and partridges rotted away in the cellars; the cinnamon tarts with ruffled edges rolled like pebbles under the flood.

But the day after Christmas the sun came peeping out again, and that evening dark ribbons appeared on the walls above the water's surface. First the width of a thumb, then the palm of a hand. The waters were slowly but unmistakably receding. Stairways rose out of the current, step by slimy blue step. Rumpled chickens and bulging rats were deposited in the doorways. The cardinals leaned out of their windows in the Vatican and listened: they could hear the noise of the deluge pouring back toward the Tiber. Soon the trickles converged into a foul-smelling delta. A herd of pestilential pools moved lazily toward the banks, and there gushed over the walls and rolled back into the river.

All night the retreat of the waters continued. The church steps rose out of their puddles, the Piazza Navona lay brown and bubbling, and a sheath of coppery mud coated the Teatro Marcello. Rome that night resembled an equatorial marsh. Snags of cypress and pine lay tangled across the streets, strange insects and worms proliferated in the ooze. A large snake was seen slithering down the nave of St. John Lateran. Everywhere hung the stench of swollen cadavers — mules and horses, even a goat or two, lay bloated in the slime of the Campo dei Fiori.

The next morning the bread carts started to circulate once more and the Cardinal Montalto sent a thousand loaves to the Borgo Vecchio, where the poor still sat huddled and shivering on their roofs. The odor of putrefying flesh grew so vile in the piazzas that the more fastidious-minded ladies moved to the cloisters up in the hills. The Pope himself left the Vatican and moved to his palace on the Quirinal. The Tiber, back in its banks, floated by with an ugly crust — flotsam and jetsam from the mountains, plows and saddles and calves and pigs, and here and there a human body, a luckless muleteer or a shepherd.

Orders were issued from the Castel Sant' Angelo for far-flung sanitary precautions. The streets were cleaned and the cellars purged; walls were buttressed; foundations were strengthened. The dead were decently buried and the tainted food was cast in the river, and with the coming of New Year's the city was sanguine again. There were prayers of thanksgiving, songs were sung in the taverns, and the dissolute slid back into their wicked ways again.

X X

Now we turn for a moment to the seneschal's wife, Plautilla.

Plautilla had been brought down to Rome by Olimpio some days before Christmas, together with Prospero the child, to stay in the house of her cousin Cinzia. Here she was when the flood burst forth in all its barbarity: a crowded hovel in Trastevere, breadless and waterless and stinking, filled with vomiting children and hysterical spinsters, and not a sign or a word or so much as a penny from Olimpio. One week she spent in this misery, hugging her boy to her breast, and finally, four days after Christmas, Olimpio's brother, the Friar Pietro, appeared at the house and took her on muleback up the slopes of the Esquiline. Here in a tiny back alley was the house of Cilla the seamstress, another relative of Plautilla's, somewhat more amiably disposed than the shrewish Cinzia; and here Plautilla lived for a while, waiting for news of Olimpio.

None came. One day, however, there was a knock on the kitchen door and a moment later Giacomo Cenci came striding into the room. It might be mentioned that during

the turmoil and confusion of the flood the various super-
visions had been considerably relaxed by the Papal authorities; and needless to say the Cenci family took full advantage of this laxity and went roaming through the city
to their hearts' content.

Giacomo greeted Plautilla, whom he had met in La
Petrella, and placed a little bag of green muslin on the
kitchen table.

The room was like a grotto: smoke-stained walls and a
low-arched ceiling, from which bottles and onions hung
gleaming like stalactites.

"Bless you, signor. You've news from Olimpio?" said
Plautilla, with pleading eyes.

"He's busy at the palace," said Giacomo dourly. "He
sends you his love and a bag of coins. He'll be looking you
up as soon as he's back."

"Oh . . . He's going away, is he?"

"Up to Lombardy. For Prince Colonna."

"For long?" whispered Plautilla.

"A month or so," said Giacomo hurriedly. "And he
strongly suggests, and I agree with him, that you should
leave the city as soon as possible, and visit your family up
in the hills."

"Is anything wrong?" said Plautilla. Her lips began to
tremble.

"You must be sensible, my good woman. The city is full
of disturbance, the bread is short, the cellars are swamped,
and there's talk of the plague in the Borgo Nuovo . . ."

Plautilla looked desolately at Giacomo, who avoided her
glance.

"He's going on business for Prince Colonna?"

"Ahem," said Giacomo. "More or less."

"He'll be perfectly safe?" pleaded Plautilla.

"Safer than here in Rome," said Giacomo. His face sharpened. "Well?" he said.

"I'll do anything he wishes," she said softly, after a moment.

"Then go out to Anticoli and wait for Olimpio," said Giacomo. "He'll be back from his trip to Lombardy and he'll follow you to the hills."

"When do I go?" said Plautilla.

"I've arranged for the carriage," said Giacomo rapidly. "You'll leave the day after tomorrow, and you'll take along the boy, and you'll stay with your family until you hear from us. And just as a precaution, and I'm telling you this in the strictest confidence, you might be wise to say nothing in any manner or form about this thing of my father's lamentable death at La Petrella . . . Do you understand what I'm saying?"

Plautilla lowered her eyes discreetly. "Quite, signor. I do." She sat silently for a while, trying to grasp the hidden trend in Giacomo's plan. Suddenly she said: "One thing I'll ask you, one small thing, Signor Giacomo."

"Yes? What?" said Giacomo dully.

"I want to see my daughter, Signor Giacomo."

Giacomo tapped the table irritably. "Ah. Quite. Well, I'll arrange it. I'll speak to my sister, and I'll see that it's done . . ."

2

The following evening, soon after sunset, a message arrived for Plautilla requesting her presence in the Church

of the Capuccini. So Plautilla set forth and groped her
way through the maze of puddles.

She opened the door and stepped through the black
flannel curtain. It was icy cold in the church, the marble
floor was damp and clammy, but the glow of candles and
the smell of incense made it seem warm and intimate.
Plautilla tiptoed down the aisle, glancing nervously left
and right. Suddenly she caught sight of Vittoria; she was
standing with Signora Beatrice in one of the chapels. She
ran up and threw her arms around the girl with a little
cry, kissed her passionately on the cheeks and choked back
her tears.

"My sweet darling, you're well?"

"Quite well, I think, Mamma."

"What a charming dress you've got on!"

"It's a gift from Signora Beatrice."

"Lovely it is . . . You've grown fatter!"

"I'm growing older, a little, Mamma."

"And taller too!" And she kissed her daughter all over
again and dropped on her knees to tighten the sash
around her waist. She even glanced with a quick humble
gratitude at the lady Beatrice, who had brought all this
terror and heartache into her life. She saw in this rapid
glance the full condition of Beatrice, and she felt a pang
of misery joined to a rush of strange kinship.

She said gently: "Yes, signora. It's just as you say. Best
for all if the girl stays with you and I'm off to the hills
tomorrow . . . And give my love to my husband if you
happen to speak to him . . . And the Lord protect you
and all the house, signora . . ."

Beatrice stood silent behind Vittoria. The glow of the
candles lit her cheeks. Her eyes brightened all of a sudden,

her hand moved forward impulsively. Then she drew back and said quietly: "God speed you, Plautilla."

3

Plautilla hurried back to her cousin's cottage, tossed her clothes in a bag and made ready to leave the next day for Anticoli. The child Prospero followed her about from room to room, tugging at her apron.

"Are we going away, Mamma?"

"Yes, dear. To your Aunt Antonia's."

"I don't remember Aunt Antonia."

"She has lovely sad eyes."

"Why is she sad?"

"She's had troubles."

"What kind of troubles?"

"I don't remember, dear. Now hush and go to bed, we'll be getting up early."

She poured some milk into a bowl and broke a crust of dark bread in it, stirred it absently and lifted the boy into her lap.

Next door a young man was strumming away on a lute. There was a clatter of kettles down in the kitchen. The candle died; the moonlight flowed through a slit in the window. Plautilla undressed and hung her dress on a hook, then slipped into the narrow bed beside Prospero.

She could see a fat little cloud floating over the Quirinal, like a silver cherub.

Prospero turned to her and murmured: "Where is Papa tonight?"

"He's going to Lombardy."

"Where is Lombardy?"

"Way up in the North, dear."

"Why is he going to Lombardy?"

"It's for Prince Colonna."

"Is Prince Colonna a bad man?"

"Not in the least. Now go to sleep."

But soon he was tugging at her elbow again. "Was Signor Francesco a bad man?"

"Goodness, child. I don't know."

"Did Papa kill Signor Francesco?"

"Hush! . . . Of course not . . . What terrible notions!"

Prospero said drowsily: "Tell me a story, Mamma."

"Which story, my sweet?"

"About the prince who turned into a frog," said Prospero softly.

And Plautilla whispered into his ear until the boy fell asleep.

4

And all this while Beatrice was riding in her carriage through Rome, peeping furtively at the black, forbidden city, listening to the fountains in the little piazzas, breathing the pine scent fresh from the Pincio. There was a great ball that night, and when they passed through the Piazza del Duca, Beatrice tapped the driver's shoulder and asked him to halt. Lanterns shone by the portico and the armorial coaches came riding, full of folk in dark velvet trimmed with arabesques of gold. The chandeliers hung ablaze from the painted beams of the ceiling and the dancers went gliding past the torch-lit windows. She caught sight of the Princess Borghese, with jewels flashing on sea-green satin; Maria Sforza she saw and the wolf-faced Giulia Colonna — all women she'd known before, when she too was a part of the singing and dancing.

She watched for a while, then tapped the driver again. "Drive on," she said. "Past the Palatine."

They rode on through the silent streets. Everything was dark and very still, except for a tavern here and there where a lamp shone dimly. Some drunken soldiers were standing outside the Pheasant, tossing bottles to and fro. Down the street shone the rosy glow of a brothel. Beatrice could see the white-faced prostitutes leaning out of their windows, gossiping with the silky-bearded grooms.

They threaded their way past the Campidoglio and down the jungle of alleys that wound through the ruins. Fallen capitals covered with moss lay helter-skelter in the starlight. A trail of ivy, like a crazy wig, hung askew from a Corinthian column. Here and there a tiny hut leaned against a derelict temple. In these days the Forum was called the Campo Vaccino: the Cattle Pasture. The medieval towers of the Frangipani loomed over the silent meadow and the weeds grew thick from the slabs of marble. There was a delicate tinkle: a cow in its stall. The rich, clovery smell of manure filled the air, and under that, darker and subtler, the tang of ancient humanity.

The coach came to a halt by the Colosseum. A strange excitement took hold of Beatrice. Vittoria had fallen asleep with her head on her shoulder. Beatrice woke her. "Come," she whispered. The girl trembled with fear as

[162   ]

Beatrice led her cautiously into the heart of the amphitheater. The huge pillars looked like a row of cliffs in a lonely gully. Strange figures moved furtively among the arches — beggars and vagabonds and such. A dull blue haze filled the giant bowl, like a cloud of smoke. The tiers of arches rising on the opposite wall looked like a vast mirage. Beatrice felt she had entered a mysterious new world — a world of black secrets and vicious old ceremonies. This was the place where the sorcerers gathered to call forth the demons. It was the sleeping place for cutthroats and outcasts and lunatics. An owl hooted in a far-off cranny, bats went swooping over the caves. There was a smell of dead rats, of centuries of refuse and excrement.

A wisp of a moon crept through the clouds. The distant walls shone like mountaintops. Down below in the arena shone a web of black cisterns, half filled with water and all sorts of floating debris.

Vittoria was crying softly. "Hush," said Beatrice. "Don't be frightened." She turned and stepped back through the inner arcade.

Suddenly she gave a small cry: something was plucking at her cloak.

She glanced down. A tiny creature held out his palm imploringly. He looked inhuman: no legs at all, only a pair of naked feet attached to his trunk, and two fingerless flippers instead of arms. A face bloated yet uncannily shriveled, like a bulldog's. He didn't speak; he kept bubbling and gurgling inarticulately. Beatrice reached into her cloak and dropped some coins in his palm. And then, on a sudden impulse, she leaned down gently and drew her fingers over the monstrous little head.

"God be with you," she whispered. Then she hurried

[163   ]

through the archway and lifted Vittoria into the coach.
The driver had fallen asleep; she tapped him briskly.
"We'll go back to the palazzo now," she murmured.

5

When she entered the hall she sensed immediately that
something had happened. Nothing dramatic or distinct: a
faint withdrawal, a smoldering stillness. She climbed the
stairs very slowly with Vittoria's hand in her own, and
suddenly the maid Bastiana came running from the gallery. She fell on her knees and flung her arms around Beatrice's legs.

"Signora!"

"Mercy! What's happened?"

Bastiana kept sobbing uncontrollably. Finally she stammered: "God help us! It's poor little Paolo . . ."

Beatrice hurried up the stairway to her brother's chamber, which looked southward toward the unlit walls of the
Ghetto. The boy lay motionless in the bed. Lucrezia was
kneeling beside him with her face half buried in the coverlet. Bernardo was weeping in the corner and Giacomo
stood motionless in the doorway. The doctor Battista and
the priest Don Luigi stood murmuring by the window.

Beatrice stood expressionless beside the bed for several
minutes. Then she left without a word and walked swiftly
down the hall.

6

A narrow corridor led through the back of the palazzo over an archway which connected it with the older wing. This wing had once been used for the children's rooms and the nurses. Now it was empty and deserted, sprinkled with cobwebs and dust.

Beatrice walked aimlessly down the hall and up the stairs that led over the arch. The moonlight drifted through the bolted windows, streaking the floor with pins of light. A door creaked; there was a familiar odor of ancient cloth, wilted leather. She entered a large square room with a high painted ceiling, lined with shelves where old ledgers were lying in dusty piles. A little cradle stood in a corner. Beatrice peeped into the cushions, which gave out an aroma of sour, rotting linen.

The light in the room was frail and powdery, like a veil of snowflakes. It fell on a chest, a spinning wheel, an old broken sofa. Beatrice tiptoed across the room and knelt on the floor beside the couch. It was littered with toys, painted dolls and stuffed animals. She picked up a woolly black horse — it was her dead brother Rocco's. It sighed faintly as she touched: a shower of sawdust poured from its belly.

She put it back and peered at the row of bedraggled little dolls. Their wax faces were blurred with years of desertion. There was a desperate air about them; they were begging for recognition. There was a devil with a long red tail which had once been Giacomo's, and a tousled queen with a copper crown which had belonged to her sister Antonina. She caught sight of a doll that she herself had fondled years ago: a curly-headed milkmaid with bright pink cheeks and a flowered apron. She took it gently; the filmy eyes looked vacantly back at her. She pressed the doll to her breast and whispered: "Costanza . . . My poor little darling!"

At that moment she heard a faint rustling sound in the neighboring room, like the sound of claws moving slowly across the tiles. Beatrice knelt motionless. A breath of wind suddenly shot through one of the windows. A door hissed feebly as it swung ajar.

A hazy glow, like that of an aquarium, filled the chamber beyond. An aisle of gray disheveled garments hung on their hooks along the wall — old-fashioned ball gowns and carnival costumes, children's dresses for communion. They stirred faintly in the breeze, a bodiless ripple of lace and taffeta.

Then she saw him: he stood frozen by the middle window, drenched in the light of the moon as though it were some inner phosphorescence. The clothes were streaked with decay. The collar hung tattered. The blood clung like a mask to his mutilated face. He seemed to throb with a fleshly radiance, like the glow of a firefly, now distinct, now fading into a dull chiaroscuro. Beatrice knelt without stirring, holding the doll to her breast, beyond panic, as it were, in the presence of such a distillation.

The breeze shifted; the door swung noiselessly shut again. For a while she still knelt there at the foot of the couch, lost in the dreamlike satiety that follows all great fulfillments. Finally she rose and walked slowly back to the inhabited wing of the house and down the dark stairway that led to the door of her bedroom.

BOOK THREE
The Witnesses

XXI

ONE BRIGHT SPICY MORNING, just a week after New Year's, three men rode out through the Porta del Popolo and crossed the Ponte Milvio and started climbing the road to Florence. The man on the gray horse was Olimpio the seneschal. The one on the black was Camillo Rosati, a young exquisite who was the Prince Colonna's private secretary. The lad who rode on the donkey was Pacifico Bussone, a moonfaced fellow who served as groom to Giacomo Cenci.

The land was liquid and lively after the devastating rains. Torrents ran gurgling through the valleys, sharp, mercurial in the sun. A light frost still lay on the slopes as they climbed uphill, but then the air lost its chill and the smell of cypresses hung over the road. Strange country this was — smooth, dark hillocks, like sepulchers; the crumbling arches of the Trajan aqueduct, like bridges from nowhere to nowhere; and the little pine groves which floated like clouds in the Etruscan solitude.

They came to Sutri and stopped at a dismal little inn called the Angel. A haunted town, thought Olimpio, all littered with rocks and old caverns. He turned gloomily to Camillo and fingered his wine glass. The two men were sitting beside the hearth while the groom Pacifico stood by the horses.

"I see wickedness in this wine," he said, holding it high over the firelight.

"Bad wine," said Camillo, gingerly. "No good wine comes from these parts."

Olimpio turned to Camillo: "So you're going all the way to Lombardy?"

"On business for my master, as I told you," said Camillo airily.

Olimpio gnawed sullenly at his bone. "What sort of business, may I ask?"

"It's about a wedding they're planning," said Camillo, stifling a yawn.

"It was Signor Giacomo, you say, who suggested I go along?"

"My master agreed with Signor Giacomo. It was felt, all in all, that . . ."

"Quite," said Olimpio, growling. "He doesn't like me close to Beatrice these days."

"Not only that," said Camillo, with a sliding glance at Olimpio. There was something blunt and bull-like, volcanic about Olimpio: the sinewy neck and bulging chest, the echoing voice, the threatening eye. Something formidable and at the same time wistful, bewildered. "Listen, my friend," remarked Camillo, in a voice both suave and incisive, "there's mischief waiting for you in Rome, I am sorry to tell you. I know little about this strange and intricate matter, but one thing I do know: you'd best keep well out of the way."

Olimpio's eyes grew small and cunning. He tossed the

bone to the spaniel. "And so they asked you to take me along up to Lombardy?"

"Precisely," said Camillo, flashing his teeth. "Don't you trust me?"

He reached into an inner pocket of his doublet, drew out a purse of black goat leather and tossed it casually on the table.

"Fifty scudi," he said. "From Signor Giacomo. A gift for the holidays."

Olimpio weighed the purse in his palm. "How long a holiday, Camillo?"

"Two months. Three at the most. Till the trouble blows over," said Camillo. He raised his glass. His voice grew liquid. "Let's be friends, my dear fellow. You're a man to my taste. Here's to a fine, pleasant journey!"

Olimpio likewise raised his glass. He looked slyly at Camillo: the delicate curve of the wrist, the languid eye, the silken hose . . . He smiled inwardly. He was beginning to understand.

"Here's to friendship," he said softly. The two men drained their wine glasses and sat staring lazily at the dying embers.

2

That night they spent in the gloomy old city of Viterbo, in the Inn of the Stag close by the Piazza San Pellegrino. Pacifico was left below and slept on a pallet in the stables, while the older men shared a small fetid bed over the taproom. They were weary and dulled with wine; they fell asleep without a word.

Once in the middle of the night Olimpio rose and stepped to the window. He had drunk too much wine; his bladder tingled and his head was swimming.

He staggered back to the bed. The starlight fell on Camillo's face: the thin, dry lips, the fluttering nostrils. A strange impulse came over Olimpio. His hand started trembling. One quick jab, one powerful thrust of the thumb . . .

He sighed. "I'm a fool," he muttered and tumbled back into bed.

3

The next morning the groom Pacifico came and shook them by the shoulders while the stars still shone in the plum-blue sky. They set out through the mist and threaded their way to Lake Bolsena, which lay covered with an iridescent haze. The sun flashed out suddenly: the pearly haze was a cloud of gold dust. The leafless beeches beside the road shone like high copper screens.

The goats were out on the hills already, tinkling softly as they stepped along. They turned their devilish green eyes as the horsemen clattered past. A great joy seized Olimpio. He started to sing at the top of his lungs. They rode on through the wintry fields and the pool-dappled pasturelands. Then they entered the woods and all was stillness again except the creak of the saddles and the clatter of hoofs.

That night they spent in the *osteria* in San Quirico dell' Orcia, and the following noon they reached Siena, which flashed in the sun, all plumed and bannered. A magnificent city, thought Olimpio; as fine as any he'd ever seen, with the campanile soaring into the clouds like a blood-red spear and the shops all spicy with great blue cheeses. They sat in the tavern above the Campo and sipped at their broth while the townsmen strolled past in velvet cloaks that shone like sable.

A shriveled harridan, a fortuneteller, came waddling up to their table. "Show me your palms, my sweet gentlemen! And I'll tell you all that's worth knowing . . ."

But Camillo was reluctant; he flicked his wrist and dismissed her. Olimpio frowned. He too was afraid to take a peep into the future.

The old hag turned to Pacifico, who sat nearby on a little stool. "Give me your hand, my pretty chick. Let's see . . . A chest of gold, maybe, or a princess . . ."

Pacifico blushed in his usual way; the guilt of youth hung on him heavily. The woman's face was a thousand wrinkles, tufted and bulbous as a caterpillar.

She fondled his hand and tittered artfully. "You've got what the ladies like, my boy. There's plenty of pleasure awaiting you . . ." She frowned and spat. "What's this I see!" And she looked up electrically, fixing her eyes on the pink, puzzled face.

"A killing! That's what I see! You'll be an assassin, my fine fellow!"

"Nonsense," put in Camillo swiftly.

"It's true," shrieked the hag, gathering her tatters. "I see it there, in his dirty palm . . . He'll end up a murderer, I tell you!"

And she scampered off, muttering hoarsely, waving her scaly old arms.

Camillo rose and flung his cape gracefully about him. "Let's be off," he said sulkily. "I've had enough of Siena."

And soon the men were on their way again, riding on through the windy sunlight, past the turreted hills and the lonely cypresses.

4

They reached Florence at sunset and rode on to the Boar, near the Duomo. Pacifico was left with the horses while the older men dusted their clothes and washed their faces and set out for an evening stroll. The light grew faint on the walls and the fountains hissed in the wintry shadows. They passed the Loggia dei Lanci and walked on to the Ponte Vecchio. The last flakes of sunlight hung over the biscuit-brown roofs. A lonely fisherman stood below on a tuft of gravel, angling patiently. The bells started tolling. Dusk was gathering over the Arno.

Camillo paused by the jewelers' stalls that lined the bridge on both sides. He fondled the golden earrings, the caskets of jade and lapis lazuli. The jewelers were lighting their oil lamps in the tiny shops, the light glimmered on rows of bronze goblets and copper bowls. And further back in the recesses hung the things of pure gold, the enameled girdles and necklaces, the braided caps and the gold-webbed slippers.

Camillo picked up an onyx box the size of a pigeon's egg; it was edged with a thread of gold, neatly scalloped around the lid.

He smiled coyly at Olimpio. "Charming, don't you agree?"

Olimpio weighed the box in his hand astutely.

He called to the shopkeeper: "How much do you want for this, my good man?"

"Six scudi," grunted the hunchback, squinting across the candlelight.

"Five and I'll take it," said Olimpio, counting five scudi out of his purse.

"Five it is," said the jeweler owlishly and Olimpio picked up the box, smiled ceremoniously at Camillo, bowed slightly and murmured:

"Do me a most gracious honor. Accept this token of loyalty, my dear Camillo . . ."

5

The following morning Camillo Rosati called Pacifico the groom and said curtly: "Signor Olimpio and I will continue alone. Take Signor Olimpio's horse back to Rome for him, and present our humble respects to Signor Giacomo Cenci."

And he hired a fine chestnut horse for Olimpio and the two men rode over the hills into Lombardy, which then included the province of Emilia and the fertile valley along the Po. They crossed the Apennines at Futa. Snow lay sprinkled in the shade of the rocks and an icy wind came sizzling through the pines. Stony vistas reached out toward the distant peaks; here and there a small castle crouched on an overhanging cliff. This was notorious bandit country, but there was no sign that day of the bandits, only the lonely mountaineers leading their mules through the woods. Finally they entered the valley and rode on toward Bologna, where they slept and took meat before starting down the Via Emilia.

Now the land was gentle and flat, webbed with tiny canals. Here and there in the distance rose a red campanile. Teams of snowy-white oxen moved indolently under the trees and flocks of sheep nibbled away at their cool brown pastures.

It was in Modena, in a little tavern, that Olimpio suddenly said: "Tell me, Camillo. Have we left the States of the Pope?"

Camillo nodded. "We have."

Olimpio sighed with relief. "Well," he said, "I've nothing to fear then."

Camillo filled up his glass. "What did you have to fear, Olimpio?"

Olimpio gazed solemnly into Camillo's face, which was bland and smiling. "Can I trust you, Camillo?"

"Of course you can trust me, my dear."

Olimpio hesitated. The veins in his eyes seemed to throb and darken. Suddenly he blurted: "It was something that happened in La Petrella."

Camillo nodded discreetly; he lowered his eyes.

"I killed Signor Francesco Cenci," whispered Olimpio with sudden intensity, fixing his hot black eyes on Camillo. "Yes. It was I who did it, Camillo." He raised his hand and held it over the table, spreading the fingers against the firelight. "I killed Signor Francesco with this very same hand of mine, Camillo!"

Camillo gazed through the leaded panes at the watery towers of Modena.

[176   ]

"Listen, Camillo," said Olimpio rapidly, leaning forward and clutching the wine jug. "It was I who did it, but it was Signora Beatrice who thought of it, and who spoke of it, and who insisted on it. It was she who forced me when I hesitated. It was she alone who caused the killing!"

"And Signora Lucrezia?" said Camillo.

"She knew, she knew," said Olimpio contemptuously. "She's a chickenhearted woman but she too was a part of it. She dawdled and trembled and wept but she too wanted the killing. And the tinker Marzio, he too was a part of it. So help me God, Camillo, they all struck him down just as much as I did!"

Camillo's voice grew low and courteous: "Did you love Signora Beatrice?"

Olimpio hesitated. Then he muttered: "Yes. I loved her, I suppose."

Camillo folded his hands and looked calmly into Olimpio's eyes. "If you did it for love, my dear Olimpio, then it's all forgivable."

Olimpio's eyes grew soft with gratitude. He smiled brokenly at Camillo. "I'm happy you've said so. You're a friend, Camillo. I was the slave of desire, and that's the truth of the matter. And so it wasn't my fault what I did, was it, Camillo?"

"No," said Camillo. "It wasn't your fault, Olimpio."

And they finished their wine and rode on through the wintry sunlight.

XXII

At rubbiera the two horsemen turned off the Via Emilia and rode down a small muddy side path toward the Po. The land was rosy and fat, all studded with poplars, with storks' nests crowding the steeples and nunneries huddling behind their walls. The little duck ponds shone in the sunlight like great copper coins. The cocks ruffled their feathers and crowed merrily from the dungheaps.

And so they came that afternoon to the castle of Novellara. They rode to the gate, where Camillo knocked at the lion's head which hung on the door. They waited; a bolt creaked on the wicket window.

"Who is it?" said a bald young fellow.

"Visitors from Rome," said Camillo.

"On whose behalf do you come?"

"Prince Colonna's," lisped Camillo.

The man vanished. A moment later the door slid open. They were led through the courtyard into an enormous hall, where they were greeted by a vivid little lady in black. She peered brightly at her guests, the suave young dandy and the massive castellan, and introduced herself: Vittoria di Giantommaso di Capua, Marchesa de la Torre

di Francolise, the widow of the Conte Alfonso di Novellara.

Camillo led her to the window and spoke to her softly.
Then the two of them departed and Olimpio was left
alone in the hall. The sun was low; threads of light seeped
hazily through the windows. Flames crackled in the enormous hearth, shedding their warmth on two great wolf-
hounds that lay grunting and twitching in front of the fire.

Olimpio sauntered toward the fire, threw off his cloak
and knelt by the flames. He reached over to stroke one of
the dogs; the beast growled and backed away. A tingle of
uneasiness crept through Olimpio.

Time passed. An hour, possibly. The sun sank and the
hall grew dark except for the slowly dying fire, which cast
its glow on the crimson tapestries.

"Signor!"

Olimpio turned; a man in a pale green shirt stood in the
doorway.

"Your supper's ready, signor, if you please."

Olimpio rose and followed the servant, who led him
down a stairway into a small timbered room.

2

A table stood by the wall, and by the table a single chair.
A candle burned in a niche by the window. There were
two tapering glasses and a bottle of wine.

Olimpio sat down and sniffed greedily at the *ministra*.
He winked at the servant. "What's your name?"

"Taddeo," said the servant, lowering his eyes.

"Taddeo. So be it," said Olimpio affably, and he sipped at the soup with a great loud gurgle.

"What soup is this?" he said with a grimace.

"Dandelion soup," simpered the servant.

"Hm," growled Olimpio. "You serve dandelions to your guests here in Lombardy?"

He pushed the soup away squeamishly and raised the lid from the meat platter. A magnificent leg of lamb, roasted to a deep golden bronze. Olimpio sighed with relief as he tore the meat from the bone.

"*Abbachio arrosto,*" he said genially. "Let's see how the Lombards treat their lambs."

He took a bite and rolled his eyes. The lamb was bad too. There was a strange aroma hovering about it, like the smell of dead roots.

Olimpio gnawed at it unhappily. Finally he dropped the bone in the platter and reached irritably for the salad. "Strange seasoning you have here in Lombardy."

But hardly had he tasted the salad than he spat it out furiously. "*Ahimè!* What's wrong with this? You eat like pigs here on the Po!" And he sipped from the neck of the wine bottle to wash away the sickening flavor.

The door opened with a creak. Camillo stood on the threshold, smiling.

"Ah," said Olimpio. "I thought you were dining up-stairs with the countess!"

"And so I am," said Camillo. "But the roast isn't ready yet . . . Do you mind if I sit and have a small sip of wine with you?"

He raised a glass and filled it to the brim, then passed the bottle to Olimpio. But as he held out his arm the bottle slid and crashed to the floor. The wine spread over the stones in a great black stain.

"No harm done," said Camillo nimbly. "Another bottle, please, Taddeo."

Taddeo went and brought forth a new bottle from the cupboard; he drew the cork and leaned forward to fill Olimpio's glass.

"Your health," said Camillo, mellow-eyed.

"Your health, dear Camillo!"

The two men raised their wine glasses and drank with a flourish.

Olimpio coughed and dropped his glass. A violent spasm shook his body. It was as though a pack of wolves were tearing away at his flesh. He clutched at his throat, which burned like fire. *"Oché, oché!"* he cried desperately. He fell to the floor, roaring with pain. "I'm dead! I'm done for! God help me!"

Two servants rushed in from the hall and knelt beside Olimpio, who was writhing in anguish, spitting and coughing with all his might. He shook his fist at Camillo.

"By God, Camillo! It's you who did this!" His knees shot up in a spasm of pain. "You toad! You traitor!"

Camillo shrugged his shoulders and glanced contemptuously at Olimpio, whose shirt and doublet were spattered with wine.

"Nonsense," he said. "You're drunk, that's all . . ." He turned to Taddeo and flicked his finger. "Please see that this man is put safely to bed."

And he went off to dine with the Countess Novellara.

3

The servants struggled and panted as they carried the powerful body into the guest chamber. Olimpio kept howling with pain and fury. The moment they laid him on the bed he leaned over and vomited violently. A foul stench filled the air. The spasms gradually grew milder. Suddenly he rolled from the bed and crouched on the floor with a groan. A flood of excrement burst out, blood-colored and nauseous. Tears were pouring from Olimpio's eyes. He was reeling with misery. He clutched at the coverlet and drew himself up on the bed again. The servants quailed and held their noses. Taddeo flung open the window. An old harridan ran up with a mop and started cleaning the floor.

"I'm dying, I'm dying," moaned Olimpio. He closed his eyes; his face kept twitching. Suddenly he cried: "Call me a confessor! For the love of God, call him quickly!"

Taddeo left and hurried back with Father Antonio, a plump man with a thick red beard, who leaned quietly over the bed and laid his hand on the sick man's forehead. Olimpio quivered; he was drenched in sweat; he opened his bloodshot eyes. The servants tiptoed out of the room and Father Antonio, speaking in a whisper, proceeded calmly to confess Olimpio, who was quivering violently with a sudden chill. The terrible tale came forth brokenly, in fits and spells.

"Repent, my son," purred Father Antonio. "And keep on praying, for soon you die."

4

But Olimpio did not die. For three hours he lay writhing, sweating and vomiting and defecating; finally he fell fast asleep. The night passed in violent fits of nausea and fever. Now and then he cried faintly: he begged the Lord to forgive him. But as the morning drew close his strength returned gradually. When the light crept in at the window he opened his eyes and he knew that he'd live. The vast strength in his body had hurled out the poison.

Soon after sunrise Taddeo brought him a bowl of clear broth and an hour later the servants brought him a platter of bread and goat cheese. Olimpio tasted each mouthful scrupulously, chewing at length before he swallowed. He kept glancing with blurred, suspicious eyes at Taddeo.

"No danger," said Taddeo wryly. "This time it's safe, signor. Eat calmly."

Toward noon Camillo peered through the doorway and tiptoed up to the sleeping man. He leaned over, touched his temples, and left the room silently.

Olimpio slept and kept sleeping; it was dusk when he woke up again. He sat up suddenly. There was a vigorous knock on the door.

"Who is it?"

"There's a gentleman to see you, signor," whimpered Taddeo.

"What does he want?"

"Come forth!" boomed a powerful voice.

Olimpio rose from the bed and flung his cloak around

him. He tottered to the door, paused a moment, then flung
it open. What he saw was a flock of elderly, ill-kempt soldiers, all armed with cutlasses; one of them was carrying a
Milanese arquebus.

Olimpio stood without moving. He started to speak. The
man raised his arquebus and brought the barrel down on
Olimpio's head. Olimpio fell; he lay stunned. A moment
later he came to. He saw the soldiers brandishing their
knives with a threatening air.

Now he was sure that his end had come. The men were
plainly about to kill him; they raised their knives, eyes
aglitter, and closed in on him swiftly. He gave a last feeble
moan and covered his face with his cloak. But the men
jumped on him clamorously, tore off the cloak and groped
at his garments. They ran through his pockets and
snatched the black leather purse from his doublet. One of
the men tore the ring from his finger, ripping the skin
from the joints. At this Olimpio struck out; he was wild
with anger at losing the ring. He hurled himself on the
man with the arquebus, struggling to tear away the
weapon. He stumbled; he sank to his knees. Then he saw
Camillo in the doorway.

"Camillo! Help me!" he shouted.

Camillo stood motionless, with his hands on his hips.

"Camillo, save me!" cried Olimpio. "I'll give you a hundred scudi! I swear it!"

Camillo looked at him frostily. "A hundred scudi?
Where do you have them?"

Olimpio lied: "They're in Rome, Camillo! Secretly buried! I'll tell you where!" And he kept on gurgling hoarsely
while the soldiers pinned him to the ground, knives raised
in the air for the final thrust.

"For the love of God, Camillo, save me! I'll give you everything I have!"

But Camillo shrugged his shoulders and plucked the ring from the soldier's hand. Then he took the leather purse and emptied the coins in his palm. Thirty-two scudi, there were. Twenty he split among the soldiers. The other twelve he dropped in his pocket. Then he turned to Olimpio and said:

"We'll talk no more of friendship, Olimpio. There's no friendship with a murderer. Here you are and here you'll stay; give thanks to the Lord that you're still alive."

"Camillo . . . Wait!"

"I'm off to Rome," said Camillo curtly, and he strode into the courtyard.

The men took hold of Olimpio by the armpits and carried him down into the cellar. Olimpio hung sagging between their arms; limp, bloodstained, bedraggled. He scarcely stirred when they reached the dungeon and the captain clamped the irons on him. He lay back on the pallet and stared listlessly through the grated window.

Clouds were gathering, brown and jagged. The wind came sweeping over the plains. An hour later the rain came rattling against the stones. Olimpio lay shivering in his cloak; but already his strength was coming back. The tremendous vitality was beginning to stir again.

The night came and passed. More days and more nights. Days of stench-ridden loneliness and sour bread and water; nights of cold and discomfort, of long, fierce brooding.

One thing beyond all others stirred Olimpio to fury as he lay there, and that was the thought of the diamond ring.

XXIII

Snow had fallen in the mountains and the air was cold after the sirocco. Up in Ascrea a sheet of ice lay over the troughs. Marzio the tinker went wandering disconsolately among the lanes with a cap of rabbit's fur on his head and Cenci's cloak flung about him. Each day he'd wander from hearth to hearth with his yellow lute, teaching the old songs and dances to the boys of the village. On wintry nights by the light of the moon he'd go forth with his band and strum away while they danced and sang and the villagers peeped through their windows. In one house if he was lucky they'd give him a bowl of soup; in another a glass of wine; in a third a slice of cheese. He spent his nights in the stables wrapped up in the dead man's cloak. He spoke little, he slept fitfully; a dark loneliness filled him. The world about him had grown shadowy and senseless, like a dream.

One morning, it was a Sunday, he walked down through the frozen hills to visit his wife, who was staying in Poggio Vittiano. He arrived at sunset at the house of his brother-in-law Lelio. His old mother Cristina threw her arms around him and started to sob. Lelio and his cousin Giovan' Angelo stood by the fire, glowering uneasily.

The three children popped out of bed and tugged at his coat. He knelt on the floor and kissed them. "Tino! What a big boy you are!"

Porzia stepped out of the bedchamber and greeted him coldly. She turned her head away when he tried to kiss her.

"Come. Sit down by the fire," she said wearily. "You're cold. I'll bring you a bowl of *minestra*."

His sister Girolima and the two young men sat silently while Marzio ate.

"You've been in Ascrea?" said his mother gently.

Marzio nodded. "Sometimes in Poraglia. I've been wandering about here and there. Playing the lute."

The glow from the fire fell on their faces: three men and three women. The steam rose softly from the bowl; the embers clucked in the hearth.

One of the neighbors, whose name was Matteo, poked his head through the door. He raised his shaggy black brows when he noticed Marzio.

"Greetings," he muttered, hovering in the doorway.

"Greetings," said Marzio. "Come and join us!"

But Matteo frowned and shook his head and hastily bade them all good night.

For a while there was silence. Then Cristina said softly: "Is it bad for you still in La Petrella?"

"There are ugly stories going about in La Petrella," said Marzio heavily.

"Tell me, Marzio, "said his mother with a trembling look. "Are they true, those stories?"

Marzio leaned toward the fire and spread his hands in front of the flames. The red light played nervously on his weak, weary face. The skin of his hands glowed dimly, like folds of parchment.

"No," he said. "There's no truth in those stories, *mamma mia.*"

"I knew there wasn't," said old Cristina, hanging her head.

"Let your heart be at peace," said Marzio, staring into the flames."

"God bless you," said Cristina, and a tear rolled down her cheek.

A little later Porzia whispered: "Listen! I hear someone coming . . ."

"It's only the wind in the ivy," said Lelio.

"It's the doves in the cote," said Giovan' Angelo.

Lelio glanced quickly at Porzia, but no one spoke after this, and a little later they went to bed.

2

The three women slept in one room, the three men in another. Marzio as usual slept wretchedly. Dark shadows moved through his dreams: enormous birds, like vultures, rolling out the dough for the *fettuccini* . . .

Toward dawn he suddenly woke up and glanced through the window: a tall shadow was moving stealthily through the mist. He sat up sharply. Two more shadows were moving silently through the olive trees. He shook Lelio by the shoulder. "Quick," he whispered. "The *sbirri!*"

Lelio sprang out of bed. The sky was still dark; they could see the stars shining faint through the early mist. There was a sound of footsteps crackling on the ground, like broken glass. Lelio ran into the kitchen and hurried back with a small black ladder. A triangular window near the ceiling of the bedroom looked out over the roofs.

"There! Hurry!" hissed Lelio.

Marzio, wearing nothing but a flannel shirt, raced up the ladder and scrambled clumsily out on the roof. Then Lelio thrust the ladder back into the kitchen, behind the spinning wheel.

There was a violent pounding on the door.

"Who is it?" growled Lelio.

"It's the constable of the court of Rome!"

"What do you want?" stammered Lelio.

"Never mind! Open the door and be quick about it!"

"Just a moment!" shouted Lelio. He hurried out of the kitchen, still in his nightcap, and unbolted the door.

The chief constable entered, followed by a horde of Papal *sbirri,* who swarmed through the kitchen and into the adjoining bedchambers. The women cried out and began dressing frantically; Porzia slipped swiftly into her long purple gown. The sergeant at arms led the search. No sign of Marzio, of course. But something about the triangular window caught the constable's eye.

"Bring the ladder," he ordered. The sergeant at arms climbed up on the roof.

"Is he there?" said the constable.

"He's there!" called the sergeant at arms.

And he turned his arquebus on Marzio, who was crawling along the eaves.

"Stop," he cried, "in the name of the law!"

Marzio turned to him miserably; his flannel shirt was flapping in the wind like a banner.

"Don't shoot," he muttered. "I'll come."

He crept clumsily down the ladder, followed by the sergeant at arms, who kept prodding him busily with the arquebus.

Marzio stood shivering in the middle of the kitchen, half naked and woebegone. The swaggering *sbirri* started to jest with their prisoner.

"Poor fellow! Well, well. Here he is, at last."

"Yes, here I am!" cried Marzio bitterly. "If I've done wrong I'll pay the penalty!" He spread his arms. "And what if they hang me? We all die sooner or later!"

And he took his cloak from the hook and slid his arms through the tattered armholes. The sergeant at arms put on his manacles, and then did likewise with the two young kinsmen. Old Cristina stood weeping silently by the fire. The boy Tino clung to her skirt, puzzled and frightened and sobbing.

Soon after dawn they started for Rome: Marzio and Porzia in front, shivering with cold, and right behind them Lelio and the shepherd boy Giovan' Angelo. They walked on foot, a pitiful quartet, clad in black, threadbare clothes, with their manacles tinkling in the wintry wind. Before and behind rode the brightly dressed horsemen. They walked over the stony mule paths with the snow blowing in their faces; down through the villages, where the crowds gathered to see them passing; through Vallecupola and Posticciola and the other bleak hamlets, where the windows swung open and the housewives gaped as they staggered by.

Soon after nightfall they reached Rome. They walked through the streets with their chains still clanking. The drunken soldiers leered from the taverns, the little whores peeped down from their balconies. Porzia and the shep-

herd boy Giovan' Angelo were placed in a house of deten-
tion on the Viminal. Marzio and his brother-in-law Lelio
were escorted to the prison of Tordinona, and there they
were locked in adjoining cells, cold, dark and alone.

3

The prison of Tordinona rose straight from the banks of
the Tiber, an immense, meandering structure built around
an octagonal courtyard. It no longer exists, but the adjoining street still bears its name. Its tiny windows on the
north side looked down over the river, toward the Castel
Sant' Angelo and the neighboring orchards called La Vi-
gnola. The southern windows looked out toward the Inn
of the Orso and the Church of San Salvatore in Lauro.

Marzio's cell was in the "poor," the antiquated part of
the prison: the wing which looked over the Via Tordinona. Here the prisoners could stare all day long through
the iron gratings and beg for alms, or gossip and joke with
the passers-by.

It was Thursday morning, still cold but a day brisk and
sunny, when Marzio Catalano was led through the corridors to a vaulted room. Three men were sitting at a table
with their backs to the window: the commissioner Giuzza,
the bespectacled notary, and between them the judge:
Ulisse Moscato, who was doctor in both of the laws, and
criminal prosecutor for the Most Reverend Signor Vicar
of Rome.

The three men were glancing over a sheaf of papers;

they continued to ignore Catalano's presence. The notary was a frail, cadaverous person; the commissioner was stout and pink, phlegmatic. It was the judge who wholly dominated the atmosphere of the room. Marzio looked furtively at Moscato: a sharp-eyed little man with a pointed skull and quivering nostrils.

The two guards stood motionless. No one spoke. The brazier hissed fitfully.

Finally Moscato raised his eyes. Without preamble he said: "What do you do for a trade, please, Marzio Catalano?"

His voice was slow and casual, deceptively mild.

Marzio said weakly: "A little of everything, as it were, your worship."

"Such as what, for example?"

"I'm a kettlemaker, your worship."

"You've been living in Poggio Vittiano?"

"No, your worship. In Ascrea."

The judge said silkily: "Did you make your kettles in Ascrea, by any chance?"

"No, your worship," said Marzio hoarsely. "I taught the boys to sing and dance, and to play on the lute . . . That's all I did in Ascrea." Suddenly his voice broke with emotion; his eyes grew blurred with tears. "I have a wife and three children, signor, two girls and a boy. The boy is five, his name is Tino, and the little girls are three and one . . ." And then he added, in a choking voice: "I'm a poor man, your worship."

Moscato waited a moment. Then he said in a compassionate tone: "Were you ever in prison before, Catalano?"

"Once," said Marzio, regaining control. He frowned with concentration. "Just for two or three days, on the complaint of Signor Francesco Cenci. For having brought some letters from Signora Beatrice to Rome."

"To whom were these letters addressed?"

"To her brother, I think, signor."

"What were their contents? Do you happen to know?"

"They spoke of her father's cruelty, signor."

The notary scribbled away. The commissioner nodded lazily. Moscato murmured: "Did you ever have financial difficulties? With Signor Francesco, for example?"

"No," said Marzio, stammering a little. "I bought a horse from Signor Francesco. It wasn't quite paid for at the time, so I gave him a gown of my wife's for security."

Moscato fixed his eyes urbanely on the tall, dilapidated man. "Why did you flee from La Petrella, Marzio Catalano?"

"I was in fear of Tirone," whispered Marzio, after a moment.

"Tirone?" said Moscato coldly.

"The commissioner of Abruzzo," put in Marzio.

"And why were you frightened of Tirone?"

"He was spreading an evil tale . . ."

"What tale, might I ask?"

Marzio shifted from foot to foot. Finally he blurted: "That I was involved in the death of Signor Francesco!"

"I see," said Moscato sympathetically. He glanced at Marzio with a ghost of a smile. "Well, let's forget about Tirone. Tell me," he murmured, puckering his lips, "exactly what happened in La Petrella. Did you ever speak intimately with this man Olimpio?"

"You mean . . ."

"I mean," said Moscato, with a sudden ferocity, "about this matter of killing Signor Francesco?"

Marzio took a deep breath. He kept staring at the judge; his eyes shone with a frozen, fascinated luster.

He began to speak in a low monotonous voice: "Olimpio journeyed to Rome one day, your honor, and on his return he showed me a bright red root and a little pellet of opium, which he said Signor Giacomo had given him for the purpose of killing Signor Francesco. And in return for this killing, said Olimpio, Signor Giacomo had promised to give him bread for the rest of his life, and a dowry for his daughter Vittoria."

"And what did you say?" asked Moscato pleasantly.

"I tried to dissuade him, my lord. He asked me to help him but I refused. Three times he asked, but I always refused."

"And that is all?"

"That's all, signor. Ten days later, more or less, Signor Francesco was found dead in the elder thicket, and the folk of La Petrella blamed Olimpio for the murder."

"What led the folk of La Petrella to suspect Olimpio? Do you happen to know?"

"It was because of some bloodstained mattresses which were found in the apothecary's house, signor."

"Who was the apothecary?"

"Gasperini, his name was," said Marzio. "And he was the uncle of Olimpio's wife, Plautilla."

"Yes, I see," said Moscato, fingering some papers.

It was not yet noon, but the sky grew suddenly cloudy and a plum-blue darkness swept through the room. A boy appeared with a lantern, which he placed on the table beside the judge. Moscato's face, to Marzio's eyes, seemed suddenly to shrivel; it grew sharp and gleaming and greedy, like a stoat's.

"Was Olimpio," murmured the judge, "on intimate terms with Signora Beatrice?"

Marzio blushed. "I'm not sure . . . Well, he might have been, signor."

"Did you ever," said Moscato rapidly, "get a gift from Signora Beatrice?"

"Very little, your worship."

"Be precise, if you please."

"The cloak I'm wearing, your worship."

"Yes. Continue. What else?"

"Twenty scudi in coins, your worship."

"Ah. Anything else?"

"Porzia's gown was given back to me by Signora Beatrice, your worship."

Moscato nodded absent-mindedly. Suddenly he thrust his head forward: "Did Signor Francesco die of poison, do you imagine?"

Marzio hesitated a little. He spoke very gently. "I think not, your worship. He was always on guard against poison. He ate cautiously. Even with his family. One might say that he had a terror of poison, your worship."

The notary wrote swiftly. The commissioner folded his hands. Moscato placed a finger against his chin and said very gently: "And that's all you have to tell us?"

"That is all, your honor," said Marzio, with a timorous smile. "After the death of Signor Francesco the rest of the family went to Rome, and Olimpio went with them with his daughter Vittoria. I haven't laid eyes on them since . . . I'm an innocent man, your worship!"

The three men had already risen. They moved past Marzio into the corridor. Drops of rain clicked in the *cortile* as Marzio was led back to his cell.

XXIV

Now the evil days began for the family of the Cenci. On the morning after Marzio's interview the Papal *sbirri* arrived at the palace. They arrested both Giacomo and his brother Bernardo and brought them to Tordinona, where they were placed in the secret, the "rich man's" wing. They went politely, almost placidly. There was nothing sinister in this event. They expected a day or two of questioning; a matter of bail, perhaps, or of bribery. They were accompanied by two servants laden with wine, roast fowl, and cheeses.

The following day — on the fifteenth of January, to be precise — Ulisse Moscato paid a smiling little visit to the Palazzo Cenci. Papal guards, armed with dagger and arquebus, were rapidly stationed about the palace. The back doors were bolted and the horses were led to the stable, and the servants huddled behind the stairs with terrified glances.

Moscato, followed by his notary, strode through the courtyard and up the stairway. He opened the door of the room where Beatrice Cenci was waiting for him.

She rose and stood by the fire. She was dressed in black velvet; her hair hung loose over her thin white shoulders.

"Good day, signora. Pray be seated."

"Good day," murmured Beatrice.

"You must forgive me," said the judge contritely. "I am forced to intrude upon your privacy."

"Quite," said Beatrice laconically. She turned back to her chair.

The judge drew his finger across his eyebrows and sat down by the fire. His face looked pensive, dejected. The notary took out his quill.

"I must ask you," said Moscato gently, "to recall a most unfortunate episode. I deeply regret this, needless to say. I am quite aware of the pain it causes you."

Beatrice looked at him coldly. "Please proceed, your honor."

"Very well," said Moscato. He leaned back and squeezed his fingers, as though he were drawing off a tight pair of gloves. "Let's go back, if you'll be so kind, to the day of your father's death. Do you recall that day clearly?"

"Clearly enough," replied Beatrice.

Moscato nodded. "Very well. Be so good as to tell me what happened."

Beatrice sat very straight, with her long hands folded in her lap. Her face was pale and composed. Her eyes were hard, clear, indifferent. The firelight fell over her shoulders, brightening the long narrow neck. Moscato's eyes caught the vein throbbing unevenly in her throat.

"I was in the gallery," said Beatrice, "when the sun rose over the hills that day. I was watching some huntsmen riding across the valley, as I recall."

"Yes," said Moscato. "And then?"

[197   ]

"I heard Lucrezia crying," said Beatrice. "I hurried across from the other room and stepped onto the balcony. My father's body lay in the thicket, way below, all in a heap."

"Did you look closely? Did you see him clearly?"

"No," said Beatrice. "I turned away. The moment I saw this hideous thing I called for the servants, who came running."

"Which servants, Signora Beatrice?"

"The butler Giorgio," said Beatrice quietly.

Moscato glanced at the notary, whose head was bent over his papers. There was a curious light in Moscato's eyes; something gentle and indulgent, and at the same time vibrant, alert. His nails clicked on the arm of the chair.

"Tell me, please," he said discreetly, "of Olimpio Calvetti. What manner of man is he? What does he look like, for example?"

Beatrice's face scarcely changed. Her voice grew dull and deliberate. "He is tall of stature, you might say; thickset rather than lean. He wears a heavy black beard. He looks . . . well, slightly coarse."

"A handsome fellow, all in all?"

"I've hardly considered the matter."

"Why was he sent from the castle?"

"How should I know?" said Beatrice coldly. "Letters came from Prince Colonna requesting the seneschal to leave the castle."

"There was no quarrel," said Moscato nimbly, "between your father and the seneschal?"

Beatrice looked into the judge's eyes. Her voice deepened. "None," she said.

"A lonely life, it must have been," said Moscato absent-mindedly. "Was your father generous to you? Did he treat you well?"

Beatrice hesitated a moment. "Of course," she said. "He was very fond of me."

"Did you ever write to your brothers in Rome, Signora Beatrice?"

"Yes," said Beatrice, expressionless. "Once or twice, I suppose."

"Did you ever, in these letters, happen to speak of your father's cruelty?"

"Never," said Beatrice, raising her brows. "There was no cruelty. Why should I speak of cruelty?"

For a minute or two they sat silently. Neither of them moved; they stared at the fire. Finally Moscato raised his eyes, which wandered over the long high room, with its ornamented ceiling and elaborately painted walls; over the tapestry which showed Aeneas kneeling in front of the Queen of Carthage; over the tall silver candlesticks which stood on the table; and at last over Beatrice's person — the slim white neck, the velvet sleeves.

"It has been asked," said Moscato casually, "why you did not visit your father's body when it lay in the church. What is your opinion on this point?"

Beatrice's voice was calm and ironic. "I gave all that the archpriest requested. I paid in full for the funeral ceremonies. I also gave some cloaks and stockings, and other objects, for charity. I did as was fitting and proper. I felt disinclined to visit the church."

Moscato kept nodding. "Yes. Quite. I understand . . . One last question, signora. What can you tell me about the wounds on your father's body?"

"Nothing," said Beatrice, cold and flat, "beyond what the archpriest Don Marzio told me."

"And what did he tell you?"

"That a large elder spine, such as the peasants call a *sterpone,* had cut into the temple beside the eye and pierced the brain. He pulled out the thorn with his own fingers, the archpriest told me. It left a deep red hole, said the archpriest, and he placed his finger in that hole . . ."

Her voice grew tense and excited. Suddenly she grew still; her eyelids quivered. A look of uncontrollable fear crept into her eyes.

The notary was busily scratching away. Moscato plucked a hair from his sleeve. He gazed at Beatrice for a moment; he seemed lost in thought. Then he cleared his throat. "Thank you, signora. I am deeply indebted to you."

Beatrice rose and glanced silently through the window as Moscato left the room and crossed the courtyard on his way to Lucrezia's apartment.

2

With Lucrezia the judge was brief and gentle and casual.

She too was all in black, but earrings dangled from her ears and a bright red stone shone on her middle finger. A cat lay purring in her lap. The scent of her flesh filled the room.

"Tell me, signora," began Moscato, "of the day of your husband's death."

"Ah," said Lucrezia, her fingers fluttering. "What more is there to tell?" She glanced at Moscato with agitation, then quickly away again. She sighed and flung open her arms: "I was moving about the room that morning, doing one thing and another. Soon after sunrise, if I remember rightly. All in the usual sort of way. And then one moment, as I glanced through the door, I saw a hole in the balcony. My heart sank, signor. I immediately suspected something dreadful. I hurried out all of a tremble, and I saw my husband lying below in that tangle of shrubbery which we called the thicket."

"I see. You saw him clearly?"

"Ah . . . not very! Tears poured from my eyes!"

Moscato murmured sympathetically: "Was he a dutiful husband, signora?"

Lucrezia's gaze grew deep and reproachful. "Alas, your worship. I'm afraid he wasn't. He was eccentric, to say the least. Most unkind to both Beatrice and myself. He held us imprisoned, as you probably know. Month after month. Quite without reason."

"Was Signora Beatrice unhappy?"

"Goodness me . . . Indeed she was!"

A wisp of a smile went flitting across Moscato's lips. Lucrezia kept stroking the cat with her jeweled fingers.

"Why," said Moscato, leaning forward in his chair and fondling his chin, "why was Olimpio Calvetti sent from the castle? Was it because Signor Francesco was angry with him?"

Lucrezia looked confused. She reflected a moment. "Why, no, your worship, I shouldn't say so. Signor Francesco desired that Beatrice and I should remain alone, with no young man in the castle, while he went riding about the countryside. That was the reason, I suppose. Signor Francesco was jealous by nature. But there was no anger, signor, not a bit of it, as far as I know."

Moscato peered at his fingernails, which were long and pink and shiny. He reached out and plucked a tiny green bottle from the table, held it up against the light, then set it down again thoughtfully. The room was warm, cypress-scented; a pale blue curtain hid the bed, and there were embroidered cushions on the chairs. A jar of rose water stood on the night table. The air of a courtesan's boudoir, thought Moscato; he glanced at the small, fat woman who faced him, toying nervously with her necklace.

"There was," he murmured, "no ill-will between Signora Beatrice and this man Calvetti?"

Lucrezia blushed and lowered her eyes. "Oh, mercy, no," she said quickly. "They rarely saw one another. There was no occasion for ill-will."

"I see," said Moscato.

Lucrezia's eyes grew pleading. "There's no cause . . . no possible ground for suspicion, is there?"

Moscato's face broke into a puckish smile. "None whatever, signora."

He rose and bowed amiably and took his leave. His heels clicked on the stones, crisp and neat, like dice in a cup.

3

Now it was Giacomo's turn. Three sunny days were allowed to pass, and then Moscato ordered Giacomo Cenci to be brought to his quarters in Tordinona. Moscato sat huddled in a voluminous black cape, his tiny head protruding, his eyes gleaming like china buttons.

His voice at first was deceptively soft, almost caressing. "I believe you realize, Signor Giacomo, that there are rumors to the effect that your father was murdered?"

"I dare say," said Giacomo aridly.

"You've heard such rumors?"

"I was aware of them."

"How did you hear them?"

"God knows," said Giacomo, with a little shrug. "One hears these silly tales. Servants' gossip and so on."

"What is your opinion of these rumors? Is there any truth in them, do you fancy?"

Giacomo glanced sharply at the judge. He waved his hands contemptuously. He had the beautiful tapering hands of all the Cenci, but he was shorter than Beatrice and somewhat angular of feature. His lips were sharp and petulant; his skin was soft and somewhat oily. His eyes, which lacked the cool, disciplined fire of Beatrice's eyes, rolled nervously under their lids; they had an oriental sheen to them.

"I've always laughed at such rumors," he said in his thin, sexless voice. "What the devil do I care about these fishmongers' rumors?"

Moscato drew his collar about his neck, leaned forward and smiled. His teeth shone white and sharp. "Tell me, Signor Giacomo. Did you ever plan with anyone to obtain the death of your father?"

Giacomo caught his breath. He sat motionless and pale. Then the blood rushed back to his cheeks; his eyes flashed indignantly.

"What's this?" he snapped. "What do you take me for? A strange question for you to ask me!"

"May I repeat it?" said Moscato blandly. "Did you ever,

Signor Giacomo, plan with anyone to obtain the murder of your father?"

Giacomo hesitated a moment. Small white bubbles shone on his lips. Something seemed to collapse within him. His voice grew frail and petulant. "I never, your honor, discussed or contemplated, or even dreamed of such a plan. Either on my part or anyone else's. The idea is outrageous."

Moscato smiled. He spread his fingers and studied them scrupulously. Finally he said: "Why, signor, did you tolerate Olimpio's presence at your table? Why, signor, did you keep his daughter Vittoria in the palazzo? Why, may I ask, did you make such unusual efforts on behalf of Olimpio Calvetti?"

"I made no efforts," said Giacomo, sick at heart all of a sudden. "Olimpio's presence in the palazzo was none of my doing, as it happens. He was a friend of my brother's and of Beatrice's as well. I had nothing to do with this ill-bred ruffian."

"And you never, perchance, made any gifts to this ill-bred ruffian?"

"Certainly not," said Giacomo.

"None whatever?"

"None," said Giacomo.

"Thank you, signor," said Moscato. Giacomo turned and walked to the door. His eyes were glazed and unseeing, like those of a man in a trance. He drew a handkerchief from his sleeve and carefully wiped his brow, and slowly followed the bearded guard down the corridor.

4

On the twenty-second of January, three Papal guards appeared at the palace and accompanied Beatrice to the rooms of the judge in Tordinona.

This time Moscato was chilly and sharp in his manner. He looked coldly at Beatrice, who stood motionless in front of his table. The red light from the brazier shone up at her cheekbones, leaving a mask of shadow around the eyes. She wore a shawl over her head; a heavy crucifix hung from her throat.

"How much longer, signora, will you insist on evading the truth?"

"I make a point of always speaking the truth," said Beatrice dryly.

"Very well. Let's have the truth. Did you ever," said Moscato rapidly, "give money, or a cloak, or his wife's gown, to this man Catalano?"

"Never. None of these things. I did nothing of the sort," murmured Beatrice.

"And if the man should appear and testify to the contrary?"

"Let him appear," said Beatrice curtly. "Let him testify as he wishes."

The door opened and Marzio was brought in from the antechamber. Beatrice at first refused to look at him. When she did she found it hard to recognize him. Unkempt and woebegone, haggard and bony under the mud-stained cloak; there was something phantasmal about Marzio's appearance.

Moscato said: "Tell us the truth, Catalano, about this cloak you are wearing."

"I've told you the truth," said Marzio humbly, wiping his nose with his forefinger. "Signora Beatrice gave me this cloak, and twenty scudi in coins, as well as my wife's purple gown. That's what I said, and it's the truth, your honor."

"The man lies," said Beatrice.

"It's the truth," cried Marzio, "and you know it, signora!"

"Nothing but lies," said Beatrice slowly. Her eyes were fixed on Moscato.

"Well, we'll see," said Moscato, and he rose with a grunt and led the way into an adjoining room, which was dimly lit by a small black oil lamp. Strips of heavy brown cloth hung over the window and covered the wall from floor to ceiling. There was a sickening smell in the air, like decaying mutton. Ropes and straps hung from the wall, and curiously shaped leather girdles. Beatrice recognized with disgust the apparatus of the torture chamber.

Moscato gave the order nonchalantly. Marzio was seized by the guards and stripped. The filthy clothes were tossed in a heap, all ripped and stained and sour-smelling. Poor Marzio, blushing with shame, covered his sex with his hands, but the guards seized his arms and held them raised toward the pulleys. The miserable, bony body was bound to the rack.

"Have you told the truth?" murmured Moscato.

"I've told the truth!" said Marzio, shivering.

Moscato glanced at Beatrice with his berrylike eyes.

"I say that he lies," said Beatrice hoarsely.

"Stretch him, please," said Moscato quietly.

The guards bent down and turned the wheels. Very slowly Marzio's body was raised by a set of bloodstained ropes while another set held his feet bound to the floor. His legs were purple with cold but the sweat poured suddenly from his face. He snarled with pain; his face grew twisted. A knoblike swelling appeared in his groin. There was a click, faint and liquid, as the bones slipped out of their joints. Marzio screamed uncontrollably. A stream of urine shot forth. Beatrice drew the shawl over her face; she caught the strong, acrid odor.

Moscato, gazing intently at Marzio, said softly: "Have you told us the truth, Catalano?"

"Nothing but the truth! Oh God! I swear it! Let me down!" screamed Marzio.

Moscato's lips moved inaudibly as he recited the Credo; the recital of one Credo was the usual duration for such torture.

Then he said: "Release the man."

The wheels were turned again slowly. Marzio's body was lowered and unbound from the rack. He sagged and sank to the floor; saliva poured from his mouth. The guards resettled his arms into their joints while Marzio kept sobbing uncontrollably. Then they left him with his bundle of gray, rotting garments.

Beatrice followed Moscato back into the room of interrogation. Her face was white and drawn; her eyes were distant and filmy.

The judge said casually: "You will sign this testimony, please, signora." And he gave her a quill and the sheet which the clerk had laid on the table.

Beatrice took the quill in her hand without a word and

wrote swiftly: *All that I have testified I hereby say that I, Beatrice Cenci, have testified to be the truth.*

Then she drew the shawl tightly around her and followed the *sbirri* out of the room.

5

It was an hour before noon when she returned to the palazzo. She took her food in her room and while the sun was still high set out alone and on foot for San Pietro Montorio. The air was sweet on the hills; instead of visiting the church she walked down an empty path and out toward the pasturelands.

A ruddy glow lay over the fields. Not a leaf was stirring. Utter calm; utter solitude; the world seemed lost in a trance. Only the clouds moved slowly on their great silver wings. For an instant the illusion of peace returned: the nameless shadows and whispers which had come to obsess her drifted away in the bright wintry haze of the meadows. She walked on. The path entered a glade littered with moss-tufted ruins. The light hovered over the old, shattered columns like a halo.

A cold uneasiness gripped her. The whole past, the world of the dead, seemed delicately, surreptitiously alive all around her: eyes watching, ears listening, tiny footsteps among the elders . . . She turned and ran down the path. The veil of pines suddenly parted and the roofs of Rome lay below her — the pearly domes and rippled tiles lost in a sea of twilight, like a thousand seashells.

She hurried on. Dusk had fallen when she finally crossed

the Ponte Sisto. The lamps were lit in the jewelers' shops and the craftsmen leaned over their glowing metals, weaving the threads of pure gold into marvelous patterns of bees and spiders, with garnet eyes flashing venomously, as though they were alive.

She turned to the left, toward Monte Cenci. A cold wind shot up from the river. Drops of rain were beginning to plant tiny kisses on her cheeks. She passed under an archway and caught her breath. Had someone called her? Was someone following her? There was an echo of distant hoofbeats: then the sound died away . . . All was still but her heart was pounding uncontrollably, ready to burst. She waited a moment, then turned the corner and darted across the street. At that moment she saw him. She recognized him instantly. The shape of her dreams: no longer a beast or a bird this time, but a man, bearded, corpulent, his face in shadow as though masked, eyes gleaming like a rat's. He stood in the shade of a portal; an instant later he was gone.

"Nonsense," she whispered. "It was nothing at all. It was only a shadow . . ."

XXV

A BITTER BLUE WIND came down from the hills that day.
The thick waters of the Tiber were littered with twigs
and dead thistles, and beyond the Castel Sant' Angelo the
cypresses shuddered in the breeze. Dark clouds hung over
the city; outside the Inn of the Bear an old woman sat
fanning the brazier under the roasted chestnuts.

A gentle-eyed man in a faded cassock followed two
guards down the prison corridor. A crisp knock; a rustle of
papers. "Enter, please," said Ulisse Moscato.

The priest entered. The notary raised his quill with a
meticulous air.

"Your name is, I believe . . ."

"Don Marzio Tommasini," said the priest.

"You are the archpriest of the village of La Petrella. Is
that correct?"

The priest nodded gravely. "It is correct."

Moscato gazed at the priest in a strange, probing way.
The priest blushed and lowered his coal-black eyes. He
was a tall, bony man, far larger than Moscato. His hair was
streaked with iron-gray and his face was gnarled, weather-
beaten. His hands were the hands of a man who has worked

in the fields, dark and leathery, with heavy knuckles and thick, short nails.

He cleared his throat, then said softly: "Before I testify, your worship, may I be allowed to state the following? I am a Mass priest and I wish to avoid any sort of irregularity. I do not intend, by anything I say, to endanger the life of any person."

Moscato nodded perfunctorily. "Quite. Of course . . . And now please tell me," he said, waving his hand, "what you saw on the day of the death of Francesco Cenci."

The archpriest sighed. "I was present, your worship, when Signor Francesco's body was lifted from the thicket and raised by means of a ladder over the wall. I saw his body brought to the fountain, and I witnessed the washing of the body."

"You saw the wounds in his head?"

The archpriest nodded austerely; he glanced at the ceiling. "I saw the wounds sufficiently clearly. I saw the woman Dorotea thrust her finger into a wound by the dead man's eye."

"Did you see a thorn in the wound, Don Marzio?"

"There was no thorn in the wound, your worship."

"No elder spike, or something of the sort?"

"Nothing whatever," said the archpriest.

"Signora Beatrice," said Moscato wearily, "has testified to the contrary. She has testified that you told her that you saw an elder thorn in the wound."

"I told her nothing of the sort," said the archpriest, in sorrowful tones.

Moscato glanced through the little window. Drops of rain were beginning to fall. The wind had died; there was a listless melancholy in the sound of the raindrops.

"Please continue," said Moscato. "Did you touch the body, Don Marzio?"

"I touched the hand and raised it slightly as the body was being washed."

"Was it cold? The hand, I mean?"

"It was cold, your worship. The body was quite cold already when it was rescued from the thicket."

"May I ask one further thing? Did you see," said Moscato delicately, "the hole in the balcony from which the dead man fell?"

Don Marzio hesitated. Finally he said: "Yes, your worship. I saw the hole."

"Was it a large hole, Don Marzio?"

Don Marzio looked forlorn. "I shouldn't say so, your worship. Not large, precisely."

Moscato's eyes grew sharp and menacing. "What is your opinion, Don Marzio?"

"My opinion," said the archpriest gently, "is the following, your worship. Signor Francesco's body, which was stout, could scarcely have fallen through so slender a hole."

"Thank you, Don Marzio. That will be sufficient," said Moscato, rising.

The archpriest turned without a word and wandered back down the corridor.

2

That same day the pantry boy Pasquale went down to the shop near the bridge to buy some tarts for Lucrezia Cenci.

The baker's wife Raffaelina was sprinkling raisins on a pie. "Well, what'll it be for today?"

"What do you have? It's for Signora Lucrezia."

"Peach patties, apricot patties . . ."

"She's weary of patties. Something new."

"How about a nice juicy honey bun?"

"With almonds?" said Pasquale anxiously.

"There's always almonds," said Raffaelina. "Come, take a peek at the kitchen."

Pasquale followed the woman into the kitchen. Mattia the baker, an ape of a man with a cauliflower nose, was pulling a tray of cinnamon wafers out of the oven. The air was sweet with wandering odors — burnt almonds and steaming cherries and fine crisp layers of buttery dough. Pasquale went mincing among the great blue platters, dipping his finger in a bowl, plucking a raisin from a tart, sniffing here and sniffing there with his long dainty nose. There were snail-shaped puffs filled with cream, ginger curls and hazelnut crescents, buns like blackamoors' heads with citron teeth and pistachio eyes, and on a shelf by the window an enormous cake shaped like the Castel Sant' Angelo, layer on layer of *millefoglie* with an extravagant icing of marzipan. Pasquale leaned over furtively and snipped a nut from one of the bastions.

"Fiend!" shrieked Raffaelina, slapping the fellow on the wrist. "That cake's going to the Orsinis! They're having a ball tonight, and I'll ask you to keep your paws out of my pastries!"

Mattia turned with a leer and jabbed Pasquale in the ribs.

"There's other sweets you can toy with — how about it, my lily? Didn't I see you in Trastevere the other day with the poet Pozzi? The one with ribbons on his cuffs?"

Raffaelina squealed with laughter. "He doesn't need to go to Trastevere to find rosebuds like that Pozzi. Right in the palazzo, I hear . . ."

"Listen," snapped Pasquale, stamping his foot, "you stop waggling your wicked tongues, you two! All day long I hear nothing but chitter-chatter about the palazzo. It's nothing but Cenci this and Cenci that from morning till midnight. It's a hissing of vipers and the Lord protect me!"

The cook regarded him placidly. "Well, what's your personal opinion on the matter?"

"My personal opinion?" Pasquale thrust his hands on his hips. "It's that folk should stop prying into other people's boudoirs!"

"Boudoirs, is it?" said Mattia with a great guffaw. "Well, I'm glad to hear it. At least there's fun being had on Monte Cenci . . ."

As soon as Pasquale had gone with his muffins under his arm, Mattia turned to his wife.

"Well, what do you think of it all?"

"I think there's mischief aplenty in that palazzo!"

"You think Signora Beatrice . . ."

"There's no doubt whatsoever. Eight months gone, if it's a day. Her belly's like a soufflé!"

"So you think the poor creature . . ."

"Poor creature, indeed! Carrying on with that low-class seneschal, like a common slut! They killed the father in a panic. He'd have martyred the girl on a cross if he'd ever found out!"

"A dreadful business," growled the baker.

"Boiling vats, that's where they belong! Till their bellies pop open and their eyes turn pink as bonbons! Hell's too good for folk like that . . ." She breathed a deep sigh and started buttering a pan. "But I know what will happen. They've got friends in the Vatican. The usual thing, it will be. A fuss and a fine and that's the end of it. Three months hence, mark my words, there'll be dancing and singing at Monte Cenci . . ."

3

The following night, which was the last of January, a midwife was hastily called to Monte Cenci. A sullen night, with a great ring of vapor around the moon and a steady tolling of bells from San Tommaso.

There was whispering and tiptoeing in the palazzo. The stable boys sat huddled in the kitchen, belching and leering; the chambermaids darted about with a brisk, mysterious air. Ludovica kept to her room with an air of stern disapproval. Lucrezia likewise kept to her room but sent the maid Bastiana scurrying about to bring her the latest bits of news. Beatrice lay in her bed with the midwife looming above her, an elephantine woman with a face peppered with warts. The only other person in the room was a little lady in coal-black bombazine who sat by the bedside holding Beatrice's hand: Caterina de Santis, this was, an old friend of Beatrice's. She was a widow; her husband had died of the Spanish plague two years ago and her beauty had faded abruptly; she looked withered and birdlike.

It was shortly before midnight that Madonna Caterina came down the stairway and took a carriage through the streets and finally arrived at Tordinona. She begged permission to give a message to Giacomo Cenci.

He was sitting beside the window, adding figures in a long black ledger.

Caterina paused in the doorway. "It's a boy," she muttered.

Giacomo's face was pinched and tense. He put down his quill.

"A healthy child," said Caterina crisply. "It will live, I think."

"Have you spoken to the nuns already?"

"I have indeed," said the widow bitterly.

"When do they come to fetch the child?"

"Tomorrow night," said Caterina.

"And how is Beatrice?"

"Well enough. It's rather difficult at the moment . . ."

"Quite," said Giacomo. "Naturally."

"Well, good night, Signor Giacomo."

"Good night," said Giacomo. The door closed softly, the footsteps died in the corridor. He sat motionless by the window with the quill between his fingers, listening to the bells tolling away in San Tommaso.

XXVI

Marzio Catalano was brought forth from his cell once more on the third of February. He looked like a corpse. His jaw hung loose and unshaven, his eyes were huge and sunken and lifeless. He was led to the icy courtroom where the prosecutor Moscato sat at the table with the senior judge, the stately and decrepit Molella. In the corner at a separate table sat the usual notary.

MOSCATO (*rather casually*): I strongly advise you, Catalano, to make up your mind to confess the truth.

CATALANO: I've told you the truth already, your worship.

MOSCATO (*more crisply*): We think differently, Catalano. We know that you were a participant in this murder. We know that you received twenty scudi and the cloak you are wearing for taking part in the Cenci killing.

CATALANO (*listlessly*): I got the money for something quite different, signor. And this cloak was given me as a gift in memory of Signor Francesco.

MOSCATO: Listen, Catalano. What do you make of the following? On the day of your arrest in the village of Poggio Vittiano you were heard to remark: "If I've done wrong I'll pay the penalty. What if they hang me? We all must die." These words, I might say, can be construed as a confession of guilt.

CATALANO: They are words I never said, I swear it, your worship!

MOSCATO: You are sure?

CATALANO: Quite sure.

MOSCATO: And if we bring in witnesses who testify that you said this?

CATALANO: The witnesses lie if they say I said this.

MOSCATO (*turning to the guards*): Please call the witnesses.

The door was flung open and the Constable Pirro Galeotto appeared, together with a younger man in a bright red doublet. They both testified verbatim to the words uttered at the moment of arrest.

CATALANO (*in a high-pitched voice*): They lie!

MOSCATO: Be careful, Catalano. I suggest that you tell us the truth.

CATALANO (*sullenly*): I had nothing to do with the killing and that's the truth, your worship.

MOSCATO: Please allow me to remind you, Catalano, that a heinous murder has been committed on the person of a most noble Roman, Francesco Cenci. You persist in denying what we know to be true. We will now accompany you to the torture chamber.

Ulisse Moscato and Pompeo Molella accompanied Marzio into the adjoining room. They were followed by the notary and two heavily armed guards. Marzio's throat muscles worked oddly when he glanced at the tangle of ropes. "Strip the man," said Moscato.

The *sbirri* proceeded to strip Marzio. He had grown grotesquely thin. His ribs hung over his belly like bars on a cage. The guards took him by the hand and bound the ropes around his ankles, which still bore the greenish bruises of his previous visit to the torture room.

There was a moment's delay. One of the wheels refused to turn. It creaked heavily, then stopped. One of the guards bent down and tugged. The wheel went spinning, the ropes rippled and writhed like a nest of serpents.

Suddenly Marzio sank to his knees and turned to the white-haired Molella: "I'll tell the truth, signor, I swear it! Free me from the rack! I'll tell you everything!"

Marzio was clad and then promptly led back into the witness stand.

"Gentlemen," he said, trembling with emotion, "I'll tell you how it happened, this terrible killing of Signor Francesco! I'll tell it from the beginning and I'll tell it with truth. The real beginning was in the heart of the lady Beatrice, who led a life of misery and imprisonment up in the castle. She longed to see her father slain in return for all his cruelty, and she begged the castellan Olimpio to help her in this plan."

MOSCATO: Did she ever speak to you personally of such a plan?

CATALANO: Yes, she spoke to me one evening, from the terrace by the battlements. She begged me to go on muleback to the bandits of Marcatelli, some of whom were old friends of mine from days when I roamed the hills, and she begged me to coax them to kidnap and kill her father. I told her I would do so, but I knew the thing would be folly. So I delayed and did nothing, and Signora Beatrice hit on her second notion.

MOSCATO: What was that?

CATALANO: She begged me to travel to Rome to speak to

[219   ]

Signor Giacomo and ask him to help her. But I pretended to be ill when the time came to do it. So it was Olimpio who took this trip, and when he returned to La Petrella he showed me a small red root, shaped like a thimble. He also had a pellet of opium which Signor Giacomo had given him.

MOSCATO: What happened to this little root and this pellet?

CATALANO: Olimpio gave them to Signora Beatrice, my lord . . .

Gradually, as Catalano proceeded with the confession, a look of passionate relief appeared on his face. His voice grew calmer; the torment fell from his eyes. And Moscato likewise spoke more and more gently; his expression grew mellow, almost dreamy.

MOSCATO: Tell me, Catalano. Did Olimpio have carnal relations with Signora Beatrice?

CATALANO: With regularity, my lord.

MOSCATO: What do you mean, with regularity?

CATALANO: I mean this. Before leaving his residence in the castle Olimpio pried open the bars in the prison window above the thicket, and near this window he placed a ladder, and outside the wall of the thicket he placed a smaller ladder, and by means of these ladders he entered the castle at night and was able to visit Signora Beatrice with considerable regularity.

MOSCATO: I see. And what of this business of the poison? What happened?

CATALANO: Nothing at all. Signor Francesco was a suspicious man, and he had the whim that his kinfolk might try to poison him, and in recent weeks all his food was tested by his daughter before he ate, and so

this queer little root was useless, and Signora Beatrice
grew desperate.

MOSCATO: Yes. Proceed.

CATALANO: Well, one night, it was a Sunday, I think . . .

MOSCATO (*glancing at a sheet*): That would be the sixth of
September?

CATALANO: It might have been, your honor. Well, that
night, soon after sundown, Olimpio and I climbed the
wall of the thicket with a small wooden ladder, and
then we took a second ladder, much longer than the
first, which was hidden in a tangle of shrubs, and we
climbed through the open window and pulled both
of the ladders after us, and we stood in the castle
dungeon, from which we passed into the wine cellar,
and from the cellar we climbed through a window
into the cloister, and from there we tiptoed . . .

MOSCATO: Was it dark now?

CATALANO: Pitch-black, your honor. Olimpio came to a
door which he opened with a long thin key, and we
came to the terrace which adjoined the rooms of Signora Beatrice, who was waiting for us, all wrapped in
a cloak, and I held a candle in my hand while she
spoke of her plan, which was for the killing of Signor
Francesco in his bed. I passed that night in a lonely
room while Olimpio stayed with Signora Beatrice; I
slept on a wooden table under a blanket which the
lady gave me. Horrible dreams I had all night, listening to the rats scampering across the floor! The next
day Signora Beatrice brought us a jug of wine and
some meat on a plate, all neatly covered with a damask
napkin, and Olimpio and I ate in silence, brooding
about this dreadful plan, until it was late afternoon

and we happened to think that our absence from the village might set some tongues wagging. So Olimpio spoke to the lady Beatrice and we hastily crept back to the thicket. We scaled the high wall and hid the ladder in the weeds and went our separate ways for a little while.

MOSCATO: What did you do?

CATALANO: Nothing of particular gravity, your worship. I sat by the fountain and played the lute, if I remember correctly.

MOSCATO: And then?

CATALANO: Night came, my lord, and that was the night that my heart burned so bitterly . . .

And the tinker proceeded with the tale of the killing: the hesitations, the recriminations, the delays and soul-searchings, the bribes and the promises, the pleas and rebuttals. And finally he told of the actual scene in Lucrezia's bedchamber, where Olimpio sent the hammer crashing on Francesco's skull; he told of the blood that poured and of the dressing of the corpse and all the frenzy and flurry of thrusting it through the balcony. He told the whole elaborate story from beginning to end, extenuating his own behavior, as was natural, and incriminating the others gratuitously: dwelling on Olimpio's blind ruthlessness, circling about Lucrezia's hypocrisy, and emphasizing the cold hard obduracy of the lady Beatrice; so that the whole tremendous crime emerged in its entirety, soft-pedaled in spots, melodramatized in others, but in its essentials following the truth with fidelity.

And it was obvious to Moscato that here at last was the truth. For the remarkable thing about this crime, in spite of all the confusion, is its strange emotional coherence, its profound human logic. Even the moments of play-acting and folly and incompetence, even the little touches of self-pity, self-doubt, self-contradiction, most of all perhaps the childish grotesquerie of the crime itself — even these carry a desperate ring of reality. The most casual details emerge as chords in a single structure. A lie or an evasion in Marzio's recital would have been as jarring to Moscato as a note struck falsely in a great dramatic aria.

So Moscato nodded and closed his eyes, realizing that the truth now lay before him; and the tinker, limp and worn, was led back to his cell.

2

A hundred yards from the prison gates stood the Inn of the Bear; some young Bohemians were sitting around the fire with their amber glasses.

"What's news today?" said Cosimo of Brescia, a fashionable painter of miniatures.

"There's been a confession down at the prison," said the poet Ugo Pozzi.

"Who's been confessing?"

"It's the tinker Marzio. He's told everything, I hear."

"You don't say," said Cosimo, running his finger over his lips. "I don't trust those confessions. They get them by torture, one and all."

The poet nodded. "It's a horrible thing, so they tell me, the *veglia*."

"Well," said Sandro, a boy with a harelip who served

[223]

as groom at the Farnese, "terrible or not, that's the way they do it. You can't hang a man without a confession. And if he won't confess willingly then they have to use torture, and that's the law, right or wrong, and there's nothing to be done about it."

"What's he confessed, this man Marzio?"

Ugo chuckled into his glass. "The whole business, from tip to toe. That's what I heard from Paolino, and he's a cousin of one of the guards at Tordinona. He confessed that the castellan Olimpio did the killing because of his lust for the lovely Beatrice, who vowed to do away with her father, and they killed him with a hammer one morning and then they hurled him from the balcony, and now it's the scaffold for the lot of them, says this friend of Paolino's."

"And richly deserved," remarked Sandro.

There was silence for a while. The firelight burned in the yellow glasses, and the jet-black velvet of Ugo's doublet shone like the hide of a panther. Eusebio of Battipaglia, a local eccentric, sat in a corner singing a song — he sang softly and sweetly, but suddenly he dropped his guitar, tucked a feather behind his ear and went loping into the night. The room was silent again.

"It's a pity, though," said Ugo suddenly. "Such a lovely lady, and so young."

"And a child newly born . . ."

"It's been taken to the nuns of Montecitorio . . ."

"A dark fate for a newborn child . . ."

"So it is," said Ugo grimly.

"It's a terrible thing to kill one's father."

"So it is; it's the sin of sins."

"Even if the father's a festering scoundrel."

"True enough. Murder's murder."

"Still, the blood in this man Cenci was the blackest in Rome," remarked Ugo. "There wasn't a lad on the Campo dei Fiori who was safe from his lewdness. Nor even a lass, for that matter. There wasn't a thing he didn't stoop to."

"Blood like that," said Sandro lugubriously, "poisons the veins of all who spring from him. All the children and the children's children and there's no end to it ever, and the scaffold's the place for suchlike vermin."

"Ah," said Cosimo, wiping the wine from his tawny mustache, "you're a cruel one, Sandro. Who are you to pass judgment?"

"Yes," said the barber Ippolito, thrusting himself into the chatter. "There's a little thing or two I could tell about you too, Sandro."

Ugo the poet kept nodding, and the light of the candle hung in his eyes, which burned like vast and melancholy sapphires. "We're all sinners, every last one of us. There's not one of us, I say, who's one whit better than the lady Beatrice. She was driven to desperation by all this cruelty and lechery, and if there's mercy in the law they'll spare her life, and the widow's too."

"And the seneschal?"

"Ah, the seneschal!"

"He'll go to the gallows," put in Sandro, whose eyes were gleaming like a viper's, "and then he'll plunge into hell, and there he'll burn in a caldron for the rest of eternity!"

And again there was silence. A pool of wine shone on the table; it leaked to the floor drop by drop, like the ticking of a clock.

[225   ]

XXVII

THINGS MOVED SWIFTLY and ominously after Catalano's confession. Three days passed; on the seventh of February the *sbirri* appeared at the palazzo and conducted the two ladies to the prisons of the Castel Sant' Angelo. Beatrice, still weak and pale, was placed in a room which faced the vineyards; Lucrezia was put into a large barren chamber which looked on the court.

2

Lucrezia was led to Moscato's quarters that same afternoon. The judge sat grimly at the table; his mien had radically altered: no longer casual and discreet but sharp, steely, staccato.

MOSCATO: You will excuse me, signora, if I insist on the truth today. Time is short. This whole matter must be brought to an end. Please tell us what you know about your husband's death, and please be clear about it.

LUCREZIA: I have told you before. My poor Francesco fell from the balcony. It was all rotten and flimsy, and many a time I said, "Francesco darling . . ."

MOSCATO: That will do. I am not interested in this fable of the balcony. What about the mattresses on Signor Francesco's bed? Were they removed at any time?

LUCREZIA (*touchily*): I don't know. I don't busy myself with mattresses.

MOSCATO: Did you see blood on any of the mattresses?

LUCREZIA: Bless my soul! Why should there be blood on them, signor?

MOSCATO (*shrugging his shoulders*): Did you continue to sleep in the marriage bed?

LUCREZIA (*rather fastidiously*): I think not, signor.

MOSCATO: Why not, signora?

LUCREZIA: I didn't care to sleep alone, and that seems natural enough, your worship.

MOSCATO: Couldn't Signora Beatrice come and sleep in your room with you?

LUCREZIA: I preferred sleeping in Beatrice's chamber, if you'll excuse me.

MOSCATO: Now listen carefully, please, signora. Did either Olimpio Calvetti or Marzio Catalano appear at the castle on the day of your husband's death?

Lucrezia glanced at her hands and then said quickly: "I don't recall. I know nothing about this."

Then she looked up again and fixed her gaze on Moscato. There was something impenetrable in her eyes; as though the greed, the obesity and petulance were only a mask, and a secret life went on beneath, tenacious, hornèd, like a reptile's.

MOSCATO (*leaning back in his chair*): Signora Lucrezia, the court is weary of all these lies. Your husband was murdered, and you had a hand in the execution of this murder, and you will now proceed to tell us the truth in full detail.

LUCREZIA (*after a moment, with great firmness*): I have nothing to say, signor.

MOSCATO: The court, signora, I warn you, possesses the truth.

LUCREZIA: I've said all I know. There's nothing further to say.

MOSCATO: You are sure?

LUCREZIA: Quite sure.

And Moscato, pale with impatience, had Lucrezia accompanied back to her chamber.

3

Now Beatrice was ushered into the presence of the judges. She was dressed in black, as usual, with a long silk shawl over her head. Cold, contemptuous, aloof as always, but a little worn, a little feverish.

This time the gentle and elderly Molella began the questioning:

"There are still some small points we must ask you about, unfortunately, signora."

"Very well. Please ask them," said Beatrice, tightening her shawl.

"Did you ever, Signora Beatrice, make any gifts to Olimpio Calvetti?"

BEATRICE (*flushing*): Certainly not. I don't do favors for a
 seneschal.

MOLELLA (*mildly*): Did the seneschal stay at the palazzo
 after your father's death?

BEATRICE: I kept to my rooms. I have no idea who might
 have stayed at the palazzo.

MOLELLA: Did you speak to the seneschal on the day of
 your father's death, signora?

BEATRICE: I have already testified on this point. You can
 go and read the testimony.

MOLELLA (*clearing his throat*): Be so kind as to answer the
 following, signora. Did Olimpio visit Rome shortly
 before your father's death, by any chance?

BEATRICE (*insolently*): I don't know. Ask him yourself, if
 it matters to you.

MOLELLA (*after a careful pause*): At what time, signora, did
 your father generally arise in the morning?

BEATRICE: How should I know? Ask him yourself, if you
 feel inclined!

Now Moscato intervened. He said sharply: "Excuse me,
signora. I suggest that you choose your words with more
discretion."

BEATRICE: I know no other way, signor, of answering these
 pointless and preposterous questions.

MOSCATO (*silkily*): I suppose you know nothing, signora,
 about a certain Lombardy hammer which was found
 in the castle?

BEATRICE: I am not a blacksmith, sir. I know nothing about
 hammers.

MOSCATO: Or a rolling pin, possibly?

BEATRICE: I am sorry. I am not a cook.

MOSCATO (*nodding*): I see. Perhaps you can answer the following question. Did you see the seneschal Olimpio on the day before your father's death?

BEATRICE (*fiercely*): I did not.

MOSCATO: Please be careful, Signora Beatrice. We are informed to the contrary.

BEATRICE: I can't help it. Your information is false, I am grieved to tell you.

MOSCATO (*placidly*): Did you ever, signora, speak to Marzio the tinker from the battlements?

BEATRICE: I am not in the habit of gossiping with tinkers, your worship.

MOSCATO: Did you ever contemplate a plan which involved certain bandits?

BEATRICE: I marvel at such a suggestion! What do I know about bandits?

MOSCATO: Listen with care, please, signora. Did the seneschal Olimpio ever climb into the castle with the assistance of ladders or other implements?

BEATRICE: I'm not a sentinel, signor. I don't keep watch over such matters.

MOSCATO: Did the seneschal ever show you a poisoned root, or a pellet of opium?

BEATRICE (*suddenly trembling*): Certainly not.

MOSCATO: Think hard, signora!

BEATRICE (*recovering her poise*): I am not a chemist. I know nothing about opiums.

Moscato sat back with a smile, placed his fingers in a row on the table, and calmly proceeded to describe the whole crime in full detail, as it occurred.

MOSCATO (*dryly*): Have you any comments to make on this recital, Signora Beatrice?

BEATRICE (*frozenly*): Whoever told you this nonsense is a liar, signor.

MOSCATO: Very well. We will now confront you with the tinker Catalano.

Beatrice glittered with rage. "Please do so," she said breathlessly. "And I'll tell the filthy scoundrel what I think of him!"

Some time passed while a messenger was sent to Tordinona and Catalano was led from his cell and brought across the river on the wooden ferry which connected that prison with the Castel Sant' Angelo. Finally he appeared, gaunt and bony, shivering with cold and coughing violently, and still wearing the dead man's cloak flung about him.

"Do you confirm all you've said, Marzio Catalano?" said Moscato.

"I do," said Catalano, teeth chattering in the cold.

"About the ladders? About the opium? About the hammer and the rolling pin?"

"Yes, my lord. It all happened exactly as I told you."

Beatrice drew the shawl still more tightly around her face, so that only her eyes were visible. "Do you realize, Marzio, what you're saying?"

"God forgive me," whispered Marzio, "and you too, Signora Beatrice, but it's nothing but His own bitter truth that I've told them!"

For a moment Beatrice said nothing. Her eyelids twitched; her eyes watered.

[231   ]

Then she said: "Remove this man. He's out of his mind. He's a lunatic."

Moscato flicked his hand. Marzio was led from the room. As he left he turned his head and cast a last look at Beatrice: a look pleading, compassionate, desperate, prophetic and final. Then he staggered into the corridor and disappeared in the darkness.

Beatrice returned with Moscato to the room of interrogation and signed in the record: *I, Beatrice Cenci, affirm this testimony to be the truth.*

4

The following day two *sbirri* came to Catalano's cell to conduct him once more to the place of interrogation.

It was soon after dawn; a heavy chill filled the corridors and the dampness from the flood-soaked masonry trickled dismally down the walls.

"Catalano! Wake up!"

But the tinker didn't stir. He lay face down on the filthy pallet, with Cenci's cloak drawn tightly about him.

One of the *sbirri* kicked him lightly.

"Wake up, Catalano!"

And still the tinker refused to budge; the guards knelt down and shook him gruffly. But the corpse was stiff and cold and no answer came forth, and not long after, the body was hurriedly removed from the cell and taken down to the prison cellar, where it was laid aside for burial.

And that is the end of the tinker Catalano, and from now on our tale must continue without him.

XXVIII

ONE WINDY EVENING the servant girl Bastiana left Monte
Cenci with a basket in which the cook had tucked a chicken,
a bottle of wine and a fine Sicilian peach, and she made
her way toward the Castel Sant' Angelo.

It was carnival time; the streets were heavy with
clamor. Down by the archway a host of ragamuffins was
watching a cockfight. They screamed and cursed as the
wild-eyed roosters went tottering about, all streaked with
blood and lunging crazily for the kill. Suddenly a terrible
howling swept through the air: it was the Jews, who were
being driven forth from the Ghetto, as happened each
year — naked and wailing they came, beards fluttering in
the wind, and when they reached the Piazza Costaguti all
the windows were flung open and the pitiful procession
was showered with rotting fruits and foul eggs.

Bastiana peeped through an archway at all this vulgar
hilarity and then turned into the narrow Via dei Fale-
gnami. She came to a small black door at the bottom of a
stairway and called softly: "Graziella!" The door opened
cautiously. Bastiana entered on tiptoe and kissed the old
woman who was holding the candle: her aunt Gina this

[233]

was, the wife of the mirror-maker Ovidio, and the mother of the newly married girl Graziella.

"Is Graziella here?"

"She's gone out," said Gina. "She'll be back in a little while."

Bastiana put down her basket and glanced about the room. Little mirrors were hanging all over the wall, reflecting a hundred candle flames; every movement of Bastiana's was echoed a hundred times.

"You're on your way to Signora Beatrice?" said Gina hoarsely. She suffered from dropsy: her legs were thick as the trunks of a tree.

"Yes," said the girl. "The cook's baked her a chicken for carnival."

"Ah. Poor lady," said Gina, sitting down by the table. "All alone on a night like this, when she ought to be singing and dancing."

There was a hubbub in the street as a group of revelers rushed by, a slapping of sticks and a blowing of whistles. They could hear the crash of a wine bottle as it splintered on the cobblestones.

"Tell me, Bastiana," purred old Gina, plucking casually at her mustache. "What does she look like, this lady Beatrice Cenci?"

"She's like magic to look at," said Bastiana wistfully. "Deep sad eyes and a beautiful mouth, with something bitter and lonely about it, and a voice that's low like the wind in the woods . . . She's the loveliest lady I've ever seen, *zia,* and it's dreadful to think . . ."

"Yes?" said Gina, somewhat beadily.

"I can't believe it," said Bastiana.

"Oh, she did it," said Gina contentedly. "That I'm sure

of, my sweet. I feel it here in my bones. She killed her father and that's the truth of it." She plucked a raisin out of a bowl and slid it into her mouth. "Have you ever laid eyes on the seneschal?"

"Oh, yes," said Bastiana, blushing. "Many a time."

"Good-looking, is he?"

"Oh, marvelously!"

Gina gurgled with relish. "Just as I thought. It's the way of the world." She added musingly: "What's the gossip these days at Sant' Angelo?"

"She'll be free in a month, that's what they're saying," said Bastiana anxiously. "There's a wicked judge who's handling the case — his name is Moscato — but with His Holiness in a gentle spirit and three great cardinals that are friends of the family, they say the thing will come to an end without definite proof. They'll never force a confession out of Signora Beatrice, that I'm sure of!"

"Well," said Gina sepulchrally, "with all the wickedness in high places, nothing but scandals among the princes and even whispers about some of the bishops, there's no point in keeping a poor dainty girl locked up in prison."

Bastiana drew her fingers along the edge of the supper basket. "Well, I think I'd better go, *zia* . . . You'll tell Graziella that I looked for her?"

"So I shall," muttered Gina, running her tongue across her lips. "Now hurry along, dear, and bring the love of the Roman people to Signora Beatrice . . ."

2

Bastiana walked swiftly down the Via dei Giubbonari and elbowed her way through the throngs on the Campo dei Fiori. The piazza was filled with masqueraders — two-headed monsters and African savages, wicked devils with lolling tongues and wild-eyed griffons and werewolves. Poor folk chiefly these were, with burlap costumes and wigs of hemp, all prancing about and wheeling wildly to the music of the tambours. The taverns were full and the wine flowed freely over the flagstones; the dancers leaped on the tables and swung dizzily in the twilit air.

One young rogue with a head like a lizard's seized Bastiana by the arm.

"Where are you off to, my hussy?"

"I'm no hussy, and I'm off to my mistress!"

"What's this?" said the lizard boy, plucking the peach from the basket. He took a bite and tossed it gaily to a high-hatted clown. "And here's some wine! *Bravissimo!*" And he lobbed the bottle to a witch who came scurrying down the alley. "Bless my soul, here's a lovely pullet!" He whisked out the chicken and ripped off a drumstick. "And here's a kiss to pay for it all!" he said, thrusting his snout at Bastiana, who burst into tears and went running down the street with her empty basket.

3

Outside the Palazzo Regis a procession of coaches had gathered. Guests were entering the palace through a gantlet of torches. Mythological gods in powdered wigs, buxom naiads in brocades, Mars and Jupiter were there, and hoary Neptune with his trident. There was Solomon with the Queen of Sheba and a phalanx of blackamoors, followed by Leda bearing a swan and Danaë sprinkled with gold dust. A black-masked Hercules came up with a lion's skin tossed over his shoulder, and two Amazon queens with a horde of brown-bellied slaves. The crowds gathered in the street to watch this shimmering assembly; humble folk dressed like sprites and gray goblins and sorcerers. Bastiana watched for a while and hurried on through the Piazza Navona, where the muleteers were having their annual donkey race, and as she followed the alleys past Monte Giordano she peered furtively into the innyards and under the archways; all sorts of orgies and quaint little depravities were going on — one night in the year they could be indulged in without fear of censure.

Down on the river one of the wealthy princes — Borghese, maybe, or Odeschalchi — had hired a houseboat and decked it with Venetian lanterns. A band of musicians dressed in scarlet were playing away on their fifes and fiddles; three Spanish acrobats were wheeling about, leaping and diving among the garlands. Bastiana gaped at the dazzle. Such a thing she'd never seen. A great clown in a ruffled collar was doing cartwheels down the deck and two little dwarfs with feathery hats were passing sweets among the crowd.

Down on the shore, in the crannies among the shrubbery, strange couples were shamelessly disporting themselves. Masqueraders dressed like birds, beasts, reptiles of every hue — a scaly crocodile was kissing a peacock, a lion was gamboling with a unicorn, two young foxes were stripping the feathers from a fat silvery swan. Bastiana blushed to see such pinchings and huggings; a kind of panic swept through her, half shame, half envy.

She hurried across the bridge and came to Sant' Angelo. A young guard in a bright red uniform with golden buckles stood by the entrance. When he saw Bastiana coming his eyes began to sparkle.

"Bastiana! Come here!"

"Carlo, listen," whispered the girl, "it's a dreadful thing that's happened!"

The soldier grinned. "Yes? What's happened?"

And she told how the lizard boy had robbed Beatrice's supper basket and there was nothing left now to bring to her mistress in Sant' Angelo.

Carlo reached into his pocket. "Here, my pet. It's all I've got, and now run down to Giambattista's and buy a dinner for the lady Beatrice. And an hour from now I'll be waiting for you at the chapel by the bridge . . ."

So Bastiana took the money and hurried down to the Borgo Nuovo and filled her basket at the *osteria;* then she returned to Sant' Angelo.

4

The lady was sitting with a candle beside the window, playing her lute.

"Play on, signora! Don't stop!"

But Beatrice laid down the lute and looked gravely at Bastiana.

"You're out of breath, my poor child."

"Indeed I am," said Bastiana, and as soon as the guard had closed the door she told the whole extravagant tale of carnival night — the fighting cocks and the wailing Jews, the thieving lizard boy and the racing donkeys. She told of the gold-braided costumes she'd seen at the Palazzo Regis, and of the kindness of the soldier, whose name was Carlo of Bertinoro.

"And he lent you the money, this Carlo of Bertinoro?"

"He did, signora. He wished you to have a lovely dinner tonight."

"And he gave you all he had, this soldier-boy Carlo?"

"He did, signora. Three scudi it was. To give you comfort in your loneliness."

Beatrice sat silently for a while. Her eyes were hard and piercing, like a wasp's. But then they softened and a new, mysterious light transfused them: they grew wide with a melting, almost trancelike tenderness. She said gently:

"You've seen Madonna Caterina?"

"Yes, signora. All is well."

"She's seen the boy?"

"Yes, she has, and she says he's a sweet little devil."

Beatrice plucked at her sleeve; she looked at the floor intently.

"I'm sorry, signora," said Bastiana brokenly, and her tears came flowing. She knelt on the floor beside Beatrice with her hands on the lady's knee.

For a while there was silence; then Beatrice murmured: "Tell me, dear. Whom did you see tonight at the Palazzo Regis?"

"Ah, signora," said Bastiana happily. "There was the Princess Caetani, the one with the squint, and she was dressed like the Queen of Egypt, and Count Altieri was

there with the Princess Pallavicini, and I saw Prince
Colonna in the guise of Mercury, with wings on his heels.
And there was the Princess Lancellotti, dressed like Cupid,
with a bow and arrow . . ."

"Tell me, Bastiana," said Beatrice idly. "How is life at
Monte Cenci?"

"Sad and empty," said Bastiana.

"They've locked my room?"

"They have, signora."

"How is Ludovica?"

"Quite well, signora."

"And the children?"

"They're well, signora."

"And Vittoria?"

"Poor little thing. She's very lonely now that you've
gone." Bastiana's voice sank to a whisper: "You'll soon be
back, signora, won't you?"

"Soon enough," said Beatrice wearily, and then she murmured good night. So Bastiana kissed her hand and went
hurrying down the corridor. Soon the gate was drawn
open and she ran across the bridge to the little chapel
where young Carlo stood in the shade with his buckles
glistening.

XXIX

IT WAS the feast day of St. Thomas Aquinas, a gusty day
with the weathercocks spinning and a hint of spring in the
wandering air. The smell of roots and red earth came up
from the Tiber; it joined the scent of the incense as the
procession passed slowly into the Church of Santa Maria
sopra Minerva.

The nave was alive with petals of flame, like a field of
buttercups. The friar Pietro Calvetti, acting as sacristan
that day, was scurrying about in the crowded sacristy.

Suddenly he halted and cried softly: "The Lord protect
me!"

A dark face, heavily bearded, turned toward him in the
shade of the transept. A hand beckoned furtively. Fra
Pietro sidled over.

"God bless you," he whispered. "Where have you been,
my dear brother?"

"In chains, by Christ!" hissed Olimpio. "In the castle of
Novellara . . ."

"Mercy! What happened?"

"They tried to kill me like a pack of wolves. That's
what happened."

"God protect me!"

"But I finally got out of their clutches . . ."

"Hush," said the friar. "Step forward a bit, here in the dark where none can see you. Just wait. I'll be back in a moment."

He scurried off and came back three minutes later with a key. "Come along," he whispered, and he led the way past the crowd in the cloister, up a stairway into the monastery and down an ill-lit corridor. He bent down and unlocked the door of a tiny cell.

"This is Fra Giuliano's cell," he whispered. "He's off on a journey to Tuscany. You can sleep here for a night or two. No one will notice." His eyes bulged suddenly with dismay; his nostrils twitched like a rabbit's. "Olimpio! Don't you realize that the Cenci are all in prison? Don't you know what the rumors are saying? You're in mortal danger, Olimpio!"

Olimpio sat back on the narrow bed and stared sullenly at his brother. Fra Pietro was a paunchy little man with a bulging nose and lips like a baby's; only the eyes, tense and inflammable, had something in common with Olimpio's.

Poor Olimpio looked dark and shabby, all bespattered with the filth of the journey: his beard matted, his eyes bloodshot, his doublet torn, his hose in shreds, his shoes muddy, and the dirt thick under his fingernails. He stank with all the days and nights in the dungeon.

Darkly and bitterly he told his tale. He told of Rosati's treachery and the poisoned supper, of the theft of the ring and the weeks in the cellar; he told of the Countess Vittoria's secret visits to his cell, of how he finally escaped one night and of his journey back to Rome, on foot and penniless. He shook his fist in a paroxysm of rage.

"Go, Pietro, and tell this perfumed lily Rosati that if he doesn't return my ring I'll come and chop it off with a hatchet!"

"Hush," said the friar, his fingers palpitating.

"Tell him I'll kill him, by God!" roared Olimpio.

"Be still!" hissed the friar. "They'll hear you!" He peered through the window into the cloister.

"Let them hear me. I don't care. Let them come," growled Olimpio. He lay back with a groan and fell suddenly fast asleep.

2

The little friar had a brother-in-law, a young muleteer, Agostino. He hurried toward the Pantheon, where the man was sitting in the Inn of the Sun, and begged him to fetch Signor Cesare Cenci as quickly as possible. The following morning, soon after sunrise, Cesare Cenci appeared in the monastery. Fra Pietro hustled him deftly into the cell where Olimpio was lurking.

"So you're back," said Cesare Cenci in his lean, metallic way.

"By God," said Olimpio fiercely, "I'm back to make trouble, I tell you!"

"My good man, don't you realize that you're the one who's in trouble?" said Cesare. "You aren't aware, I suppose, that Catalano has confessed everything. The whole tale is known to the authorities from beginning to end."

"That fool Marzio!" howled Olimpio. He threw his

hands in the air. "If I'd had my own way this would never have happened! I'd have put him out of the way. I knew he'd talk if they ever caught him! Those silly women talked me out of it, and here's a fine kettle of fish! Women, women! They'll ruin us all! They'll bring us all to the scaffold!"

"Calm down," said Cesare, fluttering his hands, "and be practical, my dear Olimpio. If you stay in Rome you're a dead man. Leave Rome. Go into hiding."

Olimpio's cheeks sank wearily. The fire went out of his eyes. He kept moaning to himself like a wounded mastiff. "Leave Rome? How, I ask you? Listen, my good Signor Cesare. Fetch me some money — a hundred scudi or so — and fetch me my horse, which the groom Pacifico brought back to Rome, and fetch me my new velvet costume which Signora Beatrice had made for me — fetch me these and I'm ready to leave. Like this"— he plucked at the tattered doublet — "I'm ashamed to step into the street!"

"Don't fret," purred Cesare, stroking his beard. "I'll do what I can."

And that same afternoon the muleteer Agostino returned to the monastery, bearing a large, puffy bundle under his arm. The friar led him clandestinely to Olimpio's cell.

"What's this?" snapped Olimpio, opening his eyes.

"New clothes!" said the gentle muleteer triumphantly.

Olimpio opened the bundle and drew out a pair of mouse-gray hose, a liver-hued jerkin and a white-striped doublet.

He spat with disgust. "Who chose these rags, in God's name?"

"Signor Cesare," said the muleteer.

"They're fit for a fancy boy," said Olimpio savagely, and he held up the doublet with a dainty air, with his hand on his hip. "Does he take me for a clown, or a sodomite, this Signor Cesare?"

"It was all he could find, I suppose," pleaded the muleteer.

The friar went off and fetched a bucket of water, and then Olimpio drew off his sweat-stained garments and started washing his body with a little white cloth. He scrubbed his legs and his belly, sponged the filth from his feet and daubed fastidiously at his groin and armpits. Meanwhile the muleteer laid out the garments on the bed in a tidy row.

"And what about my horse?" said Olimpio grumpily, as the friar scrubbed his back.

"There's no trace of it," said the muleteer. "We've searched in the stables high and low, but she's not to be found. You've been lent Signor Bernardo's lovely black mare. She's up at the Trevi stables with a fine big saddle, all ready to go."

"And the money?"

The boy grinned sheepishly. "Here it is," he said with a shrug, and laid a small red purse on the table. Olimpio took it and shook it; he emptied the coins and started counting. "Hm. He calls this a hundred scudi! Barely twenty-five, and some of it counterfeit!" He spat across the room. "What fools," he groaned. "What a horde of incompetents . . ."

He picked up the doublet and stared at it fiercely.

"Well," said the friar in gentle tones, "let's make the best of it, Olimpio. You've got some money, some clothes and a horse. Not quite what you asked for, but still. Beggars, you know, can't be choosers . . . And now, where do you think you'll go?"

"Ha!" Olimpio laughed hoarsely. "Where to vanish, that's the question. Where to wither away and die of loneliness and boredom. They pretend it's me they're worried about, these poltroons and flibbertigibbets. They just want me out of the way, that's the long and the short of it. They're afraid that I'll talk. They're afraid of the scaffold!" Olimpio's face grew dark and sad, lined with furrows of self-pity. "Listen, Pietro." His voice grew haunted, heavy with memories. "You were wise when you turned away from the world's temptations. I wish I'd done the same. But it wasn't in me, that's the trouble. I'm a rover. I'm a black sheep. One thing I've learned and only one: trust no man in this lonely, dark world, my dear Pietro. I've done foul deeds, I know it, Pietro. I'm a brute and a killer, and I'll suffer for it. But I've never betrayed a man. I've never been a coward. I've never cheated and I've never lied, and I've been true to those I loved. Mother of God! I look around me and what do I see? Nothing but thieves! Nothing but vermin . . ."

He blew his nose between two fingers and wiped it viciously on his brand-new cuff.

"Where will you go?" said Pietro softly.

"God knows," grunted Olimpio.

"Where's Plautilla?"

"In Anticoli, I think."

"Go to Anticoli."

"Well, I might."

"For a while, at least."

"I'll do it, Pietro."

"Good," said the friar. "I'll tell Michele. He's in town. He'll ride back with you."

And he scratched his buttocks and gazed at his brother compassionately.

3

Shortly before dawn — it was on Thursday, the thirteenth of March — the muleteer Agostino made his way into the cloister of La Minerva and called softly to Olimpio's window:

"Well, are you ready? Are we off to Anticoli?"

Fra Pietro leaned out of his window and called down in a whisper: "We'll meet you in the Piazza di Trevi in half an hour, my boy. Go. Saddle the horses."

And soon Olimpio and the friar slid out through a side door in the monastery and hurried off through the dawnlit streets until they heard the waters tinkling in the Piazza Trevi. An innkeeper was opening his shutters. A cart rolled by, all laden with fish.

"Here we are!" cried a voice, and they turned and came on the pool, where the water danced like a horde of imps in the pearly light. Agostino was standing beside the pool, and with him were a clear-eyed youth in a yellow doublet and an older man, all in green. They greeted Olimpio rather gingerly: they were his brother-in-law Michele and his nephew Papirio, down on a trip from Anticoli. They had heard from Fra Pietro that Olimpio was riding into the hills.

"We're going back with you," they said, and Papirio

jumped on his horse. Olimpio put one foot in the stirrup
and then turned and kissed the friar affectionately on the
forehead.

"God speed," said Fra Pietro, and a dirty tear ran down
his cheek.

"God bless you," said Olimpio jovially. "Your belly's
swollen like a sow's, dear brother, but your heart is all
gold! You'll end up in Heaven!"

He waved good-by to Agostino, and the three black-
eyed kinsmen started riding along the dew-drenched
streets.

They rode up the Esquiline and over the hill past the
Colosseum, out through the Porta Maggiore and on
through the meadows beyond. The sun rose; a flock of
sheep came wandering down the road, and the light
turned their fleece into a cool, foamy gold. They rode for
five hours — the plowboy in yellow and the peasant in
green, and behind them the handsome white-striped assassin. They stopped by an inn beneath a chestnut tree
and took bread and breathed their horses. Olimpio's spir-
its grew mellow; he joked with the cook and flirted with
the goosegirl. And not long after midday the three of
them were off again, warm with wine and chattering gaily,
and their worries were forgotten, and the darkness and
loneliness fell away from Olimpio's face.

4

It was just after nightfall when they finally arrived in
Anticoli. They could see the small yellow lights twinkling

like glowworms on the hillside, and when they rode into the village they could smell the fresh-made bread in the ovens. The horses' hoofs clattered cheerfully as they rode up to the Alessandri cottage.

There Olimpio's sister met them, tall and gray and austere. Olimpio kissed her lightheartedly.

"Where's Plautilla?"

"She'll be coming," said his sister.

"Is she well?"

"Her heart is sore and sadly troubled," said Antonia coldly.

They all sat down at the table to dine, the wine was poured and the broth was brought. Then the door swung open and Plautilla stepped into the room wrapped in a shawl. She glanced furtively at Olimpio and then quickly away again. And suddenly her grief rose up like a fountain and she burst into tears.

"Go away," she cried hopelessly. "We're lost, all of us! Go away!"

Olimpio put his arm over her shoulder; he touched her chin with his forefinger.

"Are you angry?" he whispered.

She looked at him wildly but she could not speak.

"Forgive me, Plautilla."

She lowered her eyes and started trembling.

And then the joy of seeing him again, whom she loved so intensely, welled up in the poor woman and she smiled and wiped away her tears, until suddenly they started to flow all over again. She sat silently at the table while the rest of the folk ate and gossiped. Now and again she stole a dark, torn look at Olimpio. The candles shone bright; the steam rose from the bowls; and soon Olimpio's great eyes were soft and jolly and tender, and he rose and kissed his wife on the back of her neck. And at that moment they forgot the fearful strangeness that hung over them, and Papirio got out his lute and they all began to sing.

5

Olimpio rose before dawn and peeped through the window.

"What's wrong?" whispered Plautilla.

"I'm leaving," said Olimpio, yawning, and he reached for his hose and doublet. He dressed and sat down on the bed beside his wife; he touched her cheek and drew his fingertips through her graying hair. "There's no point in my staying, Plautilla. I'll bring you trouble and nothing but trouble. The whole of Anticoli knows I'm hiding! The sooner I go the better for all."

"Where are you going?" sobbed Plautilla, seizing his arm.

"I'm not sure. Into the hills. Up to Terni, perhaps."

And he kissed her good-by — a dark, troubled kiss; then he stepped into the stable and lit the lamp and saddled the mare. He could hear the stream gurgling through the pebbles behind the house. The birds were beginning to twitter among the olive trees.

The youth Papirio, who was blond and slender, tiptoed into the stable.

"I'll ride with you," he said softly.

Olimpio glanced at him and shook his head.

"Why not?" said Papirio tensely. "There's nothing to

[250   ]

hold me here in Anticoli . . . You're joining the bandits, *zio,* aren't you?"

"No. Not yet," said Olimpio gravely.

Papirio sullenly mounted his horse and accompanied Olimpio to the village gate, where the road divided. The slopes were dappled with dew and the hills looked gray and majestic.

"Let me come," pleaded Papirio, but Olimpio only looked at him. It was a deep, probing look, and then he said quietly: "God bless you, Papirio. Farewell, and take your happiness where you find it."

And so he started heavy of heart along the Subiaco road, which wound gradually uphill through a maze of copses. It was dawn and the air was full of mountain fragrance. Once Olimpio turned his head and he saw Papirio still by the gate, astride his horse.

Olimpio waved but Papirio stood motionless, half lost in the mist; he looked like a shape in a dream — something that might have been but never was.

There was the dull, thin echo of the hoofs on the lonely road, and soon the village was lost from sight and the sunlight broke through the clouds.

XXX

Hᴇʀᴇ the hills grew cool and barren: the realm of the chamois and eagle. The path wound dangerously among the blue-walled gullies. There still was snow in the crannies and tongues of ice hung over the caves; the wind shot through the curtains of rock like a stiletto. Finally Olimpio rode into a gorge where a tangle of oaks bordered a torrent. The leaves were out on the southern slope and the woods were tufted with ferns. Once a boar went rocketing across the path with flashing tusks; once a stag drew its arc over the stream, smooth as a rainbow. He rode on toward Rieti, spending his nights in empty stables, eating the hard mountain bread and drinking the sharp mountain wine: cold and weary and purposeless, but the love of life was still alive in him.

On the third day he entered a magnificent valley. He leaped off his horse and lay down under a chestnut tree. The sky overhead was a singing blue but in his heart there was only a black, gnawing loneliness.

Footsteps came rustling through the grass. He looked up uneasily. A girl was sauntering down the path with a bowl of milk on top of her head. She was wearing a bright red dress which came down to her knees. Her legs and feet were bare and brown, well muscled, like a shepherd's.

"Holla," cried Olimpio. "What's that you've got there?"

"Goat milk," said the girl with a crafty air.

"Ah," said Olimpio, "how about a drop of it?"

"It's not for giving," said the milkmaid.

"I'll pay," said Olimpio, "if you'll let me."

She raised the bowl from her head and placed it carefully on a broken tree trunk. "Well," she said, "I see you're a gentleman. You're quite welcome to a sip or two."

So Olimpio lifted the bowl and drank of it greedily, and soon the bowl was half empty and he set it back on the trunk.

"And now," said the girl with a pout, "you've drunk almost all of it."

"I have indeed," said Olimpio jovially. He patted the grass close beside him. "Come. Sit down for a bit, my dumpling."

The girl blushed and sat down. "What's your name?" she asked humbly.

"It's a secret," said Olimpio. He patted the girl on the cheek. "I wish all the girls were as generous as you, my sweet child."

"They've treated you badly?" said the milkmaid.

"More than badly," moaned Olimpio. "I've been driven to everlasting ruin and exile!"

"Indeed? Well, I'm sorry for you," said the milkmaid sympathetically.

"It's the curse of man," said Olimpio dolefully, "that he loves a woman not for virtue, not for anything good in her soul, but for the darkness that lurks in her. So it's been and so it will continue to be, till the doom of mankind."

"What a pity," said the milkmaid.

"Give me a kiss," whispered Olimpio.

So the dear, wondering child leaned over and kissed Olimpio lovingly, and he put his arms around her and lifted her into his lap, light as a dandelion. He drew his finger along the warm brown satin of her throat, and then his hand crept lower and touched the peak of her little breast. The milkmaid shook and sighed in her innocence, and Olimpio did as he chose with her and carried her up through the wilderness. And there he left her an hour later, still sobbing and bleeding, and he mounted his horse and rode on through the singing valley.

2

On the fourth day, toward twilight, he came to the city of Terni, and suddenly he remembered the groom Pacifico who had ridden with him to Florence. Pacifico hailed from Terni, and so Olimpio stopped at the butcher's and asked the way to the house of the Bussone. He was weary and stiff with cold when he finally knocked at the door.

A window swung open and a head leaned out: it was Pacifico himself.

"Pacifico! It's me — Olimpio!"

Pacifico's face turned an anxious crimson.

"Don't be frightened," said Olimpio. "I won't harm you, my lad."

"What do you want?" said Pacifico.

"Food and lodging, that's all! Can't you help an old friend who's come over the mountains?"

Dusk was settling over the town. The bells in the tower started ringing, and Pacifico's face grew hard and surly.

"You've been in trouble, Olimpio."

"Of course I have. And what of it? Come," he shouted. "I've got money and I want a warm bed to sleep in!"

"There's none here!"

"Well, then, find me one," cried Olimpio and Pacifico stammered: "I have a brother-in-law, Marco Tullio, who lives outside the walls . . . We'll go and see."

So they went to the cottage of Marco Tullio, Olimpio riding and Pacifico following, and here it was, among the vineyards, that Olimpio found a bed to sleep in. Two days later he begged Pacifico's brother Cesarino, who had also served as groom to the Cenci, to ride back to Rome with the coal-black mare and to look for his own horse and ride back with it to Terni. Cesarino consented, and Olimpio stayed on with Marco Tullio, waiting for the day when he'd ride into the mountains again.

3

And now we come to strange and terrible happenings.

Monsignore Guerra was a shrewd, assiduous cleric, a close friend of the Cenci family and of Giacomo in particular. He lived in the palazzo of the Cardinal Montalto, which later was called the Cancelleria: a pure and splendid edifice built of blocks from the Colosseum, and in modern times the residence of the Cardinal Vicar of Rome. This man Guerra was an excessively corpulent person, pink-faced, vermilion-haired, and dressed in the finest black serge, with hose and cloak of pure silk: a bit of a dandy, as it were.

One day he had word that Cesarino Bussone, a former groom in the Cenci household, had just returned from Terni, and he had him peremptorily called to the palazzo.

Cesarino appeared, obsequious and slovenly; a weak-jawed peasant of middle age with a sharp blue scar across his cheek. He stood in front of the urbane cleric with his cap in his hand, shuffling from foot to foot.

"Tell me," said Monsignore Guerra, coming straight to the point, "have you heard of this fellow Olimpio Calvetti?"

Bussone hesitated, then nodded rapidly. "It could be, your worship."

Monsignore Guerra leaned back in the rose-cushioned chair and smiled affably. He placed his hands palms down on the marble table.

"You might," he said suavely, "be of considerable use to me."

"I should be most happy, your worship," said Cesarino.

"If," said Guerra with emphasis, "you feel sufficiently inclined, that is to say."

Cesarino looked cunningly at Guerra. Their eyes met for a moment. The peasant blushed. Then he said: "I'm most anxious to please you, my lord."

"Very well," said Guerra. "I hear that Olimpio is in Terni."

"Yes, he is," said Cesarino.

"Do you know where he lives?"

"I do indeed, your worship. He lives in the house of a kinsman of mine, Marco Tullio, where he was brought by my younger brother Pacifico."

"I see," said Guerra. He studied Cesarino's face for a moment. Then he said: "Please allow me to make the following observations. First, that your brother Pacifico and your kinsman Marco Tullio are open to prosecution for harboring a criminal, unless they take appropriate measures. And secondly, that there are certain noble persons in Rome who desire that Olimpio Calvetti be removed unostentatiously. He would make, I might explain, an embarrassing witness if he were caught. Would you be interested in earning one hundred scudi in this matter?"

The scar in Cesarino's face turned color, from bottle-blue to a deep, rich purple.

"I would, my lord," he said huskily.

"Good," said Monsignore Guerra. He tossed four scudi on the table, folded his fat pink hands and peered at Cesarino tensely. The red eyelashes hung over two bright, adderlike eyes. "You will receive in due course one hundred scudi from the Cenci family. My word will be sufficient. There's an excellent horse available for you, and you'll be so good as to ride back to Terni immediately. I suggest that you tell Olimpio that his brother, Fra Pietro, urgently requests him to travel back to Anticoli, to the house of his kinsman Alessandri, since the Papal authorities are aware that he is sojourning in Terni. I might mention incidentally that Anticoli lies ouside the Papal States, and well within the borders of the Kingdom of Naples. And what is more, the Neapolitan authorities have promised a considerable reward for the capture, dead or living, of Olimpio Calvetti, who is wanted for conspiring with the bandits some time past . . . Do I make myself clear?"

"Do you mean, my lord, that . . ."

"I mean," said Monsignore Guerra, "that if your friend Olimpio enters the Kingdom of Naples and is there disposed of, you will have an additional sum, by no means negligible, at your disposal."

Cesarino bowed his head. "You are most thoughtful, my lord."

"Not in the least," snapped Guerra. He rang a tiny brass bell. "And now you must excuse me. The servant has arranged for the horse, as I told you. I expect to be hearing from you shortly."

Cesarino carefully picked up the coins from the table, bowed profoundly, and was led into the courtyard of the great palazzo. A groom was waiting for him in the shade of an archway with a fine white mare.

"You're ready to leave now, signor?"

"Yes, I'm ready," said Cesarino.

4

Marco Tullio was a pale, thick-hipped man in his middle forties. He had lost an eye in his youth: the thrust of a knife in a drunken brawl. The remaining eye, the right one, bore all the accumulated essence of greed, vengefulness and cunning. He was the least loved man in Terni. *Malocchio*, they said of him: he had the Evil Eye.

On Cesarino's return to Terni he conferred at length

with Marco Tullio. Marco Tullio, being a litigious-minded man, desired a document. He sent a letter through a friend of his to obtain a statement from the Neapolitan authorities. This he shortly received — a memorandum in green ink from a certain Captain de Sanctis, authorizing the capture of Olimpio Calvetti alive or dead, with a note in another hand specifying a reward of two hundred scudi, and with words to the effect that the dead man's head should be sent to the authorities in Cittaducale.

Now all was ready. Spring had come, the little lime trees were in flower, the ewes were lambing, the streams were full and the fields were bright with yellow butterflies. One day Cesarino Bussone came riding through the gates of Terni and pulled up at the cottage of Marco Tullio.

"Olimpio!" he called.

Olimpio was lying in the arbor, fast asleep.

The men went out to awaken him.

Olimpio opened his eyes and snorted. "So you're back, Cesarino? Did you find my horse?"

"I didn't, Olimpio, but I brought you another. A snow-white mare, and a beauty she is . . . Look, Olimpio. There's news; there's a message from your brother the friar."

Olimpio narrowed his eyes. "A message from Pietro? What is it?"

"He begs you to leave Terni instantly. You're in danger, he says. They know in Rome that you're living in Terni. Go back to Anticoli, says Fra Pietro."

"That's what he says?"

"It is, Olimpio."

Olimpio cursed and clenched his fist. "There's never an

end to it, by God! Who's behind it this time? Giacomo Cenci, I'll wager! Or else Marzio Colonna! Someone's behind it, I'll swear. It's a world of serpents, I tell you!"

"I only repeat what your brother told me," said Cesarino blandly.

"He wants me to leave?"

"He does indeed. As soon as possible. For Anticoli."

Olympio glowered. "The horse is a good one?"

"You'll see for yourself," said Cesarino.

"I'll leave tomorrow," grunted Olimpio.

"We'll keep you company," said Cesarino.

"No need," said Olimpio, knitting his brows.

"Just as far as Piediluco," put in Marco Tullio, with an air of sagacity. "I've a cousin in Piediluco. We'll walk; you'll ride. It's a pleasant journey."

"There's wonderful trout, you know," said Cesarino cheerfully, "in Piediluco."

"Good," said Olimpio. His face brightened; his anger had died. "We'll dine on trout and fresh strawberries when we come to Piediluco!"

"Tomorrow morning, then," said Cesarino.

"Before dawn," nodded Olimpio.

And so it was. Once again Olimpio rolled up his belongings and packed them tidily in his saddlebags — a copper cup, a lace collar and a new pair of spurs. And Marco Tullio in the meantime stopped at a shop not far from the gate and bought a hatchet, small and light, as well as a knife with a slate-blue handle.

5

There was a hush before sunrise; no sounds, no colors, nothing but scents — the wonderful freshness of laurel and mountain clover.

"Wake up!" cried Pacifico, poking his head through Olimpio's window.

And a little later all four of them were out in the hills, following the road to Colle di Labro, which led toward the Kingdom of Naples. Olimpio was riding in front on the lovely white mare; Cesarino followed on foot with Marco Tullio and Pacifico.

A glorious day, with the beeches shivering like nymphs in a gentle breeze. The sun crept up through a veil of dawn-dusted saplings, and soon the colors came leaping like trout out of a stream. The larks were soaring into the far-off reaches of the sky, and once they saw an eagle rising out of the valley, with a newborn lamb held tight in its talons.

Olimpio laughed with pleasure as he sniffed the marvelous air. He looked gawdy and festive in his fashionable doublet and lace-trimmed collar; he had thrust a bright red feather in his black felt hat. He waved his arms and started singing at the top of his lungs, so that the whole valley echoed and the birds in the trees cocked their heads.

The sun grew hot and they came to a mountain pool at the edge of a cliff. Here they stripped and bathed for a while and lay basking in the sunlight. Olimpio's body was dark and massive and shaggy, like a bull's. The other three men looked pale and scrawny beside him.

There they lay, nibbling at the clover, watching the birds dart through the shrubbery, when suddenly Pacifico whispered:

"Holy Virgin!"

"What is it?"

"Look!"

Olimpio turned his head.

The grass stirred faintly beside him. He saw a queer dry slithering and then a sudden arched tenseness: a ripple of mosaic, two flat ruby eyes.

"Pretty, it is," he said gently.

"It's a viper!" said Cesarino.

"Here. Watch me," hummed Olimpio.

"Don't be a fool," gasped Cesarino.

Olimpio cupped his hand and sat still as a stone. The snake drew up its body. It gleamed like freshly poured metal. Olimpio's hand struck out like a stoat, seizing the snake behind the head; but there was a sharp lightning thrust, even quicker than Olimpio's. He squealed, *"Ay!"* The snake fell and shot off through the grasses.

"Mother of Christ," said Olimpio, peering at the dot in his forearm. He started to suck at it violently and spat out the saliva.

Then he grunted: "Who's got a knife?"

Marco Tullio reached into his pocket and took out his slate-handled knife. Pacifico ripped the belt from his jerkin and knelt by Olimpio and tied it around his arm, just above the elbow. Then Olimpio carved a neat rich X across the fang marks. The men watched quietly as the blood sprang forth, dark and alive.

They sat silently for a while. Then Olimpio rose and started to dress. "Here," he said. He tossed the knife back

to Marco Tullio. He washed the wound and drank heavily
and then mounted his horse; and they were off again,
following the path through the laurels.

6

It was noon when they came to the village of Piediluco.
Olimpio paused at the village fountain to water the mare.
He was feeling weak, a bit feverish.

"We'll eat here," he growled.

"Trout and strawberries," said Marco Tullio with a
wink. "Remember, Olimpio?"

Piediluco is a lonely town, dark and ancient and sat-
urnine. It lies at the foot of a volcanic mountain along the
edge of an oval lake whose waters lap against pebbles,
smooth and blue as aquamarine. The walls are heavy with
moss; the towers are black and crumbling; the stone stairways are scalloped with centuries of use. The little angels
above the church door are pitted and wingless and the
dolphin in the fountain has lost his fins; all else is just
as it was three hundred and fifty years ago. The streets
are crisscrossed with archways and high over the piazza
rises the delicate campanile with its mullioned windows.

It was a Sunday, and the folk went strolling through the
streets in their finery, buttons shining, cuffs and collars
all foaming with lace. Cesarino led the way to the house of
his cousin Montani, where the women were roasting a
goose for the Sunday feast.

The girls blushed when they saw Olimpio, with his
flashing eyes and powerful stature and the bright red

[263   ]

feather jutting out of his hat. Four more plates were laid on the table, which was set under a fig tree behind the house, and soon the family sat down to eat with their kinsmen from Terni and the good-looking stranger in the white-striped doublet.

The day grew hot and lazy; Olimpio grew heavy with food and wine. He lay down and slept for an hour in the master's bedroom. He woke up to the sound of laughter down in the garden. The young men were throwing dice while the women sat in the shade and embroidered. Olimpio joined them. He felt thoroughly brisk again. He knelt down on the flagstones while the bell tolled mournfully in the campanile.

"What's the stake?" said Olimpio genially, rattling the dice in his fist.

"Fish for supper," said Marco Tullio. "Trout from the lake, and a basket of strawberries . . ."

They played; Olimpio lost. He went for a stroll down to the market place. But it was Sunday, the stalls were closed. Nothing for sale, not even a minnow. He went to the shore where the fishermen had gathered, lolling idly in the sun.

"What! No fish?" said Olimpio playfully. "Not a single fish in Piediluco?"

"Ah," said the fishermen, grinning. "The fish take a rest on Sundays, just like the rest of us! They're down in the bottom of the lake, as usual, saying their prayers. There's not a fish to be found in Piediluco, my good fellow."

So Olimpio strolled back to the piazza, where a boy was playing a guitar. Some young men were batting a ball against the walls of the church. Pacifico came wandering

down the steps with Marco Tullio and Cesarino, and the
four of them sat down in the sunlight listening to the
songs and sipping *grappa.*

Olimpio's mind roved back to the days of his trip to
Novellara.

"Do you remember, Pacifico? The day we rode through
Siena?"

"I do indeed," said Pacifico.

"And the great cathedral, striped like a tiger?"

Pacifico nodded and smiled.

"And that tower, Pacifico, like a ladder to heaven?"

"I do, Olimpio!"

"And the wine we drank?"

"I do indeed!"

"And the fortuneteller?"

"Ah! Yes . . ." stammered Pacifico.

Olimpio grinned. "And do you remember what nonsense she told you?"

"They're a pack of fools, these old fortunetellers,"
grunted Pacifico.

"Well, let's go," said Cesarino, gulping the rest of his
grappa, and Olimpio tossed three coins on the table and
rose.

The sun was low and the air grew cool as the men
strolled back to the Montani house. Olimpio bade farewell
to his host and the blushing girls; then he went to the
stable and took his mare by the bridle and led her down
through the piazza toward the edge of the lake. The three
kinsmen were waiting at the southern gate.

"God bless you," shouted Olimpio, when he saw them
in the distance. "You've come this far just to say good-by?"

"We're coming along," said Marco Tullio.

"No need, my lads," said Olimpio gruffly.

"We've nothing to do," said Marco Tullio. "We'll come as far as Cantalice. It's a lonely road . . ."

And they started along the road to Colle di Labro. They entered the dusk-laden forest; the far-off peaks still shone in the sunset. But here below the light faded, darkness spread through the valley, and the lake in the distance grew black as ink.

XXXI

AN OWL HOOTED; the rustle of pines filled the darkness.
They could smell the freshly cut logs which lay stacked
in the woods. Soon they came to the gorge of Colle di
Labro and caught sight of the torrent, ax-bright under the
starlight. A wooden bridge held by ropes led over a jet-
black chasm and the smell of the Apennines rose in great
earthy gusts. The bridge crackled hoarsely as Olimpio
crossed it; his heart grew tight for an instant, but he
crossed it safely.

The path fell. They entered a dense stretch of forest,
and soon they saw a small light flickering feebly among
the boughs.

"What's this?" muttered Olimpio.

"It's the Inn of Santa Susanna," said Marco Tullio.

"Have we entered the Kingdom of Naples?"

"Six miles to go yet," said Marco Tullio.

"We'll spend the night here," said Olimpio.

"Better not," said Marco Tullio. "Better rest and ride
on into the Kingdom, as we planned."

"Well, we'll see," said Olimpio irritably, and he jumped
off his horse.

They walked to the innyard gate and tugged at the knocker. The innkeeper peered through a slit in the door.

"Who is it?"

"Four weary wayfarers," said Marco Tullio.

"Bandits, I'll wager," growled the innkeeper, wiping his chin.

"Do we look like bandits?" said Marco Tullio. "Don't fret, signor. There's nothing to fear."

"Where do you come from?" demanded the innkeeper.

"We're pilgrims from Loreto," said Marco Tullio.

The innkeeper scratched at his nostrils.

"Come," said Olimpio, full of bluster. He jangled his bag of coins. "Open the door. We'll pay well for the meat and the wine."

The latch slid back from the gate and the travelers entered. The local woodmen had gathered in the taproom. The place was full of chatter and a clicking of glasses; there was a smell of leather jerkins and rich red wine. Olimpio tossed a coin to the barmaid and the glasses were filled again. One of the men jumped on a chair and the singing began. They sang the songs of the Abruzzi, high and eerie and melancholy, and one of the boys sang a song from Naples, warm and mellow as the sea itself. Then Olimpio stepped on the chair and bellowed a song from Rome, and the tears came trickling from all their eyes.

"You sound like a man with a heart," cried the boy from Naples.

"I have a heart, great and deep, and it's brought me nothing but misery," groaned Olimpio.

"Poor fellow," said the Neapolitan, whose head was

a tangle of curls. "What went wrong with you? Was it love?"

"Love it was," shouted Olimpio tipsily, "and the unspeakable folly of women!"

"Women, women," said the boy from Naples. "They're at the root of all calamity."

Olimpio gazed at the fellow with his wild black eyes. "It's God's own truth," he muttered. And he drew the boy to his side and ran his fingers through the jet-black curls.

Marco Tullio reached over and tugged at Olimpio's sleeve. "Come, Olimpio. It's late. It's time to be off for Cantalice."

But Olimpio glared at him threateningly. "Here we are and here we sleep!"

He kept fondling the black-haired fellow while the rest went on singing. Midnight came and Olimpio stepped into the woods for a moment. The stars were brilliant, the scent of pines was overpoweringly clear and fresh, and suddenly, for no good reason, a great lump came to his throat.

He sighed; the moment passed. He strolled back to the lamplit taproom.

An hour later they all were swaying and hiccuping with too much wine, and the innkeeper led them down to the stable since the beds in the inn were full. He held the lamp while the men looked about for a place to sleep, and then they rolled up in the hay and the innkeeper left them.

For a long time Olimpio heard the sound of singing across the innyard. The scent of hay filled the stable, and the smell of horses and saddles. He heard the mare stirring uneasily in her narrow stall. His blood was full of confusion, full of yearning and sudden fear, but finally he rolled on his back and a moment later he started snoring.

2

So now we come to the next day, which was the seventeenth of May and a Monday.

An hour before dawn the host of Santa Susanna came shuffling down to the stable with his lamp and banged at the door. The sleepers yawned and stretched their legs and then got up with bleary eyes; Pacifico, all tousled-headed, went over to saddle the mare. The moon was high and nearly full when they started down the mule path.

Olimpio kept yawning; the wine had left him with a throbbing headache. They came to a spring at the foot of a cliff and they all drank deeply. There was stealth in the air. Nothing stirred, not a leaf. The moon swam like a fish in the mountain mist.

Olimpio raised his head from the spring. He looked around swiftly. Marco Tullio, close behind him, stepped back abruptly.

"What's wrong?" said Olimpio.

"Nothing . . ."

"You look worried."

"It's a gnat in my eye . . ."

Olimpio wiped his face on his sleeve and grunted:

"How far to the Kingdom?"

"One more mile. Or maybe less," said Marco Tullio.

Olimpio mounted his horse and they wandered on through the moonlit forest. The dew shone on the branches like a shower of quicksilver. The mule path turned after a while and followed a deep abyss. Dawn seeped through the trees; they entered the Kingdom. A ruined watchtower rose from the top of a hill on their left. Beyond rose the mountains in a silent chain, and the slow deep wolf-light crept through the valley.

3

Soon after sunrise two young huntsmen from San Liberato were strolling merrily down the road to Cantalice. They were singing as they walked along under the trees; they felt the blood still warm in the quail which lay flung over their shoulders.

They came to a pine hut and knocked on the door. A voice came trilling out of the window.

"Well, what is it, so bright and early?"

"We're thirsty," cried the older man.

"There's a stream down the way," said the woodman's daughter, peering through the curtains.

"It's not water we're thirsty for," cried the younger man. "How about some wine?"

"There's none in the house," said the woodman's daughter, placing her elbows on the sill.

The huntsman looked at her idly. A great smile spread over his face.

"What's your name?"

"Carolina . . . And yours?"

"Mine's Enzo. You're all alone here?"

"Well, what of it?"

"Come," cried Enzo, "and we'll have a drink down by the stream . . ."

He was a fine sparkling fellow with beautiful teeth, this young Enzo, and soon the door swung open and Carolina stepped forth. She wore a pale blue dress with ruffles, and a thin black sash around her waist.

"It's only a moment," she said quickly, "just to show you the way . . ."

"Naturally," said Enzo, but they'd hardly stepped into the woods when his fingers crept around her waist and he said, rather huskily:

"Let me tell you something, Carolina."

"Tell me anything you wish," said the girl.

"It's about your eyes," said Enzo softly.

"Well, I'm listening," said Carolina.

"They're the eyes of an angel in heaven, and I'll tell you this too, my sweet, all my life I've looked for a girl with eyes just like yours!"

His breath was hot and trembling and the smell of the earth was in the air; presently the path came to a pool which lay tucked among some ferns. The girl and the boy knelt side by side and looked into the water, and he drew her softly to him and they sank into the moss.

And the older fellow, whose name was Aldo, wandered on through the flowering elders. He came to a curve in the path and stopped abruptly.

"God protect me," he whispered.

A man's body lay at the side of the road, dressed in a white-striped doublet. Some distance away lay a black felt hat with a scarlet feather. The huntsman tiptoed closer, then stood appalled. The body was headless. The blood still oozed from the neck and the flies were settling in a thick dark pool.

"Enzo!" he cried. He ran back and found the couple deep in their love-making, half naked already among the ferns.

"Come! Quickly!" shouted Aldo, tugging at Enzo's shoulder. "There's a terrible sight I've seen! There's been a murder in the woods!"

Enzo jumped to his feet, fumbling hastily at his buttons, and the hussy Carolina came tripping behind him, and soon they came to the curve in the path where the dead man lay.

The girl stepped back in horror and started running down the road. Soon she came on a group of peasants on their way to the fields. She cried out what she'd seen, and the word spread quickly. Shepherds and fishermen and woodmen came gathering about, folk from Lugnano and San Liberato, and even as far as Castelfranco; all came in a throng toward the lonely spot by the road to look at the headless man in the white-striped doublet.

4

What had happened was this.

Dawn came swiftly that morning as Olimpio and his friends entered the valley of Cantalice. The stars faded, the sky paled. There was little time to lose. The groom Cesarino, at a signal from Marco Tullio, suddenly fell to the ground with a little moan.

"What's wrong?" cried Marco Tullio.

"It's a thorn," groaned Cesarino.

Pacifico ran up to see what was ailing him. Olimpio dismounted and knelt in the grass.

"Where does it hurt?"

Cesarino pointed to his heel with a grimace.

At that point Marco Tullio raised his hatchet in the air and brought it down with a crash on Olimpio's head.

Olimpio was a man possessed of a catlike agility. He shot forward, then dove to the side and staggered dizzily to his feet. He swung blindly with his fists, but the blood poured down his face and Cesarino leaped on his back and brought him clattering to the ground. Marco Tullio kept hacking at the back of Olimpio's head while Cesarino tried to close his fingers around the big man's throat. Pacifico lifted a stone and brought it down on Olimpio's skull, whereat Olimpio gave a muffled howl and twisted his body in a mighty paroxysm. And instantly, as the body still trembled in death, Marco Tullio took out his knife and started carving away at the neck.

When the head was finally severed Marco Tullio wiped his fingers, tucked the head in one of the saddlebags and mounted the mare. He called farewell to his cronies and set out for Cittaducale. Cesarino and Pacifico washed their hands in the stream, went conscientiously through the dead man's pockets, and started back to Piediluco.

5

Marco Tullio rode as far as Rieti before noon. He had a cousin, Isabetta, who lived in Rieti. He rode to

Isabetta's house to rest his horse in the stable, and there he took off the straps and tossed the bags on the floor. He led the horse to the manger, took the head from the saddlebag, tucked it carefully in a basket and hid the basket beneath the hay.

Then he ate in the house with his amiable cousin Isabetta, drinking cheerfully and tasting the wild strawberries from the hills. An hour later, bloated and belching, he led the mare from the stable and arrived before long in Cittaducale.

He told his tale, slightly embroidered, to the ensign Ottavio Muccini, flourishing the document which had been sent from Captain de Sanctis.

The ensign offered his congratulations. "He was wanted for banditry, was he?"

"Precisely that," said Marco Tullio.

"Where is the head?" said the ensign.

"I left it in Rieti," said Marco Tullio, with a smirk.

"Could I send for it?" said the ensign pleasantly.

"By all means," said Marco Tullio.

So the ensign sent a potbellied soldier, Zoppa by name, to accompany Marco Tullio on horseback to Rieti. Finally they rode up to the stable by Isabetta's house, and Marco Tullio reached under the hay and brought out the basket. He took the saddlebag, which was spotted with blood, and observed: "Here you are, my man. Carry this back to your ensign and tell him to send my reward most speedily."

He watched the soldier ride off toward the hills with the unsavory parcel, and then he mounted his snowy mare and set out for the city of Terni.

6

The soldier Zoppa, in the meantime, rode back to Cittaducale. When he arrived he brought the saddlebag to the ensign Muccino, who had been sent up from Naples to take strong measures in this matter of banditry. Muccino took out the head and held it thoughtfully in the air. And that same day, being eager to make a good impression on his superiors, he set off with the soldier Zoppa to arrange for a formal identification of the head. Toward sunset they arrived at the monastery of San Querico, where a group of officers was called to assemble in the refectory. The head was brought out of the bag and set on a pewter plate in the center of the table.

"Can anyone identify this head?" said the presiding officer, stroking his beard.

"Indeed I can," said the soldier Zoppa. "It's Olimpio Calvetti, whom I saw almost daily when I served in the town of La Petrella."

So this was written down verbatim by a long-nosed notary, and the ensign Muccino rode back to his post and placed Olimpio's head in a cupboard to await further instructions from his captain.

But seven days passed; no instructions arrived. The days were hot and sultry and the head gave out a powerful odor. So on the evening of the seventh day Muccino ordered the potbellied Zoppa to ride with the head into the valley of Colle de Labro, where the killing was done. And here the head was hung on a tree, between the mule path and the stream; and here it was left till it rotted away, as a warning to all that passed.

BOOK FOUR
The Plague

XXXII

The Papal Prosecutor, the Most Illustrious and Excellent Signor Moscato, had continued his examinations at considerable leisure. Porzia Catalano, the tinker's wife, was brought to the court and thoroughly examined; she expressed the conviction that Olimpio Calvetti was the killer. And then old Giorgio the butler was ushered in brusquely. He told of the hidden ladders, and the missing rolling pin, and Olimpio's amorous little visits. Giacomo's wife Ludovica was politely examined at Monte Cenci. She remarked on the cordiality that had always reigned in the Cenci family. And even the cousin Cesare Cenci was brought to the court for an interview. He proclaimed in sweeping terms the whole innocence of the family and proceeded to appeal for intervention to the Grand Duke of Tuscany.

And in the meanwhile the two ladies stayed on at Sant' Angelo. They were examined sporadically; little of moment developed. Their denials remained resolute, the questions dissolved into trivialities, and for a time it appeared that the case was caught in the doldrums. Life in the Castel Sant' Angelo was casual and confused, almost chaotic. Servants came and went as they chose, friends and acquaintances dropped in for a chat, messages and letters and baskets of food and silken coverlets were sent to the prisoners.

Thus it happened one day that Lucrezia was sitting by her window, eating a strawberry tart, when she heard a voice whispering below her window. She looked out into the courtyard and recognized Cesarino Bussone, who had served as groom for the Cenci some months past.

"Cesarino!" she hissed.

"Yes, it's me, Signora Lucrezia!"

"What on earth are you doing here?"

"I've brought news, signora!"

"What kind of news?"

"Beautiful news!"

"Well, what is it?"

"I've been in the hills!"

"And what did you do there?"

"I killed Olimpio!"

"Goodness me," gasped Lucrezia. She peered at the drab little fellow below her, with his hat in his hand and a great blue scar on his cheek. "Nonsense," she murmured. "I don't believe it."

"It's true, signora! I swear! It was down in the woods near Cantalice. I was there with Pacifico and Marco Tullio, who's a cousin of mine. And we killed Olimpio, the three of us, and we cut off his head!"

"How dreadful," said Lucrezia.

"You shouldn't complain," pleaded the fellow. "The dead keep their mouths shut — just remember that, signora!"

"Be careful," said Lucrezia darkly. "They'll throw you in prison!"

But Bussone smiled craftily. "Monsignore Guerra will protect me!"

Two guards approached at this point and Bussone went scampering across the courtyard, and that same evening the news of the seneschal's death spread through the city. The stables and fish markets were thick with chatter; the news trickled into the palaces; it spread to the Quirinal and all the way to the prison of Tordinona. And soon it came to the ears of the judge Moscato, who felt considerable mortification to see such quarry slip through his fingers.

2

Some days later the Papal sheriff arrived in the hills of Anticoli and arrested Plautilla and her sister-in-law Antonia, as well as Antonia's husband Alessandri and young Papirio. They were conducted to Rome and summarily interned in Corte Savella. And the following day the poor widow was led into the presence of Moscato. She wore a black, threadbare dress and a ribbon of taffeta in her hair; her grave, gentle face looked utterly bloodless, desiccated. She stood wearily in front of the table, limp and scatter-brained with grief; her eyes moved listlessly through the vaulted room.

MOSCATO: Did you know that your husband was dead, signora, when you were arrested?

PLAUTILLA (*wearily*): Yes. I knew.

MOSCATO: How did you learn of it?

PLAUTILLA (*frowning*): Let me think. Ah yes, signor. It was a muleteer from Anticoli who had gone to Rome one day, and there he heard this bad news at the Trevi stables. His name was Telemaco. He was deaf in one ear. He rode back from Rome and he came and told us this news. It was a rainy day, I remember, and the bread burned in the oven. And so I dyed my dress black, and I found this bit of taffeta which I put on my head, for I didn't have the money to buy the regular mourning, your honor.

MOSCATO (*nodding*): I understand.

PLAUTILLA: And so, being penniless, I stayed on in the house with my sister-in-law Antonia.

MOSCATO: Tell me, signora. What happened to you after Signor Francesco's death?

PLAUTILLA: Wait a moment. That was so fearfully long ago. I'll try to remember . . .

And since she no longer had any reason for withholding the truth, she proceeded to tell Moscato exactly what had happened. She told of Olimpio's departure for Rome with the Cenci and her subsequent visit to the house of Cinzia; the hideous coming of the flood; Fra Pietro's kindness and assistance; Giacomo's visit on the Quirinal, and her meeting with Vittoria in the Capuccini.

MOSCATO: And then you went to Anticoli at Signor Giacomo's insistence?

PLAUTILLA: So it was, my lord. And there I waited for Olimpio.

MOSCATO: Did he come?

PLAUTILLA: Yes. He came.

MOSCATO: When was that?

PLAUTILLA: Oh, long ago! He came riding along one day with my nephew Papirio and he spent the night, as I well remember, and the following morning he rode off again. And that was the last I ever saw of him, my lord.

She lowered her eyes. It seemed that all emotion had died in her. Her cheeks looked creased and brittle, like goatskin.

MOSCATO: Tell me about your life in La Petrella, please, signora.

PLAUTILLA: Ah, signor . . . It seems so long ago, I can hardly remember! All was calm in the life of the castle until the Cenci arrived. And then a shadow fell over the place. A great sadness entered my life.

MOSCATO: Do you remember the night before Signor Francesco's death?

PLAUTILLA: Let me see. Yes, that was the night that Olimpio came back so late and troubled, and he lay down beside me without a word and kissed me sweetly. I said, "Olimpio, where have you been?" And he said, "In Poggio to fetch a stallion." I knew he was lying but I said, "God bless you, my darling," for a terror filled my heart and I was happy to have him back with me.

MOSCATO (*Fixing his eyes on the edge of the table*): What happened then?

PLAUTILLA: He lay sleepless; he turned and twisted and I knew he was in torment. Toward dawn he got up to take his mare out to pasture, and I got up likewise and sat by the window to comb my flax. It still was dark and I had to light a small candle, your honor.

MOSCATO: And then?

PLAUTILLA: An hour passed, and then another. I fell asleep by the window and when I woke up again the sun was high over the hills, and my baby Prospero was on the floor with a ball of wool. So I told him a tale or two, and suddenly Paolina cries next door: "Quick! Plautilla! There's a horrible thing at the castle!" So I hurried up the path, one shoe off and one shoe on, and I came to the castle and found Signora Lucrezia in her room. She was in tears, all white and quivering, so I loosened her stays . . .

And Plautilla told the rest of the wretched tale as she remembered it — how Artemisia came to the kitchen and spoke of the ugly gossiping, and how they slept by the fire with the ladies and did the cooking and laundering, and how she went and spoke to Olimpio that night all alone.

MOSCATO: Did the ladies make gifts to you in the castle, signora?

PLAUTILLA (*reflecting*): Some dishes, your honor. And a petticoat or two, and some wool from a mattress.

MOSCATO (*casually*): Any mattress covers?

PLAUTILLA: Oh, yes, a fine mattress cover. All soaked in blood it was — I thought it was blood from the ladies, you understand, but then I saw it was rich and abundant, and I hurried to soak it in a copper basin. And then I knew there was violence in this death, your worship.

MOSCATO: Did you speak of your worry to the ladies?

PLAUTILLA: Yes, I did, your honor. I said that day to Signora

Lucrezia, "Signora, there are tales down in the village, and I'm frightened that Olimpio was a part of this killing!" But the signora said softly: "Don't fret, my dear. He had nothing to do with it . . ."

MOSCATO (*gently*): You loved your husband?

Plautilla waited a moment. Then she pressed her hands together and whispered hoarsely: "Yes. I loved him."

XXXIII

Slowly, inexorably the web was being woven around the Cenci. With miscroscopical patience the judge Moscato was completing his case: filling the gaps, illuminating the motives, brightening the details, deepening the shadows. Only two more witnesses were still required to complete the fabric.

On the twentieth of June, Fra Pietro was watering some lilies in the cloister when Fra Tommaso came up and said that the Father Superior desired to speak to him. So Fra Pietro climbed the stairway and entered the room, somewhat nervously.

"My son," said the Most Reverend Father, who was a man of feathery pallor and infinite gentleness, "my heart is heavy. A minister from His Holiness has just been with me, and he informed me that you are wanted as a prisoner by the Court. Have you fallen into some sort of guilt, by any chance?"

"No, Father," said the friar.

"Not even in connection with your brother Olimpio?"

"Not that I know of, Father."

"I am greatly consoled, my son," said the Father Superior.

Two elderly friars accompanied Fra Pietro to a carriage beside the Pantheon and he was driven through the streets to the prison of Tordinona. There he spent a sultry and verminous night, and the following day he was brought into the presence of the judges.

Moscato began with a crisp little smile: "You are a Dominican friar and a lay brother of La Minerva?"

FRA PIETRO: I am, signor.

MOSCATO: And a brother, I believe, of Olimpio Calvetti?

FRA PIETRO: Yes, signor.

MOSCATO: Tell us a bit about your brother's early life, if you'll be so kind.

Fra Pietro had all the cunning of the simple and illiterate, as well as the strange blunt loyalty and insuperable obduracy. He stood in front of Moscato in his wine-stained cassock, his cheeks bristling with beard, his nails dark with the week's gardening. His eyes shone with a velvety, doe-like candor.

"Well, my lord, he was a bright handsome fellow, this brother of mine. I was the dull one of the family but Olimpio was clever and good-looking, and after he'd been apprenticed for a year or two to the tailor Rossi he decided to go to war, having an adventurous spirit and all sorts of fine notions. So he joined the armada of Pope Pius the Fifth, and later on he went to Portugal and did considerable fighting, as I recall."

MOSCATO: Was he mixed up with the bandits at any time, Fra Pietro?

FRA PIETRO: Ah, my lord. I never got to the bottom of it, he was such a deep, wayward fellow.

MOSCATO: And what next? After this business of Portugal?

FRA PIETRO: Well, by and by it so happened, I don't know how, that he drifted into the service of Prince Marzio Colonna, and he took over the post of seneschal at La Petrella.

MOSCATO: Tell me, Fra Pietro. What do you know about this Cenci murder?

FRA PIETRO (*sorrowfully*): They're all in prison, and that's all I know about it.

MOSCATO (*wiping his nose with a scented handkerchief*): Tell me another thing. A minor matter. But did Olimpio happen to visit you one day in the monastery of Santa Maria sopra Minerva?

FRA PIETRO (*innocently*): Well, now that you mention it, I think he did, signor. And he stayed for dinner, as I recall, and spent that night in one of the cells.

MOSCATO: I suppose you chatted a bit with your brother? Of this and that?

FRA PIETRO (*blandly*): I dare say I did, my lord.

MOSCATO: Well now, let's have it, Fra Pietro, and stop beating around the bush. What do you know about this murder at La Petrella?

FRA PIETRO (*wide-eyed*): Bless my soul! Only the usual Roman gossip.

MOSCATO: In short, that your brother was the murderer, I presume?

FRA PIETRO: Well, signor, I've heard tongues wagging away in the piazza, but Olimpio himself never breathed a word of it to me.

MOSCATO (*irritably*): So that's the tale. I've had enough of

[288   ]

it, I warn you. You hide your brother in the monastery, you help him escape, you hurry him off to Anticoli, and that's all you have to say about it?

FRA PIETRO (*petulantly*): What else would you like? I'm an ignorant man, signor.

MOSCATO (*peremptorily*): Very well. We shall see.

So once more the excellent judge led the way into the torture chamber, and the simple friar was stripped of his cassock and bound to the rack. An earthy, impoverished little fellow, this friar: a sharp odor spread from his flesh, like a powerful goat cheese. The ropes were tightened. Sweat burst from Fra Pietro's temples. "Oh God! Let me down! I've said what I know! There's nothing else!"

"Tell the truth," snapped the judge, and he murmured a second Credo.

"God help me!" screamed the friar. "Virgin in Heaven, come to my rescue!"

"The truth," hissed Moscato.

"Madonna, save me!" shrieked the friar.

The wheels creaked, the ropes shivered; the arms snapped out of their joints.

"I'm dying," gasped Fra Pietro. "Let me down! Let me down!"

But the ropes were kept taut. The friar's muscles throbbed and quivered. His paunch heaved like a belly dancer's. Suddenly a great gush of feces went spraying across the floor. A sickening stench filled the torture chamber.

Moscato gave orders that the friar be released. The wheels were turned, the ropes were slackened, and the unsavory clothes were tossed to the victim.

The friar lay naked on the floor, still shivering and moaning. Suddenly he said: "I'll tell the truth now. That's suffering enough for any man."

So the notary took out his pen and Moscato said non-chalantly:

"Proceed, Fra Pietro."

Fra Pietro proceeded.

He revealed all that Olimpio had ever confessed to him: the killing of Cenci at the instigation of Beatrice, with the connivance of Lucrezia and the approval of Giacomo; the disastrous trip with Camillo Rosati, the poisoning and the beating and the theft of the ring; Olimpio's appearance in La Minerva and the purchase of the white-striped doublet, and then Olimpio's departure with the boy Papirio to Anticoli. And finally he told of certain visits he'd been paying the ladies in Sant' Angelo, and of messages and letters that were surreptitiously passed to the prisoners.

The notary sprinkled the sand across his papers and the judge took his handkerchief and wiped his lips fastidiously. And that same day, which was the longest day of the year, he gave instructions that the ladies Lucrezia and Beatrice be removed from Sant' Angelo and placed in the cells of Corte Savella under strict surveillance.

2

Now the final witness was called from the Palazzo Colonna and driven in a carriage to the Court of Savella. He looked startled, a shade offended as he strutted down the hallway, his doublet shining with a satin collar and dolphin-shaped studs. But as he stepped before the judges his *sang-froid* returned; he smirked amiably and flicked a grain of dust from his sleeve.

Moscato eyed him dyspeptically: "You're Camillo Rosati?"

"I am, signor."

"You're in the private employment of Prince Colonna?"

"Quite correct."

"Prince Colonna had a seneschal at his castle in La Petrella . . ."

"Perfectly true."

"And his name was Olimpio Calvetti. Is this accurate, signor?"

"Entirely accurate."

Rosati's face was long, flaccid; a thin layer of powder covered the pouches and fine-grained wrinkles on his cheek.

Moscato leaned back in his chair and toyed with the buttons on his cuff.

"Tell me," he said in mellow tones, "did you ever know this man Olimpio Calvetti?"

Rosati nodded. "I did, my lord. Superficially, as it were."

"What was the nature of your relationship with Olimpio, may I ask?"

"It was strictly conversational," said Rosati, with a touch of pique.

"I see," said Moscato, caressingly. "Did he ever ask you for favors?"

"Well, he hinted," said Rosati dryly, "that I intercede with Prince Colonna. To bring a halt to certain investigations that were proceeding in La Petrella."

Moscato nodded. "And did he ever make any threats?"

"He insinuated, I believe, in the presence of Prince

Colonna, that it would be wise to keep certain scandals entirely secret. In view, as he implied, of his relations with Beatrice Cenci, which he knew were disturbing to Prince Colonna."

"I see," said Moscato. "A form of blackmail, as it were."

"There is considerable mutual loyalty between these noble families," sighed Rosati.

"And did you mention these matters to Giacomo Cenci at any time?"

"I thought it best. I told him to treat this man Olimpio with discretion."

"And what did he say?"

"Well, one day in the Piazza Santi Apostoli, if I remember rightly, I happened to mention that I was making a journey to Lombardy. And Signor Giacomo remarked that he would regard it as a favor if I took along Olimpio on this little journey."

"Which you did?"

"Which I did."

"And what happened on this journey?"

Rosati's eyelashes quivered. Half coquettish, half venomous, a sheen of subtle gratification spread over his face. He paused; he moistened his lips. Then he said rather languidly:

"Well, one day, over a glass of wine in the city of Modena, Olimpio asked me all of a sudden whether we'd passed the Papal frontiers. I said that we had, and he grew marvelously confidential, and he told me a most interesting tale, your honor."

"And this tale . . ."

"It was the tale of how he killed Francesco Cenci."

"Ah. Indeed," said Moscato.

"He told me the whole hideous episode. He held his hand in front of the fire and said: 'This hand, my dear Camillo, is the hand that slaughtered Francesco Cenci!'"

"Ahem," said Moscato. "What else did he say?"

"Much else," said Rosati, "of considerable oddity and impudence. It was Signora Beatrice, he said, who had instigated the killing. And Signora Lucrezia, he added, had thoroughly approved of the crime. And at the bottom of it all was this animal lust of Olimpio's, which sprang from the carnal relations he was enjoying with Signora Beatrice . . ."

"And then?"

"We arrived at the charming castle of Novellara shortly after, and there Olimpio got drunk and behaved most disgracefully. The local guards, I regret to say, were forced to remove him to the dungeon."

"Was he searched, by any chance?"

"Well, he was, in point of fact. A few scudi were found, which I distributed discreetly. And this diamond ring which I'm wearing — I thought it wiser to remove it, under the circumstances."

"Naturally," observed Moscato, nodding. His voice grew cutting, contemptuous. "You will leave this ring with us, if you'll be so kind, Signor Camillo."

A hint of a smile appeared on the notary's lips as he scribbled away. Moscato folded his hands and gazed piously at the ceiling. Molella frowned as he listened; he cleared his throat once or twice. And finally Rosati appended his graceful signature to the testimony.

XXXIV

THE GREAT HEAT fell on Rome. Up in the hills there still was a breeze, but down by the river the air was motionless and foul, insupportable. One could smell the butchers' meat rotting away in the shops; the fruit fell apart on the vendor's wagon.

In the thick-walled palazzi the shutters were closed all day long and servants tiptoed from room to room spraying the tiles with scented water. In the piazzas the sun poured over the ground like a flood of lava; life fled into the cellars, the crannies, the caverns. The candles drooped in the churches. The oil flowed like water. Dogs went dripping with hydrophobia, donkeys curled up and died. Over the Ghetto the smell of sweat and effluvia hung like steam. The street urchins dove naked into the Tiber by Sant' Angelo and children went splashing in the *acqua vergine* of the Piazza Trevi.

In the cells of Tordinona the prisoners stripped off their rags; they lay sweating on the flagstones or clinging to the bars of their windows, and up on the Aventine the little nuns sat in their cloisters, waving their raffia fans and dipping their feet in the pools.

Nothing stirred in the city while the sun hung blazing. But at sundown a tremendous sigh of relief passed through the streets. Little by little the signs of life reappeared in the doorways, and from dusk until midnight there was laughter and gossiping around the fountains.

2

The gossip in Rome was that affairs were growing dark for the Cenci.

Bits of news leaked out from the palazzo, from Tordinona and even the Vatican. Tongues wagged freely in the Piazza Navona and behind the fruit stalls in the Campo dei Fiori. The taverns and stables, the markets and palaces were full of hints and speculations. But there was more to it than gossip. There was a powerful fascination in this thing. The people of Rome felt strangely stirred by the plight of the Cenci. Deep in their hearts, with the unerring intuition of the Romans, they knew what had happened, and why and how it had happened. But with the Roman flair for the tortuous, they toyed with every new intricacy, perpetually discovering new facets, exploring new motives, until finally the Cenci murder had been embroidered into a great dark tapestry revealing every nuance of human passion and wickedness. Perhaps they felt, these Roman townsmen, that the truth lay deeper than mere circumstance. Perhaps they felt that law and justice could never appraise this deep complexity. Perhaps they felt in their Roman way that much could be said on all sides, that evil had sprung from evil and proliferated evil. Perhaps they sensed, in this patricide, something profound and universal: something old beyond memory and mysterious and terrible which had spread its poison through the very bloodstream of humanity. Perhaps they looked into their hearts and heard strange, disturbing echoes. Or perhaps, in their shrewdness and all-enveloping cynicism, they had come to think of the Cenci as companions in human suffering, and had come in some way even to love them a little. They saw through the confusion and sullenness in Giacomo and the childlike silliness of Lucrezia. They recognized the blunt, animal feeling which lurked in Olimpio. They sensed the pathetic helplessness and weakness of Catalano. They knew quite well the bitterness of Porzia and the suffering of Plautilla, and they knew the cruelty and corruption of the murdered man Francesco. So elaborate and probing was the gossip of Rome that they even spoke of such minor participants as Gasperini the druggist and the butler Giorgio. They even knew of those delicate subsidiary threads that led into the palace of Cardinal Montalto, into the house of Prince Colonna, and into the private chambers of Clement the Eighth.

All this they knew, these inexhaustibly garrulous people of Rome. On all of it they expatiated; all of it they understood. Only Beatrice bewildered them. Here was a thing not quite Roman: somber, defiant, and a bit inhuman.

3

One day — it was the hottest day of the year — an old woman who lived on the Isola San Bartolomeo stepped into the courtyard and saw a cat lying under the archway. She leaned down and stroked its ears; but the cat was stiff as a stone and the eyes were thick with a greenish glaze.

So the woman, whose name was Adriana, picked up the creature in her arms and carried it under the fig tree, and there she dug a hole and buried the cat, wiping away a tear or two as she did so.

The next day Adriana felt dizzy and feverish. Her face turned yellow as saffron and great black rings shone under her eyes. She started to tremble with cold and crawled back into her bed, where she lay weak and shivering under the thick gray blankets. A bit later a flood of black vomit poured out of her. Adriana rolled on her side and started praying.

Toward sunset she let out a terrible scream. The neighbors came running across the courtyard. When they entered her room they found the old woman in a heap by the bed, with her face all purple and twisted, like a gargoyle's.

4

And all of a sudden a strange, uncanny stillness fell on Rome. There was no more gossiping in the piazzas. The streets were empty, the inns were deserted.

It all began in the filth-littered alleys of the Isola San Bartolomeo. The day after old Adriana was safely buried, a young fisherman named Luigi and a muleteer, Pierino, both fell ill in the same manner, at almost the identical moment. They suddenly crumbled in the street, an hour or so before sunset, one of them in front of the Ospedale, the

other near the Bridge of the Four Heads. They started
sweating and shivering, a violent pain seized their bowels,
their eyes grew filmy and their lips turned black as pitch.

The next day the plague was ablaze all over the island
and two days later it had spread to the slums of Trastevere.
Old men would sit in their arbors with puckered faces and
sunken eyes, looking as though the life were being quietly
sucked out of them; and suddenly, without warning, they'd
let out a shriek and collapse. The symptoms were always
the same: an acute fit of dizziness followed by violent chills
and spasms of nausea; reddish pustules blistering the skin;
a deep blue film covering the eyes; an unquenchable thirst
which rose to a howling delirium. And then, an hour or
two later, the final cramps which led to extinction. The
corpses were gathered together in sacks of burlap and
hooded friars dragged them hurriedly into the walled
cortiles. And there in the dead of night they'd be heaped
on the carts and carried toward Ostia, or into the fields
beyond the Pincio. Neither the doctors nor the chemists
ventured forth after dusk, and all night long there were
prayers and lamentations in the Borgo Nuovo. The housewives bolted their doors and locked their windows and the
grandmothers pinned pictures of the saints in every cranny.
The Franciscan priests passed by in the mornings, accompanied by barefooted boys who carried jugs, bells and baskets. They went about sprinkling holy water, but they
never crossed the thresholds and they held their habits
tucked up gingerly, so as not to touch the gutters. The
families of the dead put black kerchiefs around their necks
when they entered the streets, and the shopkeepers locked
their doors the moment they saw them approaching.

The squares grew eerily still, all the fishmongers fled to

Ostia and the wealthy families rode out to their villas in
Frascati and Tivoli. Even the dogs and donkeys disappeared from the lanes. The fleas and lice shed by the dead
went seething through every crevice. Filth accumulated in
the streets, for no one came to cart it off. Lonely walkers
heard their footsteps ring back from the culs-de-sac, and
iridescent flies swarmed over the refuse in little rainbows.

And the heat kept clinging to the city like a coat of oil.
Nothing stirred, the arcades along the Via Coronari were
still as catacombs. Only in the caves of the Colosseum a
cry would echo now and again: a lonely beggar suddenly
caught in the grip of the pestilence.

5

And Beatrice sat alone in her cell by Via Monserrato.
What did she feel, in these silent, ominous hours? No remorse, not a grain of it. No regret; no fear, certainly. A
strange kind of relief, after all this sickening tension; a nar-
cotic indifference which bordered on tranquillity. This
loneliness, after all, was no greater than the loneliness
she'd always known. Her mind wandered casually over the
fragments of the past — a village carnival, a storm in the
mountains, the dripping of wine in a wine cellar — but the
central violence had slipped from her mind like an anchor
cut from its chain.

Once or twice brief messages were sent from Lucrezia or
Giacomo. But the feverish intimacy of crisis had somehow
drained them of reality. They hung suspended in her fancy
like masks in a twilit room. She thought of Olimpio now

and then, but he loomed in her mind like a great shadow — features blurred, eerily remote, a natural force more than a human being. Sometimes she thought of the child that had sprung from her body, but this too grew distant and imprecise, like an aching dream. The judge and the notary and the prison warder danced about in her mind like those Neapolitan marionettes she had seen as a child — full of words and gesticulations, threats, grins, monstrous attitudes, but no more vital than a waxen head with a body of sawdust.

And when the plague came to Rome she hardly noticed the difference: a greater stillness out in the streets, a gentler stealth in the prison air. But the dying and suffering were nothing but rumors. Her life went on in a state of impenetrable secrecy, so profound that the world outside only struck her intermittently, like a splinter of light piercing a deep-sea grotto. Her lute had been sent along with her cushions from the Castel Sant' Angelo and she'd sit at night by her candle, singing the song of the demon lover:

> Oh my lord crept in by the window
> As the mist crawled through the night,
> My lord lay down by my pillow
> And his flesh was marble-white.
>
> "Oh my love, your eyes are as bright as flames
> But your lips are cold as ice!
> Oh my heart is heavy with dread," I cried
> And he kissed me once or twice.
>
> And the kisses tore at my heart like steel
> And the fire burned in his breath
> And my love flew out on his phantom wings
> And back to the fields of death.

XXXV

THE PLAGUE reached its peak toward the middle of July. All the foreigners, the visiting prelates and ambassadors had left the city and no one entered or left through the great stone gates during the day. But every night a dark procession passed through the Porta Pia and the Porta Ostiense. Great fires were seen burning in the fields by Via Appia, but no one knew who died each day, for the entire city was steeped in secrecy.

The very earth, the very body of Rome seemed defiled. The wandering friars kept to the middle of the street away from the filth-stained walls. Food grew scarce. The country folk all kept clear of the city, and not a lamb, not a chicken, not a fish was to be found. The houswives scoured through their cellars: the whole of Rome lived on noodles, with an onion or two to spice them and a bit of wine to wash them down.

The end of the month brought some storms, and the poison was gradually washed into the Tiber; and finally the deaths began to dwindle and the plague crawled southward, toward Naples.

2

And now we move for a moment to those serene, exalted quarters where the last decisions must rest and the fate of the prisoners reposes. The day is hot, the sun blazes on the gardens outside, but in these great silent corridors the floors have just been sprinkled and a fragrant coolness comes up from the marble.

A door opens noiselessly. We see His Beatitude, Ippolito Aldobrandini of Fano, called Clement the Eighth, seated at the writing desk in his cabinet. He is a man in his early sixties, gigantically fat but fine-featured, with a skin white and smooth as well-polished ivory and tufts of white hair as delicate as thistledown. The nose is vibrant and sensitive; the mouth is anxious and stubborn; the chin is full but uncertain. The hands are long, frail, vigilant.

He glances up from his desk and nods his head slightly. His nephew, the Cardinal Aldobrandini, Legate of Ferrara, has entered the room. This cardinal is a ravaged-looking man: face pitted by smallpox, covetous eyes, a sensual mouth: a man of galvanizing vanity.

He comes to the point: "It concerns the case of the Cenci, Your Holiness."

"There is much delay and incompetence in the handling of this case, I can't help feeling."

"Delay, yes. Incompetence, possibly." The cardinal glances through the window. Tiny drops shine like scales on his coarse-skinned cheeks. He suffers from asthma and his breath comes hoarse and uneven.

"There is a sharp division of feeling in Rome, as it happens. The populace, ill-informed and prejudiced as always, favors the Cenci. The noble families feel differently, in spite of an undercurrent of solidarity. The evidence, needless to say, is quite conclusive."

"There's no doubt in your mind?"

"None whatever, Your Holiness. The trial should be concluded as swiftly as possible in my opinion."

"Even considering," murmurs the Pope, "the rank and position of the accused?"

"Most definitely." The cardinal draws his forefinger over his lips and breathes sharply. "Excuse me, Your Holiness. One small thing is required, and that is the *motu proprio* which will allow the court to have recourse to certain measures to obtain a confession. These measures, I might add, have already been applied to the lesser witnesses, but the Court still hesitates to apply them to persons of noble rank."

Clement crosses his fingers and nods his Buddhalike head. "You know my feelings. I desire that the matter be brought to a conclusion."

"Quite." The cardinal clicks his tongue. "I will direct the *motu proprio* to the governor today with the request that it be sent to the court without delay."

The Holy Father keeps nodding. "A terrible thing," he whispers.

And the cardinal proceeds to other, more impersonal affairs.

Thus it was that a notification was sent to Ferdinando Taverna, who was the Governor of Rome, allowing clearly and precisely that physical torture be employed to elicit the confessions of the four imprisoned Cenci, and urging the court to proceed as promptly as possible to the sentence. This document was then dispatched on the fifth of August to Ulisse Moscato, who received the notice with gratification.

3

On the seventh of August the judges gathered in their chambers in Corte Savella and proceeded swiftly to the final examination of the prisoners.

First came Giacomo. He was brought in a carriage from Tordinona, and entered the judge's room with an air of boredom and fatigue. His clothes were tattered and stained, his chin was thickly bearded. His face was sallow and deep green rings encircled his eyes.

The illustrious Signor Molella opened the interrogation: "Time is passing, Signor Giacomo. We must try to finish this case."

"I quite agree," said Giacomo acidly.

"Well, in that case," said Molella, "could we persuade you at last to tell us the truth about your father's death?"

"I have told you often enough, signor," replied Giacomo. "You must be weary of hearing these words, and I am weary of repeating them."

"You have nothing to add to them?"

"Nothing whatever, signor."

Ulisse Moscato, who had listened quietly, now rose from his chair. He led the way to the torture chamber while Giacomo followed behind two *sbirri,* and after him walked the little notary with his bundle of papers.

Giacomo was stripped and tied to the rack. Then

Moscato inquired, stroking his palm: "Have you anything further to remark before we turn the wheel, Signor Giacomo?"

"I've said all I know," said Giacomo, quivering.

The wheel was turned gently.

"Jesu, Jesu!" shrieked Giacomo.

A veneer of perspiration burst out over his entire body. The veins in his thighs stood out suddenly like long blue ribbons.

The wheel went on turning; the bones crackled as they slid from their joints. Moscato murmured his Credo. Giacomo screamed: "Madonna! Madonna!"

The Credo was finished and the man was lowered and placed in a wooden chair, still bound and naked.

"Will you confess now?" murmured the judge.

And Giacomo confessed. His voice went on in a drab and desultory monotone, now halting, now repeating; his eyes were fixed on the floor in front of him.

"It was Beatrice, signor, who was behind this whole catastrophe. She hated her father beyond all measure. I know my sister. I know what she's like. She's tense and nervous, like a hawk. She grew frantic, signor, locked up in that dismal castle. I can see it all. She was completely beside herself . . ."

"Please confine yourself to the facts, signor," interrupted the judge.

Giacomo glanced at Moscato dimly. Ribbons of sweat streamed down his cheeks.

"Continue," said Moscato. "What about this man Olimpio?"

"Well," said Giacomo, suddenly sharpening, "I'm sure that Beatrice kept nagging at Olimpio, who was a blustering and impetuous sort of fellow. She told me herself how she finally persuaded Olimpio to do the killing, by threatening to make an end to their carnal relationship. She told me this to prevent my ordering the man out of the palazzo, for I tell you, signor, I felt a loathing for this braggart. In any case, she contrived to keep Olimpio staying on in the palazzo, and he even came to take his meals at our table."

The guards stood silently in the shadows behind the prisoner. A small lamp burned beside him, casting a glow on his arid profile, exaggerating the tendons in his throat, brightening his frail hairless body.

"Did your brother Bernardo," said Moscato with a baleful look, "know about these plans of Signora Beatrice?"

"He did," said Giacomo limply. "He agreed to the whole project when Olimpio came to the palazzo and asked our approval."

"You gave this approval?"

"What else could I do? I was fully aware of the atrocious cruelty that my father had spent on the unfortunate ladies. I was fully aware of his misdemeanors and profligacies and outrages. It was hardly fitting that I obstruct the ladies in trying to obtain their freedom, was it?"

"It's quite true then that you gave some opium and a poisonous root to Olimpio?"

"At his insistence, needless to say," said Giacomo hurriedly. "He refused to leave the palace without them. He was a brute, this man Olimpio. There was no point in trying to stop him. I deeply regret having facilitated this regrettable crime, signor, but I beg you to bear in mind that even before I purchased these costly medicaments there had been plans to slay my father through the stratagem of bandits. And of these earlier projects I had no knowledge whatever. My role throughout was wholly passive. I might almost say that it was charitable. For I assure you, signor, the life of my beautiful sister seemed more valuable than the debauched and abominable life of my father."

"It was a question of choice between these two, in your considered opinion?"

"So it seemed; for I have no doubt, signor, that if my sister's condition had been discovered, as it would have been sooner or later, my father, being the kind of man he was, a real tyrant and intolerant of every peccadillo except his own . . . well, I'm sure he would have thrown the poor girl right over the balcony."

"I see," said Moscato softly. He seemed lost in meditation. Finally he rose and left the room with the notary behind him, and Giacomo Cenci was carefully unbound.

4

Then came Lucrezia.

Her stay in prison had added a trifle to her corpulence. She looked dumpy, almost coarse. Streaks of sweat shone under her armpits and the wisps of hair on the back of her neck hung damp and straggly.

Moscato opened a table drawer and drew out a kerchief, in which was wrapped a ring with a diamond set in braided gold.

MOSCATO: Tell me, signora. Have you ever seen this ring before?

LUCREZIA: Let me look at it. Well, yes, I have. It belonged
　　to my husband.
MOSCATO: This ring, signora, was found on the finger of
　　Olimpio Calvetti.
LUCREZIA: I don't understand. I know nothing about it.
MOSCATO: You never saw it on Signora Beatrice's finger, I
　　take it?
LUCREZIA: I'm not sure. Well, I might have. Once or twice,
　　just conceivably.
MOSCATO: Very well. (*He smiled indulgently as he wrapped
　　up the ring.*) I have a rather stimulating bit of news
　　for you, signora.
LUCREZIA (*nervously*): Indeed?
MOSCATO (*to the guard*): Bring in the prisoner.

And Giacomo was ushered into the room of interrogation, dull-eyed and derelict-looking.

"Well," he snapped, when he saw Lucrezia, "this is a
fine state of affairs. You see what you've brought us to,
you two women!"

Lucrezia stared at him filmily. "I don't know what you're
talking about."

"You know only too well, signora," said Giacomo.

"Bless my soul," gasped Lucrezia. The gravity of the moment was beginning to dawn on her. "You know as well as
I, my dear Giacomo, that I had nothing to do with this
nasty business!"

Giacomo stared at his stepmother and started to tremble
with excitement. "Nothing to do with it? Good God!" He
shook his hands in the air. "Oh Blessed Virgin, let's have
the truth out of this impossible woman!" In a fit of desperation he dropped to his knees in front of Lucrezia. "For

the love of God, Signora Lucrezia, you know how helpless I was! You know where all the guilt lies! Tell the truth as you know it, I beg you!"

But Lucrezia, stubborn and insensitive as always, turned away from him. "I can't help what you or your sister may have done. I had nothing to do with it."

"You've told me the truth yourself!" cried Giacomo, gesturing wildly. "About this murder!"

"Signor Francesco," said Lucrezia primly, "fell from the balcony, and that's all I know about it."

"It's a lie!"

"It's the truth."

Now Moscato intervened. Two *sbirri* appeared and led the prisoners down the hall to the torture chamber. Lucrezia was led to the rack, fully dressed, and was bound.

"Now tell us the truth," said Moscato stonily, "before we start turning."

"I've told it all," stammered Lucrezia, "as I've known it to be."

Moscato raised his right forefinger. The wheels were set in motion. Lucrezia's face turned quite red; she remained utterly still. The men were appalled at the incredible heroism of this silly woman. They kept turning; there was a hideous little gurgle as her joints snapped loose. Suddenly she screamed: "Let me down! In Christ's name, let me down!"

So the ropes were loosened and Lucrezia fell into the chair inertly. Sweat poured from her face; violent sobs shook her body.

"Now, signora," said Moscato. "Let's have the truth."

And Lucrezia told the truth in her garrulous, incoherent fashion.

"Ah, signor, it all began with this dreadful cruelty of Signor Francesco's, and one day, after a nail had been ripped from her hand by this senseless whipping, the girl rebelled. And it's hardly surprising, is it? She's a violent girl, my good signor, and she has it from her father! She told me of this notion of the kidnapping one morning in midsummer, and I saw the utter folly of it the moment she spoke of it, and later on when she sent the seneschal to Rome, then too I saw the folly of it. These plans of bandits and so on — perfectly childish they were. But the poor girl insisted — I couldn't blame her, your worship, all she'd suffered and all the squalor and filth and humiliation, and then fretting about this other thing, you know what I mean — she was utterly desperate, your worship! She was like a fox caught in a trap! And this thing about Olimpio, excuse my mentioning it, signor, but I hadn't the heart to condemn the girl. Blind with boredom she was, being so young and so lovely, and he was a fine-looking fellow, built like Hercules, with a flashing smile. Well, in any case, Giacomo gave his approval, as well he knows whatever he says of it, and I kept on warning and beseeching, like a voice in the wilderness. I felt sick at heart, your honor, I had nightmares aplenty, and one morning I saw them tiptoeing down the hall all grim and ghostly. I snatched up the chamber pot — forgive me, signor, I'm just telling what happened — and then the bells started tolling, it was the feast day of the Assumption. So I cried, 'Get down on your knees, my piteous lambs, and pray for forgiveness!' They grew pale at this thought for the fear of the Lord was still alive in them, and put this down too, signor, for I still remember all of a sudden how the seneschal started to cough like a man possessed, and he ran down the hall holding his hand to his throat. 'The Lord be praised,' I said to myself, but little did I know that dark girl! Her will was iron and her hold on the seneschal was a passionate wicked thing, and even the tinker gave way after I'd called him to his senses. And so I saw that the evil thing was bound to happen, and so it did when those two men broke into the room with their bloody weapons. I sat in the antechamber and held my hand to my heart, half in a swoon I was, and I heard that hacking and clattering, and I whispered, 'God have mercy on us!' For what could I do, poor miserable widow that I was from that time onward?"

All this was copied on his pages by the pimple-faced notary, and finally Moscato inquired:

"Tell me one thing, Signora Lucrezia. If you were so certain of your innocence, why didn't you tell us the truth before?"

"Ah," said Lucrezia, wiping her tears. She looked swiftly at Moscato. And for a moment a diabolical irony passed like a shadow across her eyes: a look almost inhuman in its subtlety and cunning. She lowered her lashes. Her lips trembled. "I felt pity for poor Beatrice. How could I help it, signor? I felt for her shame and her motherhood, and for the honor of the family . . ."

So that likewise was written and Lucrezia signed her testimony and was courteously conducted back to her cell.

5

Then Bernardo.

There is little we have seen so far of Bernardo. He was a sprightly-looking boy, more athletically built than his brother, with heavy eyelashes and coiling hair and a silky hint of a mustache. There was something of the black Cenci vehemence in the pout of the lips, the surly chin. But his eyes were like a squirrel's: full of a soft timorous questioning. His clothes had grown spattered and ripped during the weeks in prison. A gash in his shirt showed the tawny skin and a hairless nipple.

Moscato sat quietly for a while with his gaze fixed on the boy. His eyebrows rose faintly; a shadowy smile hung on his lips. There was something gentle, almost caressing in his expression.

"Would you say, Signor Bernardo, that your father was a cruel man?"

Bernardo frowned and lowered his eyes. "There were moments of cruelty, your worship."

"Did he ever beat you?" said Moscato.

"Once or twice," said Bernardo, blushing.

"Did he beat your sister Beatrice?"

"Yes! Most cruelly, your worship . . ."

Moscato paused; then he said, "And now tell me, Signor Bernardo. Do you recall Olimpio's visit to Monte Cenci?"

Bernardo's eyes grew bright with rage: "It was the devil who sent him there, signor!"

"You were present when he chatted with your brother Giacomo?"

"Yes," said Bernardo, suddenly timid.

"And they discussed a plot to dispose of your father? Do you remember, my boy?"

"No, signor!" said Bernardo desperately.

"You're quite certain?"

"Yes, signor!"

Moscato glanced at one of the guards and raised his left eyebrow.

For several minutes there was silence. Bernardo shifted about uneasily. Then Giacomo was led into the room, still limp and wet with the pangs of the rack.

Moscato turned to him sternly. "You confirm, Signor Giacomo, what you've testified regarding your brother's complicity?"

"I do," said Giacomo wanly.

"Signor Bernardo was present, you say, at the discussion with Olimpio regarding the murder?"

"He was," said Giacomo.

Two great tears slid from Bernardo's eyes. His courage left him; he started to sob.

"You've heard what your brother has testified, Signor Bernardo?"

Poor Bernardo nodded hopelessly.

"And it's the truth?"

"Yes, signor."

"You were present when Olimpio spoke of this plot, Signor Bernardo?"

"Yes. I was there."

"And you consented?"

"Yes . . . I consented."

And that was the end of Bernardo's interrogation. He was led, still sobbing pitifully, back to his cell.

XXXVI

Aɴᴅ ɴᴏᴡ we come to Beatrice herself, our dark and enig-
matic heroine, who was conducted that same day into the
presence of the illustrious Papal prosecutor. She entered
the room, serene and insolent, ignoring the nod from the
little notary, and stood with her eyes fixed on the egg-
shaped window behind the judge.

ᴍᴏsᴄᴀᴛᴏ: The time has come, Signora Beatrice, to put an
    end to these interviews. The court, I must inform you,
    is in possession of the truth. And the truth is that you
    instigated the death of your father.
ʙᴇᴀᴛʀɪᴄᴇ: It's a lie.
ᴍᴏsᴄᴀᴛᴏ (*leaning forward*): Tell me, Signora Beatrice.
    Did your father ever beat you?
ʙᴇᴀᴛʀɪᴄᴇ: Why on earth should he beat me?
ᴍᴏsᴄᴀᴛᴏ: Was it his cruelty which caused your hatred? To
    the point of wishing him dead?
ʙᴇᴀᴛʀɪᴄᴇ: This is ludicrous. He never beat me.
ᴍᴏsᴄᴀᴛᴏ: Come closer, signora. Let me see your left hand.

    Beatrice gave him her hand: Moscato studied the
wounded finger. There was a feverish tenseness about

Beatrice, like a tightrope dancer's: eyes luminous and fixed, a floating lightness in her movements.

MOSCATO (*leisurely*): You may recall, signora, that Marzio the tinker confessed to us.

BEATRICE: The tinker lied. As I've told you before.

MOSCATO: Signora Lucrezia has also confessed, in case it happens to concern you.

BEATRICE: I am not interested in what my stepmother chooses to say about me.

MOSCATO (*reaching into the drawer*): Have you ever seen this ring, signora?

BEATRICE (*glancing at the ring*): Certainly. I have.

MOSCATO: How do you suppose we got this ring?

BEATRICE: How on earth should I know?

MOSCATO: You gave it to someone, didn't you?

BEATRICE: Most emphatically not.

MOSCATO: You gave it to Olimpio Calvetti.

BEATRICE (*smiling*): Sheer fantasy.

MOSCATO (*replacing the ring and clearing his throat*): Do you know a man, signora, named Camillo Rosati?

BEATRICE: I've never heard of the man.

MOSCATO: Well, nonetheless, I think it might interest you to hear this man's testimony.

And the notary proceeded to read the whole of Rosati's testimony, including the references to the sexual relations between Olimpio and Beatrice.

Beatrice grew pale with fury. "Well, my lord, I must congratulate you. I don't know this villain Rosati, but one thing I know. He tried to kill Olimpio Calvetti, and now that Olimpio is dead in his grave he sees fit to spill this despicable slander!" She was stammering with excitement;

her hands shot up to her throat. "I say this man Camillo Rosati is a fiend out of hell!"

MOSCATO (*changing the subject calmly*): I have a statement, Signora Beatrice, from the archpriest of the village of La Petrella. He denies that he ever told you that he drew a thorn from your father's skull.

BEATRICE: These priests and archpriests are a pack of hyenas!

MOSCATO: Listen, Signora Beatrice. Everyone but you has now confessed. Your stepmother Lucrezia has confessed, your brother Giacomo has confessed . . .

BEATRICE (*interrupting*): Bring in Giacomo. I'd like to talk for a while with Giacomo.

MOSCATO (*demurely*): Would this be seemly?

BEATRICE: It would bring out the truth!

Some minutes passed while the guards were sent to fetch Giacomo Cenci, and when he finally appeared, ill-kempt and shaggy, discolored with bruises, it was a moment before the girl actually recognized her brother. He stood facing Beatrice quietly. There was a dreadful little pause.

Then Beatrice said: "You've been telling lies to these people, Giacomo."

Giacomo said softly: "I wish with my heart and my soul that they were lies!"

The judge requested the notary to read Giacomo's confession.

"Do you confirm this?" said the judge.

"I confirm it," said Giacomo, who kept his eyes fixed calmly on Beatrice.

"He's lying," whispered Beatrice. She had grown intensely pale. "He's insane."

"It is nothing," said Giacomo, "but the plain and simple truth."

The judge whispered to one of the *sbirri* who left the room noiselessly and reappeared with Lucrezia some three minutes later.

Lucrezia's testimony was read in full by the notary.

"Do you confirm this?" said Moscato.

"I do," said Lucrezia.

"Nothing but lies," said Beatrice fiercely. "She loathes me, this woman."

"My dear child," said Lucrezia, brushing a strand of hair from her face. Enormous swellings shone on her wrists; small pink sores encrusted her eyelids. "How little you know me," she said. "How little you seem to understand. How little you know how I've suffered for you, and degraded myself for you. My only lies were when I tried to cover your shame and folly, my dear Beatrice."

Lucrezia and Giacomo were accompanied back to their cells and Moscato observed, rather wearily:

"You will be so kind as to follow me, Signora Beatrice."

2

Beatrice was led to the torture chamber and there she was bound, still fully dressed. The wheels were turned.

Moscato murmured his Credo.

Beatrice remained motionless. The veins in her temples started to swell. She kept staring at Moscato with her huge glistening eyes.

"The truth," said Moscato, breathless.

Beatrice's face grew gaunt and rigid. A queer blue shadow appeared on her cheeks. The joints clacked. She closed her eyes.

The wheels kept turning. Moscato whispered a second Credo.

Beatrice opened her eyes and said quietly: "Very well. Let me down."

"You'll tell us the truth, signora?"

"Yes. I'll tell you the truth."

It seemed that an inner fire had abruptly gone out in her. She had lost in that hour all desire for survival. She sat in a chair with her arms still bound and dislocated, and proceeded to tell in scrupulous detail the whole story of the murder: from the moment of Cenci's violent return to La Petrella to the moment that she cried from the window to the butler Giorgio. She spoke with utter detachment: with neither bitterness nor self-pity; without passion, without luster, like a woman in a trance.

Finally she signed in the notary's copy: *I, Beatrice Cenci, herewith testify that all that is written above is the truth.*

XXXVII

AFTER their final confessions all four of the prisoners were respited and given three days to prepare their defense: with the stipulation *sine prejudicio ulterioris processus,* that is to say, without prejudice to a possible subsequent trial. Giacomo and Bernardo were led back to their cells in Tordinona; the two ladies remained at the Court of Savella. And all the lesser prisoners involved in the case, such as Plautilla and the Friar Pietro, were promptly released without further ado.

This was the middle of August, and the heat was subsiding. The plague had finally disappeared from the city. Friends, relatives and servants were now allowed to visit the prisoners freely, and in the late afternoons, when the sting of the sun had left the air, Bastiana would come with a basket of nectarines and sit at Beatrice's feet while the lady plucked dreamily at her lute. The Velli family emerged from their narrow palace in Trastevere and brought platters of pastry to the tremulous Lucrezia. The old schoolmaster Poderetti, a man with undulating hips, came to chat with his wayward pupil Bernardo. And every day Ludovica would come and sit in the cell with Giacomo, telling him the gossip of the city and the household news of Monte Cenci.

On the day which followed the last confessions the cousin Cesare appeared and informed Giacomo that the most renowned and eminent lawyer in the city, the illustrious Prospero Farinaccio, had consented to undertake the defense of the Cenci.

2

There is a bust of Farinaccio over his sepulcher in San Silvestro: an intense, extraordinarily concentrated face — falcon lips, tight goatee, a set of formidable eyes. A fanatic at first sight; but then one sees the self-indulgence, the strange urbanity and lassitude behind the powerful lean features. And there were rumors in Rome that Farinaccio in years past had shared in certain of Francesco Cenci's debaucheries. One fine day, soon after sunset, he appeared in the cell of Signora Beatrice.

"Good evening, signora."

"Good evening, my lord."

"Signora Beatrice, please allow me to come to the point. Time is short and our hearings begin in eight days."

He sat on the oval stool in front of the iron-grilled window. The soft light of the summery dusk fell like a veil over his face. A face that filled Beatrice with a curious uneasiness: dry, ruthless, astute, with crepelike skin, like an aging courtesan's.

"It has been difficult beyond my expectations to summon the facts for our defense, signora. The Judge Molella has presented me with a transcript of the examinations as well as the last confessions. It is, I am sorry to tell you, an intimidating set of documents."

Beatrice looked at him silently; then she stared at the ceiling, where a wasp was buzzing in a tangle of cobweb.

Farinaccio continued: "I have interviewed some of the witnesses. I have explored some new evidence. A case of sorts has been prepared for Signora Lucrezia as well as your brothers. It is your own situation, Signora Beatrice, which disturbs me. We will require — forgive me, signora — a rather dramatic stroke of luck."

"Yes. I see," remarked Beatrice.

"Have you any suggestions?" said the lawyer.

"None," said Beatrice. "There is nothing to add to my testimony."

There was something wayward, almost jocular in Farinaccio's eyes. "Perhaps I have failed, Signora Beatrice, to make myself clear. As I have said, your brothers and your stepmother provide the possibilities of a defense. But I have tried in vain to discover an adequate approach to your own position. It would embarrass me, signora, to see you suffer unduly . . . Do I make myself clear?"

"You do," said Beatrice, folding her hands in her lap.

"Very well," said Farinaccio. "I have thought up a stratagem."

And he expounded his scheme to her, choosing his words and developing his points in a crisp, metallic tone. Beatrice closed her eyes and listened: horrified at first and then bored, and in the end almost hypnotized. She felt no interest whatever in prolonging her existence, but there was something contagious in Farinaccio's cunning and energy. She experienced the strange sensation that an effigy

had been created, a dark, gesturing shadow of Beatrice
Cenci herself, and that this image, this illusion must be
rescued at all costs.

And finally she said: "Quite, signor. I understand. It is
most ingenious."

3

Petitions were sent to the Cardinal Sforza, the Cardinal
Caetani and the Cardinal Aldobrandini. Two additional
advocates were enlisted: the venerable Coronati and the
sly Altieri. New witnesses were ferreted out from the farms
and the piazzas. And finally, on the twenty-eighth of August, the hearings for the defense were begun in the
breathless chambers of the Court of Savella.

The first witnesses were simple folk from the village of
La Petrella: the cobbler Baldassare and the pastry cook
Ambrogio. They testified to the sexual outrages per-
petrated by Francesco Cenci all over the countryside, and
likewise to the lunatic imprisonment of the two gentle
ladies, the monotonous squalor of their existence and their
desperate pleas for release.

The second witnesses were a bevy of prostitutes, both
male and female, from Trastevere: a noisy crew of gesticulating hussies, leering street boys, cantankerous shrews.
They testified, with colorful phrases and vigorous imagery,
to the incurable profligacy of Francesco Cenci.

The third witnesses deposed regarding the boy Bernardo. His fidgeting schoolmaster, Americo Poderetti, and
his pusillanimous uncle, Mario Fano, produced evidence

to the effect that the boy was dull-witted, clumsy of speech, slow in his studies, and not responsible for his behavior.

Further witnesses testified to Signor Giacomo's sobriety and piety; to Signora Lucrezia's delicacy of instinct and humility of manner; to the boy Bernardo's generosity to beggars and gentleness toward animals; and to Beatrice's frequently expressed desire to enter a nunnery.

Then came the last and most surprising of the witnesses for the defense: and these were the cook and the chambermaid who had traveled across the hills to La Petrella — the loquacious Girolama and the acidulous Calidonia. They testified to certain equivocal scenes that occurred in the castle, and as they spoke the whole purport of Farinaccio's defense finally emerged.

4

Three old women are kneeling on the sands by the bridge of Sant' Angelo, scrubbing their shreds of tattered laundry with leathery claws.

"Well," says the first, "what do you think of it?"

"Ah," croaks the second, "it's a gamble. Who's telling the truth, that's the question, and we'll never know the answer."

"Now I tell you," says the third, a skeletal creature with one eye, "it's many a time I've chatted with Girolama about Signor Francesco Cenci, and many a time she spoke of his lecherous ways. But never once did she breathe a word about this strange new wickedness . . ."

"Incest," says the first of the women, dressed in green.

"It's the worst of all the sins. It's the darkest of all desires."

"All things I understand," says the second with pungency. "All sorts of naughtiness I've seen. But here's an evil beyond forgiveness . . ."

"And I tell you this," says the one-eyed hag, "if it's true that he lusted for his daughter, it's only natural and human that she struck in revenge . . ."

"It's a rotten age," snaps the woman in green, "that we've come to live in these days, and it's rotten blood that runs in the veins of the Cenci. When a full-grown gentleman begins to hanker for his own pure daughter . . ."

"It's a fearful tale," mutters the second woman.

"So it is," says the one in green.

And they rise to wring their linen on the sands by Sant' Angelo.

At the end of the bridge, just off the piazza, stands the Inn of the Swan. The air out in the streets is breathless, asphyxiating, but here in the cellar there is coolness in the wine-soaked flagstones. Two country bumpkins from the Abruzzi are sitting at a table with a jug of claret.

"It's no use, I'm telling you now," says the pastry cook Ambrogio, wiping his chin. "I saw the look in the judge's eyes, and there's not a word of it he credited."

"Wait. You'll see," says the cobbler Baldassare. "There's a devilish skill in these lawyers."

"They'll end on the gallows, that's my feeling," says Ambrogio in a whisper. "All that talk of Girolama's — sheer nonsense, if you ask me. I've talked to Don Marzio and he thinks as I do. Signor Francesco was a villain, there's no end to the evil he did, but he wasn't the man to defile his own blood."

"You heard what Calidonia said," growls the cobbler

peevishly, "and I tell you, it's the plain unvarnished truth. He went strutting through his rooms all naked and shameless, and each day the poor ladies had to bring the pisspot and the closestool, and each evening he forced his daughter to rub his legs with a towel, and it's easy to see that one night the old rascal might have seized her . . ."

"I dare say," says Ambrogio. "Calidonia swore she found the girl by her father's bed one evening, with a broken wineglass . . ."

"And Girolama saw her rushing into the kitchen, white as a ghost, the poor creature . . ."

"It's a lurid thought," says Ambrogio, drawing his thumb through a puddle of wine. "Maybe it's true and maybe it isn't. But the judge thinks little of it, that much I'm sure of, and there's doom in the air, and my heart is sick for the lovely lady."

In the Campo dei Fiori there is gossip among the stalls. It's market day and the men from the hills are down with their carts — pyramids of fennel and celery, purple parsnips and yellow beans. The scents of the countryside and the farmyards hover about the whole piazza.

"Here's a fine one. Fat as a goose," says the poultry vendor briskly. He plucks a duck from the cage and holds her up by the legs.

The maid Bastiana runs her thumb through the feathers, probing the flesh.

"Well," says the vendor, "the plea comes up to His Holiness today. We'll know the verdict in a day or two, and they'll all be free in less than a week."

"Ah," says Bastiana with tears in her eyes, "I hope you're right, Antonello."

"There's only one thing," says the egg dealer, who has

joined the circle. "There's great profit for the church in confiscating the Cenci properties. And to confiscate these properties there must be a verdict of guilty. And the only sentence for such a crime, if you'll excuse me . . ."

"Please remember," puts in the vintner, a bearded man with a wooden leg, "there's a great desire in the Holy Father to achieve the love of the Roman people. And the Roman people desire that the Cenci family be spared. And the Holy Father is aware of this desire of the Roman people. And his desire for popularity will guide him in the direction of lenience."

"You forget," chimes in the fruit merchant, popping an almond in his mouth, "that the Cardinal Aldobrandini is the power behind His Holiness. And the cardinal is deeply concerned about the matter. There's vice been spreading through the whole peninsula. All of Umbria is infested with lechery. There've been similar killings in Sutri and Civitavecchia. Mark my words: there's anger in the cardinal. There's a fine example to be made of the Cenci."

"Yes," says the egg dealer judiciously, "and bear in mind this thing of the advocate. The excellent Farinaccio was a crony of old Cenci's, they tell me, and it's not in his heart to rescue the murderers. Now, this case he's drummed up about the violation of Signora Beatrice: it's a deliberate absurdity, I can't help feeling . . ."

"Still, she's a pitiful fine lady," growls the vintner, shaking his fist, "and what she did, if she really did it, and we all know that she did it, was more than justified by her father's cruelty. I've got a cousin, and his name is Curzio, and he'll tell you what he's seen: there was a demon in Signor Francesco, and the sight of virtue drove him to a frenzy . . ."

[326   ]

"So it goes, so it goes," mutters the poultry dealer cynically. "The people bleed while the men in power go tricking each other for their own advantage. There's no such thing as justice. There's only self-interest. Whatever happens, the innocent suffer and the devil takes the hindmost!"

Bastiana listens to all this chatter while the tears go trickling down her cheeks. Finally she pays for the little duck and hurries back to Monte Cenci.

5

And Beatrice herself is still alone in her cell. She is sitting motionless by the tiny window which looks out on Via Monserrato. Dusk falls; the street darkens; the light of a torch glides through the bars. It glistens momentarily on the dim gray ceiling. Beatrice closes her eyes: and once again the setting sun sheds its dazzle on the blue, depopulated slopes of the Abruzzi. The radiance pours from the cliffs of Staffoli like a cataract of gold, hurling its steam through the valley, clouding the sheep with a tremulous aureole, tipping the wings of the little blackbirds with feathers of fire. And that same landscape which once had imprisoned her like the walls of a nightmare now lies illuminated with all the splendor, the oracular majesty of a long-lost dream.

XXXVIII

W HAT is the truth? What is crime? What is evil? What is justice? Ulisse Moscato was a cold and ambitious intellectual, and his approach to the Cenci was that of a chess player toward his pawns. With inexhaustible zeal and ingenuity he set his mind to deciphering the truth and disentangling the facts as they gradually emerged.

But the senior judge, Pompeo Molella, was a gentler person altogether. A man of doubts, of anxieties, of deep moral scruples; and during his interminable examinations in the case of the Cenci there were moments when his purest principles, his most fundamental premises, seemed in danger of falling apart and dissolving into chaos. Something evil had occurred; the whole truth must be established; the crime must be judged; and justice must be done. Simple enough. Of these necessities he had no sort of doubt. But there were moments in the relative coolness of dusk, as he sat in his garden by the Via Giulia and listened to the pigeons among the eaves, or to the tinkling of a guitar in the Piazza Ricci, when he felt that with the steady accumulation of facts the truth itself grew forever more shadowy, more elusive; when the very horror and violence

which surrounded life like a vast penumbra made the identification of evil a task complex beyond mere human wisdom; when even the crime itself seemed to exist not only in
the heart of the criminal but in the endless periphery of
relationships — fathers and sons, friends, lovers, enemies,
kinsmen, debtors and creditors, cooks and grooms, fishermen, muleteers, priests and princes and cardinals — so that
the act, like a pebble dropped in a windless pool, cast out
ripples through the whole tremendous fabric of society,
and the crime ceased being an individual thing but was a
part of humanity itself, past, present and to come; and the
administration of justice, the award and the punishment,
seemed a task almost hopelessly gratuitous and arbitrary,
and even in its essence a fearful confession of inadequacy,
a capitulation to the universal and unalterable injustice of
nature itself.

Such matters, made poignant by the cries and sufferings
of the miscreants, kept passing through Molella's patient,
circumspect mind. The more he pondered, the more profound grew the mystery and the tragedy. And late at night,
when he rose from his bed and stepped on the balcony to
feel the air from the Tiber and see the starlight on the
dome of San Giovanni dei Fiorentini, he felt that legality
and order were brittle, combustible things indeed, frail and
wayward as thistledown, episodic as a spark from a fire;
he felt that the sentence to be passed would be nothing
but a cry of desolation, and that the only truth and the
only comfort were in the heart of the beholder, in his
compassion, in his terror, in his forgiveness and his love.

2

And in the meantime the lawyer Farinaccio prepared his plea for the defense in collaboration with the venerable Coronati and the crafty Altieri; and this plea was presented to the Pope on the first day of September.

First they spoke of the lady Beatrice:

"Let Your Holiness please deign to contemplate the inhuman provocations in this most unhappy case. For though Beatrice Cenci has confessed to plotting the death of her father Francesco, it is equally true that this same Francesco had mistreated her abominably, held her imprisoned in the castle, and attempted to violate her virginity. And all that Beatrice may have done sprang from her danger and her fear, and it may be said that she committed the crime in defense of her honor, as well as in vengeance for the wrong she endured."

Then they turned to the boy Bernardo: "May we lay before the eyes of Your Holiness the point of his unusual youth and immaturity? For at the moment of the crime he had not yet reached his seventeenth year. And furthermore, being slow and retarded of wit, it is hardly surprising if he consented to those impious projects which his brother discussed with the murderer Olimpio. And consequently, in view of his minority and debility of mind, it would seem proper to exempt him from the customary penalty."

They passed on to Lucrezia:

"May Your Holiness reflect on her attitude as well as her acts, as fully testified. For though at first she consented to

[330   ]

the parricide, at the insistence of Beatrice, she later with-
drew her consent and tried to prevent the commission of
the crime itself. And under the circumstances, though there
be punishment for the failure to reveal the conspiracy,
the facts would hardly seem to justify the extreme penalty
of death or exile."

And finally they spoke of Giacomo:

"There is much, Your Holiness, which must unfortunately be omitted in this plea through lack of time. But
it must be remembered that Beatrice Cenci, for pardonable
reasons in our view, was the prime instigator and chief
mover of this crime, and Giacomo was only a partner and
a cognizant; and thus he cannot be punished with greater
severity than his sister."

And they concluded:

"O Holy Father, in the dreadful brevity of time remaining, let us plead that Your Holiness allow some mitigation
of the penalty, and employ his clemency and commisera-
tion toward the unfortunate prisoners. They cannot look
to the judgment of God nor to the mercy of the law, but
only to the wisdom of Your Holiness, to whom they kneel
and submit themselves."

3

Three days passed. An ominous silence followed the de-
liverance of the plea, and the petitions to the cardinals remained unanswered.

Now it was clear to the prisoners that only a miracle
could save them, and late one morning Beatrice called a
notary to her cell and made her will.

I, Beatrice Cenci, she declared, *daughter of Francesco Cenci, Roman, of happy memory, being sane of mind and sound of body, and fearing that I soon may die, make my last will and testament in the following manner and fully signed:*

I begin with my soul, which I commend in all humility to the Most Glorious Mother, to God, to the Seraphic Father St. Francis and to the whole Court of Heaven. And I will that my body be buried in the Church of San Pietro Montorio, to which I leave for my burial one hundred scudi, to pay for the purchase of a stone and the usual obsequies, the remainder to go for alms to celebrate Masses for my soul.

There followed a list of thirty odd beneficiaries — churches, monasteries and nunneries, prisons, hospitals and charitable brotherhoods, in each case with the stipulation that a hundred Masses be said for her soul. Money was left to the servant Bastiana as well as to Sister Ippolita, who resided in the Monastery of Montecitorio. And she chose her confessor, Fra Andrea Belmonte, who lived in San Pietro Montorio on the Gianicolo, to act as the chief executor of this will.

And a codicil was added: *I leave to Madonna Caterina de Santis, widow, a further five hundred scudi with the obligation to put them to interest and to spend the fruit in sustaining an unhappy boy as her ward, as I have instructed her personally by word of mouth; and while this boy shall live she shall be obligated to sustain him, and if she die and the boy attain the age of twenty years, he shall become the free master both of the interests as well as the principal, with the obligation to pray for the good of my soul . . .*

And in her own casual, undisciplined hand she appended the words: *I, Beatrice Cenci, state and declare the aforesaid disposition to be my last will and testament, and I order, leave, dispose and institute all things contained herein, and in good faith I subscribe with my own hand all the foregoing.*

I, Beatrice Cenci, as above with my own hand.

4

We are drawing very close to the end of our tale. Dusk falls: only a single day remains. Fra Andrea Belmonte has been sitting with Beatrice for over an hour. Now he rises and says good night. The door clangs shut; the footsteps die.

For a while Beatrice Cenci sits alone in her cell. The bells are chiming in the Church of Santa Maria di Monserrato. Faint echoes come drifting from the Piazza Farnese — a mare neighing, the splash of a fountain, the dull rumble of a vintner's cart.

Her head nods. For a moment she falls asleep.

A great plain spreads out toward a rippled horizon. A glow rises from all around, as though the sun were setting on every side. A smooth tower, like black glass, rises in the middle of the plain. Below stand thousands of watchers, like a vast swarm of ants.

She is a bird without wings now. She struggles to climb the black tower. Her claws scrape at the wall like tiny steel forks. Her feathers fall one by one and drift through the air like leaves from a tree. Now she is naked and pink;

suddenly she turns into a fish. She leaps and dives in an ecstasy of happiness and liberation. She swims through a forest of corals, a wilderness of opalescent branches, clipping the blossoms from their limbs with her knifelike fins.

Gradually her movements grow more difficult. The water thickens; it freezes. She is trapped in a sea of ice. Her scales grow brittle and split. And now she feels herself floating out of her skin like a newborn moth, shedding the terrible chrysalis and fluttering off without a sound, deeper and deeper into the cool abyss of the night . . .

5

The door opens again; Beatrice wakes up and turns quickly. It is the widow, Madonna Caterina de Santis. She has brought Beatrice's supper in a neat little basket. She draws off the damask napkin. There's a trout still steaming in the pot, a bottle of claret, a bowl of salad, a nest of chilled fruit. The candle is set on the sill by the table. The scent of the wine sauce flows through the cell.

"How is he?" says Beatrice.

"He's been crying, poor angel," says Caterina. "But he's healthy. He's full of mischief. I sat in the garden with him earlier, and he laughed when he saw the sparrows hopping across the grass."

"You've seen Sister Ippolita?"

"Yes, I have. She's been praying for you. She loves you with all of her heart, my pet, and a powerful heart it is . . . My darling Beatrice, all of Rome is talking of nothing but you!"

There is a pause. Beatrice is plucking the bones from the fish. Finally she murmurs:

"What did Coronati tell you?"

"Nothing at all," says Caterina hastily. "Not a word of news. Cardinal Montalto's been seeing the judge this morning. It's in the lap of the Holy Father and his thoughts are still a mystery. Don't worry, my dear. The Duke of Tuscany has written a letter. The Cardinal Sforza has done his best. You'll see. All will be well."

"Yes," says Beatrice absently. "All will be well."

Caterina's eyes are fixed on Beatrice; there is something feverish about her. "Really, my child. I've never seen you so lovely. Look — The candlelight on your cheeks! Why, I'd almost swear that . . ."

Beatrice looks at her emptily.

"Its like magic. It's almost . . ." But the words remain unsaid. "You look happy," says Caterina, placing her hand on Beatrice's wrist. "You're at peace. That's the only thing that matters."

The two women sit silently, Beatrice with her hand in Caterina's. The smell of the night seeps down from the piazza. A late summer sweetness: raw wine and ripening fruit and the pine logs heaped in the nearby cellars.

There's a crackle of hoofbeats in the courtyard. Then silence again. The gnats go swirling around the candle.

And then the door of the cell swings open without a sound: a faceless man in a coal-black hood stands on the threshold, holding a lantern.

BOOK FIVE
The Scaffold

XXXIX

On the tenth of September, in the second hour of the night, the Pope's courier delivered the sentence to the authorities in the Court of Savella. The document was signed by Moscato: *Ita pronuntiavi ego Ulixis Muscatus locumentens et judex deputatus.*

And this, in its terrible simplicity, was the sentence:

On the following morning, which was the morning of the eleventh of September, justice would finally be done for the murder of Francesco Cenci, Roman. Giacomo Cenci would be brought on a cart to the Piazza Sant' Angelo, and there his flesh would be torn from him with a pair of red-hot tongs. Thereupon the executioner would strike his head with a great hammer, and then his body would be quartered and hung on hooks beside the bridge. Thereupon the two ladies Lucrezia and Beatrice would be beheaded. The boy Bernardo would be spared; but he must witness the executions, and later be sent to Civitavecchia to row in the galleys till the end of his days. And all the properties of these four culprits would then be confiscated in their entirety, including fiefs, estates, domains, jurisdictions, rights and shares, offices and benefices and pledges, in whatever quarter existing, and would pass into the hands of the civil government and the Apostolic Camera.

2

A notification of the sentence was immediately sent to the Brothers of the Florentine Company of St. John the Beheaded. It was the special task of this charitable brotherhood, on the eve of an execution, to attend and console those who were sentenced to death. Four comforters and a chaplain, together with a sacristan and a steward, were promptly dispatched to the cells of Tordinona.

All was still beside the Tiber when they entered the prison. They wore long black cassocks with a rope around the waist and pointed hoods which covered the face, with narrow slits for the eyes. They walked noiselessly down the corridors, each of them carrying a lantern and a painted tablet portraying the Crucifixion of Christ.

First they came to Giacomo's cell. He was sitting by the window, lost in a daydream. He glanced up wearily when the seven black figures entered the cell. A look of animal panic shot through his eyes. Then the truth suddenly dawned on him: a terrible stillness froze his features.

"We've come to help you, my son," said the chaplain very gently.

Giacomo nodded vacuously. "Yes. I see."

The lanterns were placed on the floor, the tablets were laid by the candlestick, and Giacomo's horror gave way to a strange rush of gratitude. It seemed, now that death was so close and inescapable, that some deep residue of humanity

had suddenly been released in him. His eyes grew pleading, his lips quivered. He lowered his head; he started to
sob.

One of the comforters walked toward him and stroked
his head. "Take heart, signor."

There was silence for a little while and gradually
Giacomo stopped sobbing. He looked at the faceless
Brothers and said, "Please forgive me."

"Are you resolute?" said the chaplain in his slow, gentle
voice.

"Yes," said Giacomo.

"And are you prepared to die as a true Christian?"

"I am," said Giacomo.

"Do you accept this death in penance for your sins?"

"I do," said Giacomo.

"Do you ask pardon of all whom you have wronged?"

"I do," said Giacomo.

"And do you forgive those who have wronged you?"

"Yes," said Giacomo.

"You have made your testimony, and you confirm it?"

Giacomo nodded.

"Think, my son," said the chaplain. "Is there anything
else you wish to tell me?"

There was a queer, dull calm, a childlike earnestness in
Giacomo's face. He thought for a moment. Suddenly he
said: "There's one small debt I forgot to pay. I owe the
jeweler Turchetti, who lives on Via Coronari, nine scudi
for a ring . . . Would you see that this is paid?"

The chaplain nodded gravely. "I will see to it, my son."
He touched Giacomo on the shoulder. "And now we will
accompany you to the chapel."

3

A little later these same comforters visited Bernardo in his cell. Assuming that the boy had likewise been condemned to death, they prepared to comfort and confess him in the usual manner, and at half-past four in the morning he was led to the prison chapel where Giacomo was praying. Here Mass was now celebrated and the two brothers received the Holy Sacrament.

It was an hour later, when the light of dawn was already seeping through the chapel windows, that a messenger, Ambrosini by name, arrived from the general prosecutor and informed the chaplain that there had been a slight misunderstanding: namely, that the boy Bernardo, who was kneeling in the darkness nearby, had been spared by the clemency of the Holy Father, but that he was to accompany his brother to the block and witness the execution.

And so the chaplain went to Bernardo and whispered in his ear. But the boy merely looked at him with his huge, puzzled eyes.

"Do you understand what I have said?" repeated the chaplain.

Bernardo nodded his head. His cheeks were spotted with tears.

"Your life has been spared by His Holiness, my boy."

Bernardo kept nodding. "Thank you, Father."

"God bless you," whispered the chaplain very softly.

And Bernardo lowered his head and kept on praying.

4

Another group of four comforters, as well as a sacristan and a chaplain, had set out simultaneously for the prison at the Court of Savella. First Lucrezia was led to the chapel and there was confessed and consoled. Then one of the Brothers was led by a guard to Beatrice's cell, where she was sitting by the window with Caterina de Santis.

Beatrice glanced at the hooded figure which loomed in the doorway. Her eyes brightened all of a sudden; she nodded and rose without a word. A muffled cry broke from the widow Caterina, but Beatrice kissed her on the cheek and raised her finger to her lips. Then she followed the Florentine Brother down to the chapel.

The chaplain was a very old, very exhausted little man. His creaky voice was scarcely audible. He leaned tremulously over Beatrice.

"Do you ask the pardon of God for your sins? And do you confide yourself to His Holy Will?"

"I do," said Beatrice, lowering her eyes. "And I forgive all who have harmed me, and I ask forgiveness of all whom I have harmed, and I beg the Company of Mercy to say two hundred Masses for my soul . . . Some of them before I am put in my burial place, if you'll be so good to remind them of it, Father, and the rest of them after . . ."

Her voice dropped suddenly. The chaplain gazed at her through the slits in his hood and waited a moment.

"Is there anything else?"

"Nothing else," said Beatrice.

"You have made your testament?"

"I have made it," said Beatrice.

"You have nothing to add to it?"

Beatrice hesitated. "No," she whispered. But then she said in a hoarse, shy tone: "One small thing I'll add to it, Father. There's a soldier at the Castel Sant' Angelo and his name is Carlo of Bertinoro. He did me a kindness one day, and I wish to repay him. Will you see that he receives the sum of eighty scudi with my gratitude?"

The chaplain repeated the name. "I will do so," he whispered.

Holy Mass was celebrated in the Chapel of Corte Savella at half-past five; and from that moment until their departure the two ladies kept praying while the Florentine Brothers knelt beside them, murmuring gently.

The light of the candles grew dimmer. A glow crept over the ceiling, like a cloud of sunlit dust in a stable. The bells started ringing in Santa Maria di Monserrato, and a moment later there was a bright, diminutive echo. Beatrice recognized the sound: it was the fishmonger from Ostia, beating his gong as he dragged the cart toward the Campo dei Fiori.

X L

AT HALF-PAST NINE on the morning of September 11, 1599, the ministers of justice arrived at the prison of Tordinona. A brilliant day; feathery clouds went drifting across the sky. The tingle of autumn was in the air, the leaves danced on the Gianicolo and puffs of foam went galloping down the Tiber.

All over the city there was an air of festivity. People came hurrying from the hills toward the labyrinth of lanes along the river. The fishmongers covered their stalls, the vintners and butchers locked their shops, and all went scampering through the crowded alleys. A horde of tailors and carpenters, haberdashers and silversmiths, basket weavers and saddlemakers were converging on the Piazza Sant' Angelo.

A long procession had formed near the prison of Tordinona, and two carts were waiting outside the doors. The gates finally swung open. A low gasp rose from the crowd: two black-hooded comforters appeared on the threshold.

They stood motionless, waiting. The crowd began to mutter.

"Where are they?" cried someone.

"It's a scandal!" cried someone else.

"Hush," said a powerful voice. "They're coming!"

The chaplain and the steward stepped through the prison door, carrying the gold-framed tablets of the Crucifixion.

A moment later Giacomo emerged from the darkness, followed by Bernardo. Their heads were lowered. They walked forth haltingly. A ripple of panic swept through the crowd.

The chaplain and the humpbacked steward stepped stiffly into a cart. They were followed by Giacomo, who was bare to the waist and heavily bound. Two comforters followed Giacomo into the cart. Then came the chief executioner, a massive man in a crimson doublet.

The boy Bernardo was led into the second cart. He was wrapped in a great black cloak which covered his head and body; and he was followed by the last two comforters and the sacristan.

Now the procession started to move. First of all, in a narrow column, marched the Brothers of the Sacred Stigmata, who wore sandals of wood and ash-gray cassocks, with a crown of thorns tied to each girdle. After the Brothers came the bright-spangled guards and *sbirri,* with a flutter of pennants and a flashing of swords. Then came the members of the court: Ulisse Moscato and Pompeo Molella, as well as Boezio Giunta, the substitute prosecutor, all in ceremonial robes. They were followed by the Brothers of Mercy in a black silent phalanx. Then came the carts: Giacomo in the first and Bernardo in the second, both kneeling, with lowered heads, with the hooded Brothers beside them. Then came a column of various religious fraternities, friars from the Hospital of San Giacomo, from

[346   ]

the Brotherhood of Good Deeds and the Company of the Most Blessed Trinity, as well as the Church of the Fathers Ministering to the Sick, all singing litanies as they marched through the narrow streets. Last of all came the Roman populace, a multicolored rabble, young and old, women and men, cursing and praying, laughing and weeping, and thus the mighty cortege wound slowly across the city.

They followed the Via dell' Orso into the Street of the Golden Lily. Then they entered the Piazza dell' Apollinare. Here the chief executioner took out his tongs, which had lain in a bucket of red-hot coals, and the mutilation began.

A dull moan rose from the crowd. Some of the men shouted furiously. An old woman on a balcony gave a scream and fainted away. The pincers dug into the arms and tore at the tendons on Giacomo's back; then they probed into the muscles of his chest and shoulders. An ill-smelling steam rose from the burning flesh, but Giacomo knelt motionless, without uttering a sound. And the procession in the meantime wound through Via dell' Anima, past the Church of the Agonizante and through the Piazza Pasquino. Slowly it passed the Palazzo Regis, where there had been such gaiety on carnival night, and it passed the Palazzo Montalto, which was the dwelling place of Monsignore Guerra. More and more of the rabble joined in the great parade as it crossed the Campo dei Fiori and entered the Piazza Farnese, which was called in those days the Piazza del Duca. They passed the Church of San Tommaso and entered the Via Monserrato. Finally they came to a halt in front of the prison of the Court of Savella.

2

Bastiana the maid and the pantry boy Pasquale had slipped away that morning from the Palazzo Cenci. They were standing under a gateway near the court when the Brothers of the Stigmata emerged from the crowds in the Piazza Farnese.

"There. They've come," said Pasquale.

"God protect us," said Bastiana.

They saw the flashing swords of the *sbirri* and heard the clattering of the cartwheels. The doors of the court were thrown open and two comforters entered the street, bearing aloft their tablets and lanterns. They paused a moment; a powerful cry burst forth from the crowd. Lucrezia and Beatrice, both in black, appeared in the doorway. Lucrezia was sobbing; her face was lowered. Beatrice had her eyes fixed stonily on the tablet of the Crucifixion which one of the Brothers was holding in front of her. Neither of them glanced at the cart in which Giacomo was kneeling. They stepped into the street in front of the executioner's cart, first Lucrezia and then Beatrice, each flanked by two comforters, and the procession was under way again. The litanies were resumed, the cartwheels creaked desolately, and a strange dark heaving flowed through the mob.

"Did you see her face?" whispered Bastiana; tears were streaming down her cheeks.

"She's seen a vision!" hissed Pasquale. "I've never seen her so lovely!"

"Poor sweet lady," said Bastiana brokenly. "She never did it. I'm sure of it . . ."

"Wait," said Pasquale; "there'll be a miracle! The Hand of the Lord will intervene!"

And they joined the great procession, shouting and groaning with the rest of the crowd, which swarmed through the narrow quarters of Via Monserrato. They moved past the Banchi Vecchi and down the Via San Celso; the windows and doors and even the rooftops were black with mourners. The passion of the mob was steadily rising. The murmuring grew to a sullen roar. Ladies were waving their tear-soaked handkerchiefs; they shook their fists as the judges passed.

The men started to growl: "Down with Moscato! Kill Moscato!" Others were muttering against the governor and Cardinal Aldobrandini. There were even whisperings, tense and covert, against His Holiness himself. Like a great muddy torrent the throng went surging behind the procession. Beggars in rags, all sorts of riffraff and gipsies had joined the ranks. The balconies of the great palazzi were crowded with noble ladies — the Orsini princesses were watching, and the Bolognetti and the Sforza: some of them weeping, others cold and hard and vituperative.

The clouds shriveled away, the briskness died from the air. A stifling heat fell on the city as the sun rose higher. It was almost noon when the carts finally rumbled into the piazza in front of the marble angels of the Ponte Sant' Angelo.

3

A high scaffold has been erected in the middle of the piazza. A line of *sbirri* surrounds the square and guards the entrance to the bridge. The bridge itself is bristling with a densely packed multitude which clings to the parapets and squats on the statues. The Castel Sant' Angelo is like a great amphitheater; the bastions and galleries are peppered with watchers. The river is seething with boats, rafts, canoes.

The heat sharpens. The tumult and desperation accumulate. There is a perpetual undertone of muttering and wailing. Some are struck by the heat of the sun; they faint and collapse. Others fall from the parapets and drown in the rush of the Tiber. Three old women are caught in the thicket of bodies in Via Paola; they shriek as they fall, the mob flows over them: they are trampled to death.

The whole place suddenly glitters. The Papal guards have arrived. Spears crackle and blaze; banners flutter like roosters.

The judges of the court step forth and come to a halt below the scaffold. The Brothers of Mercy divide and form an aisle on each side. Beatrice and Lucrezia wander past them, like a pair of sleepwalkers.

Someone is screaming: "Save them! Save them!"

"She's innocent!"

"She's a martyr!"

"She's a saint!"

A sudden hush falls over the crowd as the carts roll into the square. They come to a halt by the wooden scaffold. There is a small gray chapel just to the right of the bridgehead — the same chapel where Bastiana once met Carlo of Bertinoro; this the comforters now enter, leading Lucrezia and Beatrice. The guards unbind Giacomo and carry his mangled body into the chapel. Bernardo goes stumbling after them with his hands in front of his face.

The guards and the comforters emerge again. The four Cenci are left in the chapel. They are hidden from view. The crowd wonders: What is happening? Giacomo is writhing with pain; Bernardo is weeping continually. Lucrezia is kneeling in front of the Virgin, limp and inert. Beatrice stares at the ceiling in a trance; then she kneels between her brothers and kisses them both very tenderly. Mass is said for the last time and the victims gaze at one another and whisper their last, unfathomable farewells.

4

The last ripple of wind has faded from the air. The Tiber oozes along its banks, sleek and ill-smelling. The stench of the mob begins to thicken in the piazza: sweating bodies packed in the sun, eyes glazed, jaws sagging. The whole city is in a trance. No one stirs; no one speaks. Terror or pity? Neither, quite. The faces are drained of emotion. All that they show at this moment is a kind of mute and hopeless animal suspense.

Smoke rises in a thin green feather from Tordinona. A flock of pigeons comes swinging down the Gianicolo, flaps idly across the river, swirls about over the piazza, and burrows its way into the sun-baked eaves and cornices.

The faces turn solemnly, hypnotically as they watch the birds. It seems that all of Rome is about to suffer retribution for some vast and hideous composite crime.

The door of the chapel opens again and Bernardo enters the piazza. He is led to the scaffold in his great black cloak. He kneels down and begins to pray, and the final ceremony begins.

Again the door opens. Two comforters come forth, leading Lucrezia, who stumbles and falls at the bottom of the scaffold. They carry her clumsily up the steps to the executioner's bench. She sinks in a faint and lies unconscious, and the executioner leans over her body; he has trouble in placing her shoulders properly. The crowd stand breathless. The ax falls and the head is severed.

The door of the chapel opens a third time. A dark ripple moves through the crowd. Beatrice climbs the steps to the scaffold with a quick firm tread, kneels down and lays her head on the block. The blade flashes. The head falls, and a strange, low sound fills the air, like the far-off bellowing of a herd.

And now Giacomo appears in the doorway, borne in the arms of the comforters. His head lolls over his shoulders, wolflike with pain. The Brothers carry his lacerated body up the steps. He reels forward blindly and places his head on the block. The executioner turns it gently, adjusts it, measures the distance. He raises the iron hammer and brings it crashing. The body quivers, collapses, and quickly the headman slits the throat. The crowd watches with a kind of stupefied horror as the man in the crimson doublet strips the corpse and scrupulously proceeds to chop the trunk into four separate parts; and finally hangs the bleeding quarters on the butcher's hooks which have been driven into the top of the scaffold.

The Brothers of Mercy gather into a line once again. They march down Via Paola, singing their thin, high litanies. The three judges turn away and disappear in the crowd. The officers and guards go strutting in a column across the bridge. Two of the *sbirri* lead Bernardo, who is staggering like an idiot, back to his lonely cell in the prison of Tordinona. And the shattered bodies remain on the scaffold, Giacomo suspended on the iron hooks and the ladies placed on biers and surrounded by torches, which are lit by the Brothers of the Sacred Stigmata.

5

The sun is low. The heat has gone from the air. The flames shine more brightly as dusk creeps over the hills. All passion has died in the mob, which moves about aimlessly with a kind of listless puzzled dejection. The Brothers come back and prepare for the removal of the bodies. First Giacomo is reassembled and placed on a bier; he is carried off by the Company of St. John the Beheaded to be delivered to his relatives for burial in the Church of San Tommaso. Then Lucrezia is gathered up and delivered to the hands of her family for burial in the Church of San Gregorio.

And now a vast and clamorous cortege is formed. The mourners have gathered from the entire city and the surrounding countryside. The streets are dark. Thousands of lanterns are flickering along the bridges. Noble ladies in their coaches, suddenly moved to compassion, have formed a long procession in Via di Panico. Monks and friars, companies of charity, doctors and scholars, scullions and chimney sweeps, all gather behind the bier of Beatrice Cenci in a tremendous column lit with candles and torches, and move through the shadows of Via Giulia.

More and more candles are lit. Flowers are tossed through the windows. Silver amulets and beads fall in a shower over the bier. The murmur of prayers, the chanting and wailing melt into a single deep rhythm. They cross the Tiber at Ponte Sisto and climb the dark fragrant path that winds through the pines and ilexes of the Gianicolo.

Finally they arrive at the Church of San Pietro Montorio. The bier is set in front of the altar, surrounded by candles. The great procession moves silently past the body.

Midnight comes. The last remnants of the crowd have finally gone. Fra Andrea Belmonte places the head on a silver platter and the four Brothers of the Stigmata lower the body into the appointed place, which is in the apse of the church, a bit to the left. A stone without a name is placed over the grave. The candles keep burning. The Brothers depart. Only Fra Andrea Belmonte remains in the church.

Certain folk still linger in the wooded paths of the Gianicolo. Bastiana, still sobbing, is waiting for the soldier-boy Carlo. Pasquale is hurrying to the bridge of the Quattro Capi. Madonna Caterina, with a lamp in her hand, is peeping into a small dark alcove. Fra Pietro pauses near the Pantheon on his way to La Minerva, and Sister Ippolita is praying in the nunnery of Montecitorio. The moon rises, all is still in the city of Rome. Only the fountains are flashing and shivering in the empty piazzas.